AT THE END OF HER TETHER

'I've been meaning to talk to you about your clothes,' Patrick said.

'Don't talk about them,' she retorted bitingly. 'Just bring them.' That sounded firm enough to her.

'I can't,' he said. 'They've been locked up for the duration of your stay. They'll be returned when you leave. House rules, you understand. All of our guests have to wear uniform, which your clothes weren't. You really shouldn't be wearing even that poncho. You're quite overdressed, although I congratulate you on your ingenuity.'

AT THE END OF HER TETHER

G. C. Scott

This book is a work of fiction.
In real life, make sure you practise safe, sane and consensual sex.

First published in 2003 by
Nexus
Thames Wharf Studios
Rainville Road
London W6 9HA

www.nexus-books.co.uk

Typeset by TW Typesetting, Plymouth, Devon

Printed and bound by
Clays Ltd, St Ives PLC

ISBN 0 352 33857 1

You'll notice that we have introduced a set of symbols onto our book jackets, so that you can tell at a glance what fetishes each of our brand new novels contains. Here's the key – enjoy!

cp (traditional)

cp (modern)

spanking

restraint/bondage

rope bondage/hojojutsu

latex/rubber/leather/enclosure

fem dom

willing captivity

medical

period setting

uniforms

sex rituals

One

Jan Norris, née Graham, forty-two, rose early on the Monday her husband was due to go away on a business trip. She looked forward to being on her own while he was away, even if she never went anywhere herself. It was nice to be alone doing whatever she liked. She looked at Sam, asleep in their bed, and wondered briefly how they had reached the point where seeing as little as possible of each other was a source of relief. Surely, she thought, other married couples stayed close even after some twenty years of marriage. Or so they said.

Jan put on her favourite candlewick dressing gown and went to make her morning coffee. Let him sleep, she thought. She wondered whom he would meet on this trip. Jan was certain he was having affairs, perhaps had been for years, though neither ever alluded to them. She preferred it that way. She didn't want to be touched by Graham. Not any more. Which meant, she realised, that he'd have to look elsewhere and she certainly couldn't berate him for that. Besides, that path led to rows and divorce, and lawyers and public shame. And she did not want to appear as 'the wronged woman'. At least he wasn't always after her for sex, though once was too often. Jan thought that she could no more help her attitude than Sam could help his.

As she waited for the kettle to boil, she looked out of the kitchen window at the brightening day. Dewdrops hung from the rose petals in the back garden, and the grass was rich green with moisture. It was going to be sunny and cool, too nice to stay indoors. A shopping trip to nearby Guildford would combine the pleasure of a spending spree with being out and about. She made her first cup of coffee and sat at the table to collect herself, liking the quiet time.

The mood was broken when Sam came downstairs and made for the kettle and his first cup of coffee.

'Where are you going?' Jan asked. Politeness demanded that at least, even if she really wanted to ask him *when* he was going, and for how long.

Hearing the unspoken question, Sam replied, 'Scotland.' No details. He understood that she needed none. 'I'll be away for a week or ten days. I'll call when I arrive with the telephone number.' He knew that she would not call unless there was an emergency. Jan had become adept at coping with his absences.

She sat at the kitchen table for nearly an hour after he had gone, enjoying the return of quiet, and eventually rose and went upstairs to get ready. She showered and shampooed her hair. The bathroom lacked large mirrors because she did not like to see her naked body. It was a nice body, her husband used to say. And still was, even if she said so herself. Trim. Athletic without being stringy. Slender waist. Full breasts. Long legs. Angrily, Jan stopped herself. She was beginning to sound like Sam, and that annoyed her.

She shaved her legs carefully, admiring them as Sam did, but without the sexual overtones he always managed to inject into the process. They were just . . . nice. Better than the sticks most fashion models got about on. Good legs. Woman's legs.

This morning, as usual, she chose to wear tights rather than the stockings and suspenders which Sam preferred. Whenever he asked her not to wear tights, she replied that they were more comfortable. The tights were a light powdery blue, glossy and smart. She smoothed them up her legs and pulled the waistband into place, fitting the gusset firmly into her crotch with the air of a virgin donning a chastity belt. The silk pants and matching bra were also light blue. The bra lifted and separated her full breasts, emphasising her deep cleavage.

Always slightly embarrassed by her bosom (never her tits), Jan plunged hastily into a full slip and quickly got into her light cream-coloured dress. She felt so much more comfortable when dressed, and never walked around naked except when bathing behind the closed door in her mirrorless bathroom. She selected high-heeled shoes to match her outfit.

Downstairs again, Jan tidied the kitchen. The ringing of the doorbell interrupted the washing-up. With a small frown she carefully took off her apron and hung it up. She laid the rubber gloves on the draining-board. Expecting a neighbour, she was instead confronted by a nicely dressed young woman wanting to sell double-glazing. She had red hair and couldn't have been more than twenty-five. Jan thought she was immodestly dressed: her skirt was too short, her blouse too tight, her breasts large and visible. A bit like her youngest daughter, Leslie, Jan thought, with just the faintest tinge of envy for the girl's youth and obvious attractiveness. The visitor was persistent, as only double-glazing reps on commission can be. It required several firm refusals before she went away. Going back through to the kitchen, Jan noticed that the back door was slightly ajar. Before she could even register alarm, they were on her.

The surprise was total. A pair of strong arms shot around her waist from behind, pinning her own arms to her sides. Before she could begin to struggle or summon the wit to scream, a second person appeared from the kitchen and thrust a hard rubber ball into her open mouth. He wore a black balaclava. Her knees felt weak. He tugged the straps of the gag around her head and buckled them tightly. Jan tried to scream, but could barely make a sound. The straps were cutting into the corners of her mouth, and she felt as if she would choke on the ball. Then the other man slipped a noose over her head, pulling it down below her breasts, knotting it tightly behind her back, locking her arms to the side. They yanked her hands behind her. She felt the bite of the rope as her wrists were tightly bound. She could not believe that this was happening, in her own home, in the middle of an ordinary morning. And the sun still shone brightly on her back garden.

Jan's terrified gaze travelled around the kitchen, noticing again the open rear door, the way they'd gained entry into her ordered world. She saw the tidy washing-up, the carefully hung-up apron, the bright yellow rubber gloves laid neatly together. Amid these signs of her normal, structured life, suddenly and bizarrely, she was bound and gagged and struggling.

As the man in front held her upright, crushing her breasts against his chest, Jan felt her ankles drawn together with more rope. It was passed swiftly around them and knotted tightly. More rope encircled her knees, pulling her legs tightly together. Utterly helpless, unable even to stand, they forced her down on a kitchen chair. Strangled grunts came through her gag, but no intelligible words. Waves of fear swamped her thoughts. What could they possibly want? Surely they could see the terror in her eyes, but they just looked silently at her through balaclavas. Her skirt had been pulled up her thighs during the struggle. When she saw them staring at her legs she wished she could tug it down. She knew what they were thinking.

Then one of the men produced a black leather bag, which he pulled down over her head. He tied the strings around her throat. Blind, helpless, terrified by the loss of sight, she struggled to free her hands and legs and shake off the gag. They lifted her arms up and pulled her wrists down behind the chair. Still struggling, Jan felt them pull her ankles under the chair and join them to her bound wrists with a short piece of rope. More rope at her waist pulled her against the back of the chair. Unable to move, see or speak, Jan felt terror strangle her, squeezing her stomach. She grew still.

One spoke. 'She'll be all right now. Get the van. I'll get some of her things.' She heard retreating footsteps, and the sound of the closing door. She froze in terror. She was going to be abducted. The gag muffled her emerging scream. Jan began to struggle again and the chair creaked as she heaved against the ropes binding her to it. Her hands twisted wildly behind her back but there was no slack, no escape. Her exertion and desperation made her breathless and the ball in her mouth prevented her from breathing properly. She began to feel dizzy and faint as she fought to breathe and scream.

At the sudden touch of a hand on her shoulder, Jan abruptly stopped struggling. She was sweaty and panting. He was back. 'I heard the chair creaking from upstairs,' he said conversationally, as if he was accustomed to hearing people struggle to escape. 'Good thing they're sturdy chairs,' he went on, 'otherwise you might have broken it and done yourself an injury.'

'Mmmmmmmmmmmmfffffffff,' Jan grunted.

When the hand moved from her shoulder to her breast, Jan froze. So this was to be the way of it, she thought. I should have known. Oh God, make him go away.

'Nnnnngggggg!' Jan screamed into her gag. She jerked abruptly, trying to free her breast from the hand that cupped it so familiarly. But she was too tightly bound. She could barely move. She was forced to endure the hateful exploration in silence.

When the hand moved to her thighs, exposed above the hem of her dress, she struggled. The man paid no attention. He continued to stroke her thighs through the smooth sheer nylon of her delicate blue tights. The caress reminded her of Sam's attempts to entice her into bed. But the same thing from a menacing stranger. She tried to resist but couldn't.

The hand moved higher, right between her thighs. He forced his fingers between. Then inside her. She clenched her thighs tightly together, but could not stop them going deeper and deeper inside her. And as he continued to probe, his free hand cupped her breast. He was clearly excited by the struggling. With a thrill of fear Jan realised that he was going to have his way with her. The Victorian phrase escaped her entirely. That was how she thought of it. The word rape was too terrible.

But he'll never get to me, she thought desperately, as long as my legs are tied. And I'm wearing pants and tights. Then she imagined him ripping them off. Think of something else. And still he continued to caress and probe her body while she tried to turn her thoughts to other things – to Leslie at work; to Sam and his awful demands; to redecorating the spare room. But her mind refused to be distracted. And then Jan suddenly sensed an entirely different sort of feeling sweep through her. A tingling between her legs gradually spread all over her body. She realised that she was flushing, growing hot, in a way she had never done before. Her skin felt sensitive and tingly. Her clothes felt tight and uncomfortable. An alien frightening thought came to her, am I beginning to enjoy this? She did not know how to deal with this sudden warmth and *loosening* between her legs and in her stomach. Her breasts felt hot and heavy, ready to burst, held in by the silken cups of her bra. Was this, oh God, how an *orgasm* began? Am I going to *come*? She had no way of knowing, or of escaping the touch of those maddening and hateful caresses.

Tied as she was and helpless, Jan could not stop him from touching her, nor, more importantly, could she stop her suddenly rebellious body from responding to his touch. And respond it did. Her back arched and her hips rose as far as the ropes allowed, as if she were offering herself to him. She gave a low moan. He's actually touching my . . . sex, she thought. I want him to do it *again*. No, no, she told herself, remembering how she had repulsed her boyfriends whenever they had got too close. She had firmly removed the roving hands and said keep away. But she could not remove these hands.

Jan was torn between the desire to cry 'Stop' and say absolutely nothing. And then he was touching her clitoris and her twinges were getting stronger and stronger. Amazingly, she knew almost nothing about her clit. She was, in the orgasmic sense, a virgin. She had no way of knowing whether he was close to touching the trigger inside her. Then her mind took over. She couldn't get rid of this image. Her legs were free, spread wide, her lips exposed, and she was completely naked. No, she told herself, no. But her body was not going to obey her. For the first time it was slipping beyond her control. The next *twinge* was much stronger. She couldn't hold back. Oh my . . . cunt, she thought, my *cunt*. And it was the first time she'd ever thought that word. What's happening to me? Was this what her friends meant by orgasm? Jan had never been able to ask, partly from shame and partly from reluctance to reveal her own abysmal ignorance. This must be . . . it. Her belly was afire, filled with liquid heat that turned her legs to jelly and made her body heave and strain against the ropes. No one had ever hinted it could be like *this*. Why had she ever held back, denied herself this indescribable pleasure? She had never known that her body, the thing she had worn all her life and kept under such rigid control, could do *this*.

Jan knew in an increasingly distant part of her mind that she should not yield but she could not act on that knowledge now. This stranger was doing something to her that no man had ever been able to do. But then none of her suitors had tied her up before beginning the assault on her frigidity. None of them had gagged and blindfolded and terrorised her either, but then none of them had ever suspected that she might respond to all this. *She* had not known that she would.

Abruptly the next twinge became a bursting spasm as her first-ever orgasm swept through her. She thought she was having a heart attack. She could feel her pulse racing and her heart thundering. If she had not been held fast by the ropes, she would have curled her body into a tight ball and hugged the strange and marvellous sensation inside herself. But being bound, her release was evident only in the shuddering of her body and in the moans that forced themselves past her gag. She felt her face redden under the black leather bag and was glad that no one could see her.

Then she felt the beginnings of a further eruption in her belly. She couldn't believe she could feel that yet again, so soon after the first. But she did, moaning and shuddering and fighting the ropes that held her. Her body, so long controlled by her inhibitions, took over. The normal part of her could only stand aside, appalled but interested, while her desires – so long denied – had their way. She was so terribly glad that her captor could not see her face, nor she his. She could not have borne being seen in the throes of, yes, passion. It must have been an orgasm, she thought, striving to avoid, even in her own mind, such words as ecstasy and joy.

But her captor showed no signs of stopping. Was he going to make her come again? Jan wished he would stop, and at the same time willed him to go on. She had never felt such confusion in all her ordered life. The sound of a vehicle pulling up outside the kitchen door interrupted her tumbling thoughts. The door opened, and the second captor returned.

'Ah, I see you've got her started. How is she doing?' he asked his companion.

'A bit reluctant, but she got there in the end. Didn't you, Jan? Come on, own up. We won't tell anyone.'

He spoke lightly, teasingly, but his words stung like a whip. How could he be so casual about what he had done to her, what he had forced her helpless body to do to her? She had been tricked into this amazing response. She felt herself flushing again, and she resolved never to surrender again, no matter what they did.

A mocking voice inside her head asked, and just how do you intend to hold back the next time? You didn't do so well this time, did you? They tricked me, Jan replied, took me by surprise. She was alarmed by the voice in her head. She was beginning to talk to herself.

'Let's get her into the van,' the second man said. And to Jan, 'There'll be plenty of time to enjoy yourself when we get you to the other end. You'll soon feel right at home.'

Home? This was her home, and they were taking her away from it. Hands untied the ropes that held her to the kitchen chair. They were taking her away, taking her God knows where. She felt herself lifted between her two captors, one taking her shoulders and the other her ankles. She was carried through the door of her kitchen and deposited on the floor of a vehicle. They lay her on her side, before bending her knees and drawing her wrists down to her ankles.

Jan recognised her awkward position as a hogtie, and flushed at the undignified image the word conjured up. She guessed that she was in a van, from what they had said, but she had no idea what kind. She idiotically hoped that it would be a closed vehicle. If any of her acquaintances saw her, Jan Norris, trussed and being driven away, she would die of embarrassment. But a more rational thought made it clear that unless one of her acquaintances saw her being abducted, and raised the alarm, she might die of something more painful than embarrassment.

Jan struggled to free herself, tugging against the rope that joined her wrists and ankles and trying to twist her hands free. The doors closed and she heard the motor start. Oh God, they're taking me away. What did they mean? Struggling, terrified, she was borne away from her normal life toward an unknown future. They weren't going to kill her, were they? No, they had spoken of 'time to enjoy yourself'. She froze as she thought of what they might do to make her 'enjoy herself'. More of what she had already begun to enjoy in her own kitchen, she surmised.

No, that couldn't be. Women were not simply taken from their homes and forced to have sex, not in this day and age. Were they? Her present experience suggested a chilling answer to the question. At the same time, a deeply buried part of her wondered if she would again feel those strange twinges and spasms of pleasure when they got to wherever they were going. She struggled and then gave up. She lay still on the floor of the van. She had time to reflect on the recent past, the uncomfortable present, and the uncertain future. With a horrified wonder she recalled her ready response to the stranger's hands on her body. I was made to . . . come, she thought. I've had an orgasm, she corrected herself primly. At least that is what it must have been. She could think of no other experience that had felt quite like it.

And she had *liked* it. No, that was not the word. She had been overwhelmed by the pleasure that had swept through her as he touched her more intimately than Sam had ever done. Than she had ever allowed Sam to do, she corrected herself again, trying to be fair. She, Jan Norris, respectably if not happily married, mother of two, a housewife had felt . . . ecstasy. Her mind supplied the word. She knew it as an abstract concept, but had never applied it to herself. Jan had in fact once felt very queer in the stomach and between her legs during sex. The feeling had alarmed her. She had thought there was something terribly wrong with her. She had sprung from the bed, much to Sam's annoyance, and fled into the bathroom, locking the door and investigating her body in as far as she could bring herself to. She hadn't come out for a long time. Sam, to her relief, had got up and gone when she emerged. It had been a long time before he could talk her into sex again.

What have I been missing? she asked herself. And recoiled in shame from the answer. She had been denying her needs for so long, she had forgotten their existence and their terrifying power when released. But a lapse like that frightened her, made her grow hot with shame. She tried to deny the pleasure but a part of her had welcomed those hands and *those* feelings. Something in her had been awakened.

It seemed to Jan that they drove forever. She rolled from side to side as the van went around corners. When the turns stopped, she guessed that they were on a motorway. Her struggles, and the aftermath of her orgasms, had tired her out. She drowsed. Then woke to struggle briefly again. To reflect on her situation and on her frightening response to her captor. And to drowse again. Helplessly bound and gagged, Jan knew her fate was in the hands of others. They had taken away her freedom of choice. And her responsibility, she suddenly realised. The loss of responsibility for her actions was entirely new.

The loss of responsibility meant that she could not be blamed for responding as she had. And so she felt less guilty about her enjoyment. Her mother's reproving image said, you enjoyed that. They forced me, she replied. They made me . . . come. Yes, the image said, but you didn't have to enjoy it. I didn't co-operate, Jan replied. She had been overwhelmed, she insisted, by the ropes and then by her body's helpless reaction to the stranger who had touched her so intimately. Her mother's image was not convinced.

The van slowed. Turns became more frequent. Jan guessed that they were nearing their destination. A stab of fear forced her to struggle and then the van finally stopped and the doors opened to let in cool air. It did not smell like city air. To her ears came the sound, not of feet on pavements or cars in streets, but

12

the distant lowing of cattle and the sound of magpies. No one will ever find me, she thought as she was untied. They stood her up but she fell to her knees, the impact softened by the arms that caught her just before she reached the grass. Her legs refused to obey her. Jan's captors left her kneeling for several minutes. She imagined them staring at her as she knelt before them, and hated the idea. She struggled to rise to her feet, and fell onto her side with a thud. She struggled to rise but could not.

She felt the cool air on her thighs, and knew that her dress must be around her waist. She knew that her captors were enjoying the show, staring at her in her humiliation. She hated the idea, and them. She wanted to weep in frustration. If her hands were free, she would . . .

Jan lay on the ground for a long time. No one touched her. Had they gone away? She remembered reading about a woman who had been abducted and left bound in the snow. She had frozen to death. But this wasn't winter. Wildly, Jan fought the ropes that held her hands and arms behind her back. She sought to eject the gag once more. Finally, exhausted, and filled with mind-numbing panic, she lay still. It was fruitless. She was not going to get free on her own.

'Feeling better now that you've got it out of your system, Jan?'

The nearby voice jolted her. That was the second time they had called her by name. How could they know that? Had they been stalking her? Jan thought back over her recent movements but could not remember being followed or studied by strangers. So, how had they chanced upon *her*? Why her? Oh God, why her?

'Up you get, old girl,' said the voice, kindly. Jan felt hands under her arms lifting her, an arm around her waist steadying her as she was propelled forward. With some relief she felt her skirt cover her thighs. They led her into a house. She could tell she was indoors because the rural sounds were muted, and she no longer felt the cool air. She only knew that they had bundled her into a lift when she felt the sudden dropping sensation in her stomach. They took her along some sort of passageway, or into a very long room. She stood still, in a strange place, afraid to move. Then hands, freeing her wrists and arms, and a new voice told her to keep the hood in place until she heard the door close.

Jan froze, even after they left her. For long minutes she did nothing, trying only to calm her fears. At last she fumbled at the string that held her hood in place, finding the knot, loosening it and pulling the bag away. Her eyes were dazzled by the sudden flood of light. It felt like ages since she had been attacked in her kitchen. The gag gave her more trouble than the bag. The strap was very tight. Finally she got it unbuckled, and removed the hard rubber ball that had filled her mouth and held her jaws apart. She let that too fall to the floor as she surveyed her surroundings.

Two

Jan was in a bedroom with a closed door. She guessed that it was locked but that really didn't matter since there was neither a handle nor keyhole on her side. Nevertheless, she tried to open it. Her nails went into the crack between the door and frame, but she couldn't get any leverage. Hopeless, she decided. Jan turned back to the room. It was a bedroom, like a hotel room, she thought, seeking reassurance. There was a bed, a nightstand with a lamp, an armchair and a tall wardrobe with wide mirrored doors. Against one wall was a low cabinet with a television and a video recorder. There were no clues as to where she might be. This could be any of thousands of anonymous rooms. No one would ever find her, she thought.

Jan glanced again at the mirror and saw a dishevelled and frightened woman staring back at her. There were smudges on her face, her hair was disarranged, and there were grass stains on her dress and tights. The red marks from the ropes stood out plainly on her arms and legs. Her eyes were wide in fear. Not liking what she saw, Jan turned away.

There was a door across the room from the wardrobe. Nervously she walked toward it, afraid that someone would spring out. It proved to be a bathroom. She went in warily and drank some water in cupped hands from the tap, washing away the sour taste of the gag. She ran cold water over the red marks on her wrists. Her face was still flushed and sweaty, and there were marks at the corners of her mouth and across her cheeks where the straps had been.

Jan looked more closely at the room, and saw the usual amenities though there were no towels. She found a washcloth and began to repair some of the damage to her appearance, feeling some confidence return as the more familiar Jan stared back from the mirror. She would have liked a bath but was very reluctant to undress. Instinctively she felt safer in her clothes, more her usual self. When she had done the best she could, she dried her face and hands and went back into the bedroom. Jan sat in the armchair, not trusting the bed. To lie there in her present circumstances might give her captors the wrong idea about her.

As she sat in the chair, Jan tried again to think about how she had been chosen for this . . . whatever it was, and what would happen. She could not imagine why they had abducted an ordinary housewife whose life had been normal in every way for as long as she could remember. She was still busy with her fruitless thoughts as the sky outside darkened.

The sound of the door opening startled Jan from a light doze. She had a fleeting thought of escape, followed by renewed terror: they were coming for her. But it was only a dinner tray, pushed through the door before it closed. She heard the lock. She had not eaten anything since breakfast. She had made a long trip bound and gagged. She suddenly felt tired and weak and hungry. The food was tempting, but she was reluctant to eat it. By eating the food her captors provided, she was acknowledging that she was

16

dependent on them for everything. But she was, wasn't she? And by eating she was sustaining herself. And her rebellious body. But what if the food were drugged?

In fact the food was good and plentiful. Jan ate, suppressing her feelings of caution and guilt. She took stock of herself as she ate, discovering no blurred vision or sudden sleepiness. The food had not been drugged. Then she left the tray behind the door. She had a vague idea of making a run for it while they picked up the tray, she thought. She sat in the armchair, watching the door.

But no one came for quite a long time, and she began to feel sleepy, as she often did after eating. Even her bizarre circumstances could not alter that long habit. And she would have to sleep anyway sooner or later, she reasoned. Just a quick snooze then, she promised herself as she rose and removed her dress. She didn't really want to sleep in it, in case it got creased. And she was accustomed to sleeping in a night-dress, but there wasn't one. She laid the dress carefully on the chair, removed her high-heeled shoes and got into bed. And, not surprisingly, slept, though her dreams troubled her.

Just before dawn she snapped awake. The tray had gone. She had not heard anyone enter the room. A cold dread came over her. They – whoever they were – had been able to enter her room without awakening her. If they could do that, they could do anything.

The thought of escape came back. She got hurriedly out of bed and went to the window, hoping that she might be able to open it. There was a sloping roof, some kind of shed no doubt, just under the window. She could reach the ground easily from there. The open fields beyond the room beckoned. Then she discovered that the window was locked. She would have to break it. Jan went to the bathroom for a towel, wrapping it around her hand as she had seen actors do when they wanted to avoid being cut by the glass. She hoped the noise would not attract her captors. Only the glass didn't break when she struck it. The glass barely quivered in the frame. Jan struck again, harder. This time she hurt her hand without making any impression on the glass. When the side of her hand stopped hurting, she searched the room for something heavier. My shoes, she thought. They had steel caps on the heels. She grasped one and struck the glass with the heel. Again nothing. She struck again, harder, then began to hammer frantically at the glass, oblivious of the noise. She wept in frustration when her frenzied efforts produced no effect. No one even came to investigate.

Jan collapsed weakly on the bed, the shoe still in her hand. Daylight grew stronger. The shoe dropped to the floor and she folded her arms protectively across her breasts. Sam would be waking up now in his hotel room, she thought. Would he be waking alone? She wished that he were here. She needed someone to rescue her from this waking nightmare. Leslie would soon be on her way to work at the antiques magazine which she edited.

She was a prisoner of she did not know who, in a house she had never seen, in a part of the country she couldn't identify from her limited view. She still did not know why she had been taken, nor how long her captors intended to keep her prisoner, nor what they would do to her. It was a fine parade of negatives when they were stood end to end. But the sum of these negatives was a strong feeling of disorientation and fear.

Jan shivered in the warm room, listening for approaching footsteps. The gag and blindfold lay on the floor where she had dropped them the day before. They reminded her of her abduction, of how she had been snatched from the comfortable and the familiar and plunged into this . . . this . . . She couldn't think of a word to describe what had happened to her. She felt as if she were going insane. This didn't happen to ordinary people, she kept telling herself. But it had undeniably happened to her.

And then there was the small matter of her orgasms. She shied away from the word, but could think of no other. Yes, well then, her orgasms of the day before. That had been shattering in a different way. But the new, strange voice in her head said, that was great. We need to try that again.

The pre-abduction Jan grimaced in distaste. She felt as if there were two of her, one rooted in the past, the other a modified version that had begun growing – yes, that was the right word – growing, since yesterday. The newer Jan was both disturbing and interesting. The newer Jan wanted to learn more about these disturbing feelings. The older Jan was in a panic, feeling herself being driven toward something she had avoided most of her life.

She sat on the edge of the bed, watching the light grow outside. It was going to be another warm, sunny day. If she were not a prisoner, the older Jan might have been thinking about taking her horse for a canter along the bridleways near her home. Instead, she paced the room, examining the wardrobe, door and the bathroom. She saw nothing to help identify her place of imprisonment, nor suggest how she could escape. But why run away before you know what'll happen next? It might be even better than yesterday. The voice inside her began whispering its subversive ideas.

Jan shook herself, both physically and mentally. She forced the subversive new Jan to the back of her mind. She simply could not afford to go about in two minds, muzzy and confused. She might have to act swiftly and decisively if the opportunity arose. She did not need the new Jan suggesting that she might be acting too hastily, asking if she really wanted to run away from *that*. Jan did not want to use the word again, or even think about it. Things were confused enough already, so confused that she just sat on the side of the bed in nothing but her underwear, a prisoner in a strange place, half-undressed.

Jan stiffened in alarm as she heard footsteps approaching. They stopped outside her door. A key turned in the lock. She came back to the present with a jerk, grabbing her dress from the chair. There was no time to get into it. The door was opening. She held the dress in front of her like a shield as a strange man entered the room.

He seemed pleasant enough, and youngish. Certainly younger than she was. He was tall, well over six feet, with fair skin and dark hair. When he smiled she could see the amusement in his eyes and mouth. Was he laughing at her? Jan wondered with a flash of anger. But it was quickly swamped by renewed alarm.

'Who are you? What .. what do you want with me?' she stammered, angry at the quaver in her voice but unable to stop it. She clutched the dress tightly to her body.

'You may call me Patrick. And what would you do if I said that I just wanted you?' The man flashed an engaging smile. 'I mean you – your body – to play upon like a musical instrument, to wring responses from it that would make yesterday's experience seem a mere prelude.'

Jan did not appreciate the irony. She shrank away from him, still clutching her dress and wishing she had had the presence of mind to put it on before he had entered her cell. Her worst fears were going to be realised, it seemed. But . . . he had used the subjunctive. Was he asking her permission?

Jan rallied. 'I would say no, certainly not,' she retorted, proud of the firmness in her voice. 'I would add that I want to be released at once and returned to my home. If that were done, I might not report this outrage to the police.' There. She had given him the choice.

He shook his head ruefully. 'I expected you to say something like that, Jan. Everything we have learned about you suggested that you'd be a tough nut to crack. But we decided to accept the challenge. And here you are, on the threshold of the greatest sexual experience of your life, still hesitating.'

He waited, watching her in a way that reminded Jan of a cat watching its prey. She decided to ignore his outrageous suggestion. 'You must let me go at once. And get out of here while I get dressed.'

He shook his head again. 'What would it take to make you give me your clothes and your body? For the next fortnight, that is. I promise to return the clothes clean and unharmed before you leave. And we will return your body enhanced and unharmed, unless you count yesterday's overture as harm.'

Jan could hardly believe her ears.

He held up his hand as she opened her mouth to reply. 'The enhancement I have in mind is a fine-tuning of your sexual responses. We intend to make your body responsive to sexual stimulation and irresistible to men. Your bonus will be the ability to have sexual orgasms like those you had yesterday, and even better ones than that if you put your mind to it. We want to take away your aversion to sexual contact and allow you to enjoy your marvellous body, and come out of denial.'

21

Jan was speechless. His audacity amazed her. Who was he to say what was good for her? And how could he decide what she would enjoy? This mysterious stranger was suggesting things that she had absolutely refused to do even with her own husband. Then the new Jan spoke up unexpectedly from the corner of her mind. How about it, Jan, orgasms like the ones that made you almost faint with pleasure yesterday? We both now know what you can do, and he's promising you even more.

Jan shook her head in confusion. He saw it. 'Listen to your better half,' he urged.

How could he know of the split in her mind when she had only become aware of it a few hours ago? His insight unsettled her.

'Many of the women who come here are like you. They just need a bit of encouragement to throw off their puritan beliefs and turn into modern, fulfilled lovers. We specialise in turning uptight ladies into courtesans. And with the really willing we can put a marvellous polish on their new skills. Or many satisfied customers have told us. If you like, I can even show you the glowing recommendations from former students.'

Jan had learned what little she knew about sex from her mother, who believed that it was a necessary but regrettable part of childbearing. Mrs Graham, red-faced and stuttering, had lectured Jan just before her wedding about what she called 'marital duties'. It was the first and only time her mother had said anything about sex. Children, she had told her, were a woman's reward for submitting to a husband's desires. It was her duty to submit. To be fair, though, Mrs Graham had not told her to lie back and think of England.

'And were these "glowing recommendations" extracted from women you'd abducted and terrorised?' she asked with what she hoped was withering scorn.

He was completely unphased. 'Some of them,' he replied. 'The others came to us voluntarily, on the recommendation of *alumnae*, some of whom were abducted like you, but who had had their eyes opened by the experience. As we hope you will be. Your body is too good to waste.'

Jan reddened at his continual reference to 'her body,' as if it were a specimen, as he seemed to think it was. But it wasn't. It was . . . her. Sam had often said the same thing about her body, but she had never listened to him. Could he have been right?

The other Jan smirked silently, wriggling suggestively in the far corner of her mind. How about it, eh, Jan?

She hesitated for a fatal second. And as she hesitated, she realised that she was not quite the same woman who had been bound and pleasured in her kitchen just yesterday.

Patrick again saw her doubt. His smile seemed to strip her naked. But he said nothing.

Jan reddened. 'I want to leave,' she said as firmly as she could. 'And I want to take a bath and get dressed. So please leave me alone.'

He looked disappointed, but said nothing more about 'teaching' her 'body' new responses. 'The bathroom is yours,' he said. He left the room, closing the door.

Although Jan did not hear the key being turned, she knew that she was a prisoner in the room once more. Nevertheless, she tried to pull it open, shrugged and turned away. At least I told him what I felt, she told herself.

Did you? asked the other Jan, advancing from the background of her mind and challenging her.

23

Jan hesitated on her way to the bathroom to study herself in the mirror. She saw a mature, full-bodied woman in her underwear. She took a second, more critical look, smoothing the slip against her body and studying the effect. Her flat stomach, slender waist and full breasts were pleasing. Below the hem of the slip her legs were visible from just above the knee, rounded and full, the ankles nicely turned, as Sam often said.

This was the body which Patrick had said was 'too good to waste'. It was a compliment, she guessed, and she went pink with a curious mixture of pleasure, embarrassment and trepidation. No stranger had ever assessed her as he had, boldly, openly, and then pronounced such a flattering judgement. She pulled the slip over her head and let it drop to the floor. She studied herself again, her breasts pushed up and out by the bra, her long legs sheathed in blue nylon, visible now from crotch to toe. Pleasing, she decided. Jan took off her pants and bra, and peeled the tights down her legs, giving herself a brief, assessing glance before she turned hurriedly away, stricken by her old embarrassment at being naked.

She went into the bathroom and closed the door. There was a deep tub, a shower, toilet and bidet. Her captors had thoughtfully provided an assortment of bath salts, shampoos and aromatic oils for their 'guests'. There was even a full-length hot air drying device, which explained the lack of bath towels. There was a conventional hair dryer too. Everything you could expect at a high-class hotel. She locked the bolt on her side of the door, put in the plug and ran a hot bath. She added Radox, taking care of her other needs, as she coyly described them to herself, while the tub filled. She avoided looking at the bidet as she crossed to the bath and sank into the hot, scented water. This was a luxury she had always enjoyed. Her mother had said it was a duty as well, quoting those lines about the kinship between cleanliness and godliness. As she soaked, Jan remembered with a smile her mother saying to her, when she was a little girl, 'You'll never get to heaven if you keep playing in mud puddles like those horrid little boys across the street.' At the time, she had thought of mud puddles as a kind of heaven.

Her knees, nipples and head stuck above the water. Below the faintly green water she could see her pubic mound with its thick curly hair. She looked quickly away. Since her long chestnut hair was mostly wet, she decided to wash it as well. She would have pinned it up as she usually did, but hadn't thought of it in time. Yesterday had been an unsettling experience. It might take some time for her to settle back into her old habits.

Sure you want to settle back into *all* of them? her alter ego asked sardonically.

Jan tried to blot out the question, but it came back again. She was beginning to realise that there are some hours which, once lived through, change the rest of your life. Yesterday (though it was too soon to be sure) looked like being one of those experiences. That explained this split in her personality. Jan had never had to engage in internal debates in matters sexual, nor in most other aspects of her life.

She looked down again at her pubic mound, the source of most of yesterday's disturbing feelings. She was surprised to see that her left hand had crept down quite close to her mons veneris, as if it had a life of its own. She jerked it back abruptly and she reached for the soap to distract herself from the disturbing idea that she had actually been going to 'touch herself,' as her mother had warned her not to do.

25

Why not? asked her alter ego. Yesterday was dynamite, wasn't it?

Jan stood up and soaped her body vigorously, rubbing her suddenly treacherous flesh with the rough washcloth as she strove to think of neutral things. Her bizarre situation did not help her mind to settle.

This bathroom, unlike hers at home, had a mirror nearly covering a full wall. As it was on the wall behind the door, she had not noticed it as she came in. Now she did, and she saw herself in it, her breasts slippery with soap and with bubbles running down between her legs, just like those pictures she had seen in Sam's magazines. They had alarmed her, but she had never said anything to him about them. She admitted grudgingly that a man needed his secret vices as much as a woman did. Hers tended more toward the odd extra glass of sherry.

Jan flushed bright red and did a quick Venus de Milo with her arms. The pose seemed even more provocative, and embarrassing, than merely standing up straight. She averted her eyes and sat down again. She ran more hot water, and the bathroom slowly filled with steam. When she looked at the mirror again, she saw with relief that its surface was clouded over. The bathwater, too, was not as clear as before. Her pubic mound was still visible, but not now in alarming detail. Her nipples and the upper slopes of her breasts, however, stuck up as before. Jan was surprised to see that her nipples were erect. And they felt funny. She touched them with her hands. They were as tight as she could ever remember them, and she was not in a cold room.

Her alter ego, which Jan now imagined as a tiny, devilish figure with faintly dusky skin, horns and pointed tail, urged her to touch them again. Jan Two, she thought, with a wry smile, giving her alter ego a name. In her mind's eye, Jan Two wore thigh-high boots with stiletto heels, but was otherwise naked.

She made me do it, Jan thought, as her hands seemingly of their own volition rose from the water to slide down the slick upper surfaces of her breasts and rest on her nipples.

Give them a pinch, Jan Two urged. And she did. One of those twinges she had felt yesterday passed from her nipples to her crotch so quickly that Jan pressed her thighs tightly together as if in denial. But she pinched her nipples again. 'Oh,' she said softly as another electric shock went to her crotch. She was on the verge of continuing the experiment when her real self cut in. She was actually 'touching herself'. Jan quickly let go of her nipples and finished washing but her nipples stayed erect throughout, begging to be touched.

Afterwards, Jan dried her long hair with the dryer while the full-length dryer warmed her body. It was a superior way of drying oneself, she admitted, soft and sensual. I'll have to cut it shorter, she told herself. A woman of forty-two should not have long hair. People might think she was trying to look like a young girl. Sam always opposed her wish to cut her hair. Jan dismissed his opposition as a typical male fantasy: long-haired women were supposed to be sexier and younger. Would he be less inclined to pester her for sex if her hair were short? Maybe she would try it out now and present him with a *fait accompli*. But this was no time to cut her hair, and instead she brushed it until it shone, and then carefully plaited it. The tail, thick as her wrist, reached well below her shoulders, almost to the middle of her back. That would have to do until she got home.

Smelling of soap and shampoo, she unbolted the bathroom door and went back to the bedroom to dress. She wished that she had clean underwear but imagined that she would only have to wear what she had for a short time, until these preposterous men took her home.

After the warmth of the bathroom, the bedroom seemed cold. She glanced at the armchair where she had laid her clothes, and suddenly the room seemed colder than before. Her clothes were gone. With hindsight she realised that she should have taken them in with her. Damn them.

Jan turned to the bed, intending to drape herself in a sheet until someone came to her. She would demand the return of . . . dear God, what was that? A pair of leg irons and a heavy leather belt with handcuffs attached lay on the bed. The manacles were open, and there were no keys. With a thrill of fear and excitement, Jan realised that they wanted her to put these on, make herself helpless, submit to them when they came for her.

No, she decided, no. She would not do that. She would go home instead.

How? asked the tiny red devil inside her. You're in a worse position than before. At least then you still had your clothes. But maybe you'd get a lift home sooner if you stand beside the road completely starkers. Want to try?

Jan flushed hot and cold as she realised the seriousness of her new predicament. The devilish figure was right in one respect: she was not, definitely not, even going to attempt to leave the house naked. Not unless the place was on fire, and even then she'd take a sheet to cover herself with. She jerked the bedclothes aside, dislodging the manacles. They fell to the floor with a heavy, chilling thud as she frantically pulled off a bed sheet to create a kind of toga. It seemed so simple in the movies, but she found that hers had an annoying habit of sliding off one shoulder or the other, baring her breasts by turns, or of falling off altogether. A poncho, she thought, picking the sheet up for the fifth time and looking for something with which to make a hole for her head to go through. In the bathroom she found a manicure kit, with a tiny pair of scissors. She also found that the mirror had cleared, and she was treated to another full-length nude view of herself.

'Damn', she said in exasperation.

Progress, Jan Two said sardonically. At least you're not blushing this time. At which Jan blushed anew, and made a hole in the sheet, enlarging it painstakingly with the small scissors. After several trials it was possible to get her head through the opening. Thus covered, she went back into the bathroom to inspect the result. Better, she thought, but there was still the matter of exposing herself every time she lifted her arms. She made two further holes to accommodate them, and inspected herself again. Still better, but a belt of some sort would help. She knew that there were none in the bedroom. A drapery cord, she thought in a burst of inspiration. She drew the drapes across the window and cut off the cord, knotting it around her waist.

A further inspection in the bathroom mirror revealed that her nipples were erect again, plainly visible beneath the sheet. She did not know what to do about that except blush once again. At least she was covered. She began to feel more comfortable. Clothes make the man, but they make most women comfortable.

When Jan returned to the bedroom, she found that a tray had been placed just inside the door. A note on it said, appropriately enough, 'Eat me.' 'Damn,' she said again. She had missed her first chance to tell her captors that she did not find their little joke funny, if it was a joke. Nevertheless, she was hungry, so she took the tray to the armchair to eat in relative comfort. She wished that the damned sheet wouldn't rub on her nipples as it did. They were going up and down like yo-yos. A bra would be nice, she thought, and pants. And tights, a slip and dress and shoes. Might as well wish for everything, as she was unlikely to get any of it.

Jan left the tray behind the door as before and returned to the armchair. She turned it to face the door so that she would not be caught unawares and settled to wait for the next development. But she felt drowsy. She shook her head in annoyance, wishing she had not eaten the food because she was always drowsy after meals. She dozed then woke with a start. Dozed again, woke with a jerk as the door opened.

It was Patrick. Good, she thought. He already knew her position, so they would not have to go through that again. She drew herself up to her full height in order to confront him.

'Your nipples are erect, Jan. That's a good sign. They're very nice too. Have you been playing with yourself?'

Jan flushed as red as the proverbial beetroot. She spluttered and stammered, put completely off her stride by his outrageous opening remark. It was some time before she regained enough poise to demand her clothes and her freedom, in that order. This time, she added, they had gone too far. She was definitely going to the police.

'Yes, I've been meaning to talk to you about your clothes,' he said.

'Don't talk about them,' she retorted bitingly. 'Just bring them.' That sounded firm enough to her.

'I can't,' he said. 'They've been locked up for the duration of your stay. They'll be returned when you leave. House rules, you understand. All of our guests have to wear uniform, which your clothes weren't. You really shouldn't be wearing even that poncho. You're quite overdressed, although I congratulate you on your ingenuity.'

Jan thought her ears were deceiving her. Over-dressed? Uniform? When she realised what he was implying, she paled. Surely he couldn't mean . . . No. Impossible.

He means stop stalling and get naked, dearie, Jan Two advised. So we can get down to the real business that much sooner.

Patrick crossed to the armchair as Jan was trying to think of what to do next. He took her hand and urged her to stand. Dazed, she did so automatically.

Awareness of where she was and of what he wanted returned when he unknotted her improvised belt and began to lift the poncho away from her body. 'No,' she wailed, clutching at the sheet. 'Let me go. You said you were going to let me go. Give me my clothes and let me go.'

'I never said I was going to let you go, Jan,' he said as he unwrapped her arms and lifted the poncho still further.

Jan felt the cool air on her bare stomach and legs and on her . . . This was not happening. Couldn't be. She fought to keep her improvised clothing, was dismayed to hear the sheet tear, feel the cool air caress her entire, *naked* body. She was naked in front of a stranger. A stranger who had promised, who had threatened, to teach her how to have sex . . . and . . . and other things.

Patrick continued, 'I, we, know it won't be easy, but believe me,' he said sincerely but lasciviously as

31

he admired her nude body, 'in the end you'll be glad you stayed.'

Jan was in her Venus de Milo pose again, shaking her head, her eyes wide and frightened. 'Let me go,' she repeated. Even to her own ears, that sounded more like a plea than a demand.

He shook his head. 'We won't give up on you, Jan. We think you're worth the effort. But we don't expect you to see that all at once. Like most new things, this will take a bit of getting used to. But if you'll just slip into those –' gesturing at the chains lying by the bed, '– I'll give you a tour of the campus and let you watch a demonstration which I believe will be informative,' he said uninformatively. 'You may even find it . . . stimulating. Do stop being difficult, please.'

Jan tried to cover herself, still shaking her head, no, no. Patrick shook his head sadly, with the air of a wise teacher faced with a promising but recalcitrant student. He picked up the leg irons and handcuff-belt and returned to Jan's side.

The jingle of the chain alerted her to his intentions, but she was no match for him. She was more unnerved than she realised by her ordeal and her nudity. And her strength was no match for his.

Patrick pulled her right arm away from her breasts and closed one of the cuffs around her wrist.

The click as it locked gave her new strength. 'No!' she shouted, trying to pull her arm away. But the cuff on her wrist was inescapable. Even as she fought, she felt her left arm pulled away from her sex, and the second cuff was locked around her other wrist. With her hands cuffed together Jan fought a losing battle with him as he pulled them irresistibly against her waist, and buckled the wide leather belt behind her back, out of her reach.

The struggle took place in a silence that seemed eerie when she thought of it later. She should have

32

been screaming at the top of her voice, but she had done no such thing. Later, she realised that screaming would have done no good. No one was going to come to her rescue. She was on her own. Belatedly, she thought she should have tried to use her hands to fight him off instead of just trying to cover herself. Now it was too late. She pulled strongly against the belt that held her cuffed hands against her belly. And made a discovery. Unlike the ropes that had bound her earlier, the steel handcuffs cut into her skin if she fought them. They fitted snugly around her wrists and prevented almost all movement. Certainly she could not cover her nakedness.

Jan was still struggling with the handcuffs when Patrick knelt to lock the leg irons onto her ankles. She tried to kick him, but he grasped her ankle and lifted her leg, threatening to topple her onto her back. As Jan fought to keep her balance, he closed the steel band around her left ankle. He kept hold of the chain that joined the leg irons. One tug would cause her to fall. He locked the other iron onto her right ankle and Jan was helpless once again, her ankles joined by a chain that allowed only very short steps. Kicking was definitely out of the question.

Looking up, Patrick grinned at her. 'That wasn't so terrible, was it?' he asked. And suddenly he ducked his head to plant a kiss on her mons veneris, perilously close to the place where, yesterday, her other captor had touched her – with those unexpectedly dire results.

'Oh!' she exclaimed in surprise. And then 'Oh' again as she tried to step back. The chain between her ankles prevented her. With her hands cuffed she could not push him away. The kiss went on, and Jan felt his tongue licking her and threatening to slide inside.

Patrick put both arms around her bottom, cupping her cheeks and holding her still as the intimate kiss went on *and on*. Jan tried to twist her hips away, but his hands tightened, holding her still. This time she felt his tongue slip into her sex, the tip finding what she guessed must be her clitoris. Jan felt the same *loosening* in her belly and thighs as she had felt in her kitchen when that man had . . .

'Oh!' she cried again, this time in astonishment as she felt the same *twinge* that had preceded yesterday's internal earthquake. 'Ohhhh.' This time it was a groan, a combination of dismay and anticipation.

It only took one lesson to teach you that, her alter ego said. Relax and enjoy it, she advised. You enjoyed it yesterday, didn't you? Practice, practice.

Jan saw herself in the mirror, a naked woman in chains with a man kneeling between her legs, kissing her cun . . . her sex. She moaned again, her knees loosening and thrusting her pelvis forward, offering her cun . . . sex to him. Jan tried to stiffen her knees, but couldn't keep them straight. She wondered what this would feel like if she were lying down, not having to struggle to stand and resist. 'Oh, ohhhhhhh, oh God!' Her body was going to betray her again. She couldn't stop herself from tumbling over that precipice. Didn't want to stop herself. Her thoughts whirled in confusion.

'See how easy it is?' Patrick said, raising his face to look into her downward glance. 'Just stay with us and you can do that anytime you want to, even if you're alone. But it's so much nicer to have help.'

'Don't . . . don't do this to me,' Jan groaned equivocally. Do I mean, don't keep on arousing me, or don't stop arousing me? she wondered. Then said, 'Please let me go,' weakly, pulling against her handcuffs.

Tugging, too, against the inclination of her newly aroused body. Her weak knees thrust her hips forward, offering her centre to his mouth. She swayed as she tried to stand straight. Patrick bent again to her crotch, kissing her crisp pubic hair, biting her, sliding his tongue inside to tease her clitoris. In her mind's eye Jan saw the devilish figure in the thigh-length boots and heard her alter ego urging her on: Good, innit? See what you've been missing all those years?

Jan thought she would faint. 'I'm going to fall down,' she groaned weakly. 'My legs . . . my legs won't . . . Please stop!'

'All right, if you insist,' Patrick said unexpectedly.

Jan felt a stab of dismay as he stood up. She hadn't expected him to stop, hadn't really wanted him to stop, had made the usual protest from habit, had expected, awaited with trepidation and eagerness, the internal fireworks she had first felt only a day ago.

Jan Two spoke to her again. Why couldn't you keep yer mouth shut, you stupid cow? Now look what you've done to us.

Jan felt the turmoil inside her: a mixture of regret and relief. Once again she felt as if her personality was split between the old, familiar, comfortable Jan and the devilish figure that inhabited a recess of her mind and would not go away.

She fought her way to the armchair, trying not to stagger. She didn't want Patrick to see how much he had moved her. Dignity, she thought, behave with dignity. One should never be a slut, nor look like one. Jan turned and collapsed into the chair. She would really rather have sat down slowly, but her weak knees gave way, and with her hands out of action she could not break her fall. So she collapsed.

'Was it that good for you?' Patrick asked.

Jan blushed and shook her head. He looked at her and shook his own head, not believing her.

'Think of that as merely the overture. The serious music starts tomorrow. We will begin fine-tuning your responses.'

Once again his audacity left her breathless. But it looked as if she was not going to be set free. She would go through the 'course' willy-nilly. She felt confused, divided against herself. But the deciding factors were locked around her wrists and ankles. She could not escape them. Catching sight of her naked body in the mirror, Jan looked quickly away. She looked down at the real thing, seeing her nakedness and the handcuffs and leg irons that accentuated it, and looked away from that too. The handcuffs held her hands down against her belly, with the result that her breasts were compressed between her upper arms. They looked as if she were offering them to him. She did not know where to look. Everything was new and alarming and embarrassing.

Exciting too, the inner voice remarked.

Patrick was looking steadily at her, which also unsettled her. She looked back at him, but could not meet his glance. She looked away again hurriedly, blushing a bright pink.

The uneasy silence was broken by the entrance of a nicely dressed young woman who looked vaguely familiar to Jan. Finally she placed her: she had come round the day before trying to sell double-glazing.

The young woman looked at Jan with a friendly smile. 'Hello. I'm Robin. I see you got here all right. I hope you enjoy your stay as much as I'm enjoying mine. Just dropped in to see how you were getting on. You look much nicer today. Must dash now. I'm on in a few minutes. See you later.' She paused only long enough to hand Patrick a riding crop. Jan recognised

36

it at once, and wondered if the demonstration would include horses, or if the crop was intended for her.

Jan felt bewildered and frightened and weak in the knees all at once. She was beginning to accept that they weren't going to let her go, and that they had gone to a good deal of trouble to get her here. She tried to stand, as if somehow she should confront this on her feet, but she could not get up easily without her hands. Patrick came over and helped her to her feet. Jan blushed and trembled, and he led the way out of the room. He left the door open. He motioned Jan to precede him down the hall. 'I want to see how you move,' he told her, covering her once more with confusion and blushes. Taking short, careful steps because of the leg irons, Jan moved ahead of him, feeling his gaze. She felt fluttery and weak with apprehension, moving jerkily, as if she was in one of those nightmares in which she tried to escape something dreadful but her legs would no longer obey her.

Suddenly Jan felt a sharp sting across her bottom. She yelped and almost tripped on her leg irons. There was a loud smack as he lashed her bottom again. She half-turned to see Patrick draw back his arm for another blow. She flinched as it landed on her hip, crying out in pain and surprise. He motioned her to go on, and he drove her before him, lashing her bottom and the backs of her legs as they went. She wanted to run, to get away from this terrible pain, but her leg irons wouldn't allow that.

Every time she turned to plead with him to stop he struck her harder. By the time they reached the stairs at the other end of the hall Jan was weeping and pleading. Her bottom and the backs of her thighs were on fire. She wanted to cover them, protect them from the lash, but her hands were held uncompromisingly to her waist in front of her.

Finally he stopped. 'Did you enjoy that, Jan?' he asked.

At first she couldn't believe her ears. Enjoy *that*? She shook her head, the tears running down her cheeks. 'Please don't hit me again,' she begged.

'Just testing. Some of our guests like a touch of the whip. We never know for sure until we test them.'

She could not believe that anyone would enjoy being whipped. She shook her head.

'They do, you know. Maybe you'll see later today, or tomorrow. And we will test you once or twice a week to see if you develop a taste for it. Robin, for instance, positively loves it. She claims she comes like a bomb when she's being lashed.'

All she heard was the threat of further tests. 'Please, no! Please don't. It hurts too much. Oh God, it hurts!'

'You needn't make up your mind now, Jan. But let's get the demonstration going. You need to see what the possibilities are. We're a little short on demonstrators this week, but we'll make do.' Patrick pointed to the stairs, and Jan began to descend slowly and carefully, taking short steps, putting both feet on each step. A fall without hands to break it would be serious.

Her skin felt as if it were burning where he had struck her. Jan could not believe that women actually liked being beaten, but she had seen pictures of it in Sam's books. Did he want to whip her? Is that what he did with those . . . those women she knew he was seeing. Jan imagined him whipping Robin. What would *she* do? Then he was whipping her. No, it was too much. Sam wasn't like that. Yet there were those pictures, the ones he kept secret even from her. Because you wouldn't allow him to touch your body, Jan Two interjected. He has to take what he can find.

Suppose, Jan thought, he decided to take up with one of his paramours and left me?

It'd be your own fault, Jan Two said. Spread your legs and live a little.

Jan pressed her thighs tightly together as she descended those endless stairs, not wholly for fear of a fall. He was right behind her with that dreadful riding crop. God, she wished she were dressed, or that she could at least cover her nakedness with her hands. Her cheeks flamed as she imagined Patrick behind her, watching her. He could see every detail of her body and she couldn't prevent him from staring, or worse.

Jan Two, smiling sardonically, wondered how bad that worse could be. She conjured up images of Jan impaled on a huge cock, the shaft deep inside her, writhing and gasping as she had orgasm after orgasm.

Jan blushed at her own immodest thoughts and at the way they roused her libido and weakened her knees. Her riotous thoughts and weak knees almost made her fall. She grasped frantically at the handrail, her chains forcing her to grab it with both hands. She stood for a moment regaining her poise and balance. But her breath was faster now, her naked breasts rising and falling. And that was not wholly attributable to her near-fall. Her heart hammering in her chest, Jan finally reached the bottom. Gratefully she held onto the newel post with her hands, as a drowning person will clutch at anything to save herself. Am I drowning? she asked herself breathlessly. Am I going to be engulfed by a sudden tide of pleasure like yesterday?

In novels, she knew, women were swept away by sudden uncontrollable passion. But not her. How could anyone be so . . . well, so infatuated, like those girls in novels? By now she was hopelessly confused.

She couldn't recover her poise. Jan Two snickered. Live, she said. There are plenty of men around who'd love to grab you and save you from drowning.

Patrick guided her to a large room that took up almost half of the ground floor, as near as Jan could judge. Another woman was already there. Jan wondered briefly if she were going to be forced into a three-in-a-bed lesbian orgy. Perhaps, helpless as she was, Jan was to be the target of their attentions. She shuddered. But Patrick had spoken of a 'demonstration'. She was to 'watch and learn'. She was to be a spectator only – this time. Jan wanted to flee, but he had shut the door. And locked it. She wondered if there were any doors in this place that didn't lock.

Three

She looked at the other woman, her fellow captive. A 'student' like herself, she assumed. Next to her own nudity, the other woman's costume, though extremely provocative by any standards, made her seem positively well-dressed. She gave Jan a grimace which was probably intended to be a smile of greeting. Jan noticed that her mouth was open wide. Why does she keep it that way, she wondered. The other woman did not wave. Could not wave. Like Jan, she wore leg irons and a leather waist belt, but her hands were cuffed behind her back. With a start Jan recognised her fellow captive as Robin.

Jan had seen her upstairs only minutes ago. Somehow she had gotten down here and into those ... clothes, Jan thought, for want of a better term. How had she done all this so quickly? Then Jan realised with a kind of dull shock that there must have been someone to help her. To chain her. The other man. Her heart sank. Patrick would be hard enough to escape from, but two men? And suppose they decided to share her?

Patrick, observing the two of them, saw her shock and wonder. 'Robin', he said, gesturing to the redhead, 'is here for a refresher course. What would, in more orthodox institutions, be called post-graduate work. She's just back from a tour around several areas spotting other prospective students and, er, distracting them for a few vital minutes.'

Robin managed to look guilty without actually looking repentant. She looked, in fact, like someone who would go on distracting prospective 'students' for as long as Patrick or one of his colleagues wanted her to. Then Patrick added, 'Robin is gagged, otherwise she might have more to say. Perhaps you can get better acquainted later.'

'Gagged?' Jan asked. 'How?' Her curiosity overcame her fear. She moved nearer to Robin, who obligingly turned so that the inside of her mouth was visible. Jan peered closely but could not see much beyond a stainless steel rod inserted vertically in her mouth.

Patrick called this a 'dental gag', explaining that there 'is a plate that covers the roof of the mouth and is hinged to the lower plate that covers the tongue. The rod holds them apart and keeps her mouth open. Behind the front teeth, at the top and bottom, is a curved plate to hold the whole thing in Robin's mouth. Once the rod is extended and locked, she can't push it out.'

Robin obligingly turned this way and that as he pointed out the features of the device. She seemed proud of her strange accessory. Jan was fascinated and horrified, but she could not look away. 'But,' she objected, 'that's like an animal. Like a bit to control a horse.' She had never imagined until now how a horse must feel with a bit in its mouth. She did not like to think about wearing the same gag herself, but she guessed that she soon would.

'Some women like it,' Patrick told her. 'Robin, for instance. Others prefer a more conventional gag like the one you wore yesterday.'

Robin made noises which were probably meant to signify agreement.

As Patrick spoke, Jan looked more closely at her fellow 'student', confirming her earlier estimate of her age: about twenty-five, not much older than Leslie, in fact. Jan wondered with a pang what her daughter was doing. Did Leslie know what had happened to her? It was strange to think of the rest of the world going about its business while she was a prisoner in this 'school', naked and in chains and about to undergo a sexual 're-education' against her inclinations. It sounded like something the Vietnamese did to their former enemies, slightly less unpleasant than executing them.

She brought herself back to the present. Robin, alert, pretty, with short-cropped red hair that fitted her head like a helmet. Robin, wearing leg irons, her hands cuffed behind her back, gagged with that steel device. So normal, so pretty, so eagerly awaiting something which horrified Jan. Was this young woman crazy, or was she?

Now this looks interesting, Jan Two interjected. How'd you like to dress up like her? Eye-catching, eh?

Yes. That was one way to describe Robin's costume. Jan could hardly think of it as clothes. Robin wore a tight red satin bra with openings that left her nipples exposed. Her pert breasts were held up and out, and her nipples poked invitingly from the middle of the cups. The bra was too tight, compressing her flesh and emphasising her cleavage. Jan clearly saw the veins leading down to Robin's erect nipples: imagined the blood making them stand up so prominently.

With a curious detachment Jan thought the detail . . . sexy and provocative. Inviting touch. Jan felt a curious urge to touch those nipples. She had never

43

studied her own nipples when they were erect. If only her hands were free ... Jan gave herself a mental shake. What was she thinking of? What was happening?

Jan Two smirked at her. Jan One blushed and looked away, down, anywhere but at those nipples jutting into space. And saw her own. They were erect, the veins in her breasts pulsing, sending blood to her breasts, making them hot and heavy. A curious tingling spread from her nipples to her belly, to her ... sex.

Jan looked at Robin. The young woman wore a suspender belt of matching red satin, and long stockings that came almost to her crotch. The shortest of elastic suspenders held them up. This was how Sam had once wanted her to dress, and she had flatly refused. Seeing how it looked on another woman, Jan was suddenly envious.

Robin's mons veneris was shaved bare, allowing the plump mound to stand out with unusual prominence, almost as if she were offering herself to whomever might pass by. With a start Jan noticed a silver chain that tethered Robin to a ring in the wall. The chain looped from the ring, over the sheer nylon of her stockings, and vanished between her legs. Surely she can't be chained by her sex, Jan thought, appalled at the idea. But she was.

Patrick lifted the chain and tugged on it, showing beyond doubt that it was somehow fastened in the young woman's crotch.

'Robin likes body piercing. In fact she's come back for a bit more this time. This chain leads to the rings in her labia. Show Jan, my dear.'

Robin obediently spread her legs as far as the leg irons allowed, and Patrick lifted the chain to give Jan a clear view of a series of delicate, shining steel rings that had been somehow passed through her labia, four on each side. They were held together by a curved bar of the same material that passed through each ring and was locked to the chain by a small, gleaming padlock. The bar looked as if it had been made specially. Lovingly, Jan would have said, if such things could be fashioned in love, especially to follow the shape of the young woman's body as it curved away to the secret place between her legs. The alien look of the steel next to Robin's bare mound was strangely disturbing. Such a contrast between hardness and softness.

'The bar has a ball at the other end to prevent it from passing through the rings. It can be fastened with the padlock at either end. One has merely to thread it through the rings in the desired direction. And then lock it,' Patrick added.

Jan shivered, not entirely in horror. How would such hardness feel next to her softness, her secret place? How would it feel to have her sex locked up, beyond Sam's reach, and her own? The thought was jarring. Although Jan never touched herself there, the idea that this part of her body could be locked away from her was disturbing.

As if reading her mind, Patrick said, 'It is a chastity belt, so long as the wearer has no access to the keys. Her owner gave them to me when he dropped her off, and I will return them when she leaves. He and I are the only men who can unlock her sexual riches. And she so loves to be unlocked and fucked. Don't you, my dear?'

Robin nodded enthusiastically. 'Ehhhhs,' she said around her gag. Jan could see that she was speaking the truth. But she could not understand Robin's liking for being owned in that way, and concluded that her sexual desires were obviously different from, and greater than, Jan's own.

Jan Two remarked that it was not very hard to have greater desire than zero.

In reply to the taunts of the inner voice, Jan found herself thinking, *I do* have sexual desires. The response both shocked and surprised her. She examined it again, and found a certain eagerness that was new. Nothing like Robin's unabashed lust, she reassured herself. More a quivering, tactile curiosity.

Progress, Jan Two observed.

But the internal split was disturbing, hinting at things Jan would rather not have known. And then Patrick touched Robin's nipples lightly. Obviously used to being handled, the young woman shivered, reminding Jan of a dog's quiver of pleasure when it is caressed. She herself hadn't quivered the day before. Had she?

Shuddered in delight, is more like it, Jan Two observed.

Once more Jan looked at her own nipples. They were still undeniably erect, the veins feeding them clearly visible under the skin of her out-thrust breasts, just as Robin's were. Jan had never paid such particular attention to her nipples before. Her hands stirred restlessly in the handcuffs, as if they would like to touch those taut buttons.

Instead it was Patrick who touched her nipples, and Jan jerked in surprise. Had he read her mind, she wondered. She tried unsuccessfully not to think about her nipples. She tried to move away but Patrick followed, leaving Robin's taut nipples. Robin looked disappointed, but she was unable to do anything about it. The chain from her crotch came up tight and she could not move any further.

Patrick had both hands on Jan now, one cupping her right breast and the other teasing her left nipple, pinching and rubbing until it stood erect and, oh

God, so sensitive. Electric tingles burst from her nipple to her sex. Jan suddenly stopped trying to escape the touch, without, she hoped, indicating that she wanted more. The touch was both arousing and reassuring, as though he wanted her to know that he appreciated her body. *My* body, Jan thought in surprise. *My body.*

Suddenly Jan realised that this was the first time anyone had actually touched her naked body in months. When her abductors had aroused her the day before, though bound and gagged, she had been fully clothed. This time she was in chains, equally helpless. And naked. It made a difference. She could do nothing to prevent Patrick touching her wherever he liked. The part of her that did not want to stop him was growing stronger. If it continued to grow, Jan could foresee a time when it would overwhelm the old familiar Jan she had lived with all her life. And then what would become of her?

But that was later. This was now, and Patrick had moved behind her, from where he could put his arms around her, hold her, prevent her escape or retreat. And from where he could use both hands to cup her breasts, now oddly hot and heavy and throbbing. From where he could use the fingers of both hands to tease and pinch and rub her swollen nipples and send delicious tingles to her sex, promising so much more now that she was naked to his touch.

Jan blushed at her delicious thoughts, closing her eyes in shame but making no further attempts to escape. Where could she go, naked and in chains? Could she open locked doors? Could she run from the house where people would stare and point and laugh at her? No. Better stay here, where her strange condition was normal. No one here would laugh and point at her. So, rationalising, she allowed Patrick to handle her, fondle her, arouse her, weaken her knees and her will. And make her feel so dreadfully good in her belly and breasts and cunt.

The word slipped past her mental guard, but Jan was almost past caring. What's in a word? What did it matter if she called it her sex or her cunt? She was forgetting the need to resist and how good it felt to become an animal, pawed, handled, caressed. Those tingles coursing through her body.

Jan opened her eyes. Robin was staring at her, the chain tight across her thigh, indenting the skin and the nylon stocking as she strained toward the older woman in the throes of passion. Robin seemed eager to be in Jan's place. But having an audience, even a silent one, was like a dash of cold water to Jan. She thrashed weakly in Patrick's arms, moaning, 'No. Please, no. Please let me go.' Patrick sensed the change at once, and he released Jan's breasts, though he continued to hold her upright until her legs were under control once more. He leaned down to whisper in her ear, for her only, 'That was a good beginning, Jan. Next time we'll take you even further. Be patient. It won't happen all in a day.'

There was no disappointment or reproach in his words, and Jan felt oddly grateful, as she had done when one of her teachers had offered her encouragement. Yes, next time she'd do better.

No. What was she thinking? 'Let me go, please! I don't want to be here.'

'I'm afraid we can't let you go, Jan. We have so much work to do yet. We've only just begun. Be patient. We'll get there in the end. Are you ready to stand on your own now?'

By way of answer Jan stiffened her knees and stood upright, and he removed his supporting arms. Jan felt oddly disappointed at that, but could not admit it.

Patrick steered her over toward Robin, who had never taken her eyes off them. Robin strained still at the chain that joined her cunt to the ring in the wall. Jan felt more comfortable now with the word, now that she did not apply it to her own body. Patrick bent down to kiss Robin's wide-open mouth. Jan was shocked. How could she want to kiss someone when her mouth was held wide open like that? But she apparently did, tilting her head slightly sideways so that her mouth could fit more closely to his, moaning in her throat as the one-way kiss went on and on. Jan was miffed. Not two minutes ago she had been in his arms and in the throes of her own passion. Now he was kissing this other woman right in front of her, and she was making the same sounds that Jan had made.

Robin clearly did not care what Jan felt. She was shameless, Jan decided. If her hands had been free, Jan knew the young woman would have been embracing Patrick.

Not that you'd want to do that yourself, would you? asked Jan Two.

Jan tugged unconsciously at her handcuffs, and found them as unyielding as ever.

At length the kiss ended, and Patrick stood back. Jan saw that Robin was breathing rapidly, almost panting. Her breasts, inside that too-tight bra, were rising and falling in an agitated fashion, and her nipples, poking out through the openings in the cups, were taut and erect. Jan again saw a whole network of veins leading down Robin's breasts to her nipples. The veins were swollen, standing out plainly just beneath the skin as they fed blood to the young woman's nipples.

Jan glanced down at her own breasts, noticing the same veins, seeing how they made her own nipples

49

erect. And they were becoming erect now, again, just from her staring at them. She quickly looked away, and saw Patrick watching her. Jan was furious and ashamed at being seen comparing her breasts to Robin's.

'Robin is here for a pair of nipple rings to be fitted in a day or two. That's one of the things I want you to see, so you'll be familiar with the process when we come to fit yours.' He spoke matter-of-factly.

Jan could hardly believe her ears. They were going to 'fit' nipple rings to Robin? And to her? No. Not possible. She shook her head weakly. 'No,' she whimpered, looking again at her nipples and trying to imagine what they would look like with rings through them. 'No, please, no.' She felt faint.

'Don't worry about it now,' Patrick told her.

How can I not worry when he's planning to 'fit' rings to my nipples? Jan looked down at them again. They seemed very vulnerable.

But Patrick had turned back to Robin. He kissed her taut nipples before he unfastened her chain from the ring in the wall and led her toward a workbench which Jan hadn't noticed. Looking at it now, she saw that it resembled a tool cabinet in a workshop. She shivered in dread and fascination as she imagined what 'tools' it might contain.

Robin followed Patrick on her lead, taking the same short, careful steps in her leg irons as Jan had done. She seemed eager, unafraid. Jan was drawn closer as if she too were on a lead, the chain joining her ankles clinking on the floor.

Patrick helped Robin to sit on the edge of the workbench, her legs hanging down in those long red stockings. The handcuffs held her shoulders back, and that too-tight bra offered her breasts to Patrick. He bent to kiss her nipples again, and Robin moaned softly as his lips brushed them. When he took one into his mouth, she shuddered and groaned, the sound coming out hollowly around her gag. Jan could not look away, though all her instincts urged her to avert her gaze. *Oh God, what's happening to me?*

Nothing like what's happening to Robin, Jan Two sniggered. Like to swap places with her? Go on, ask Patrick to do you instead.

Jan got as far as opening her mouth before she realised how she would appear. And what could she say? 'Please, please, leave her, fuck *me*, make *me* come, drive me wild, shove your cock into my . . . my cunt. Bite my nipples, fondle my breasts. Please.' No. She would not do it. Never in a thousand years.

But maybe in the next few days, Jan Two suggested.

Jan gazed in horrified fascination as the arousal of the younger woman went on. Patrick said something to Robin which penetrated the haze of lust. She nodded her head weakly. Then to Jan he said, 'Robin thinks you'd get a lot more from this if you had something to occupy you pleasurably. She has agreed to wait a bit so I can fix you up. Don't you think that's generous?'

'Fix me up?' Jan asked weakly. 'What do you mean to do to me?'

'Nothing final. Just give you a lollipop to suck on before I do the job on Robin.'

Dear God, was she going to have to watch him screwing her? No. She would close her eyes. Look away. Ignore the sounds that were sure to go with the act. And did he think that if she saw another woman being had then she would want the same? He did not know her at all if he thought that.

Jan Two snickered.

51

But now he was coming toward her. Was that a leer? What does he see when he looks at me, she wondered.

Naked prey in chains, Jan Two said. One who has already abandoned half her scruples and is about to have the other half severely strained.

Jan noticed the bulge in his trousers for the first time. For me, or for Robin? It looked huge. Threatening. He steered Jan toward the workbench. She went because she couldn't do anything else. Struggling was useless. She watched helplessly as he opened drawers and cupboards, laying out a selection of equipment which made her heart sink. A short chain with swivel snaps at each end. Two black rubber cups, nipple shaped. It didn't take too much imagination to guess where they would go, but why was he going to cover her nipples? She should have felt relief, but she did not. The next object banished all hope of relief.

Jan had never seen one in actuality, but she had no trouble recognising the hard knobbly dildo which Patrick laid on the workbench. Dear God, was that for her? She clamped her thighs tightly together. She could never accommodate all that. Could she? And what would it feel like to have that inside her?

Relax and find out, Jan Two suggested. You might like it.

Jan shuddered. Never.

Very soon, said Jan Two.

Patrick seemed to think she would have no trouble. He looked at Jan with a smile as he laid the dildo on the worktop. The last item he selected was a bottle with a screw cap and a brush. Jan recognised the spirit gum that actors used for attaching moustaches and wigs. She had used it herself in Little Theatre productions in Godalming. It seemed so out of place here. This wasn't the Little Theatre. This was really happening. To her.

Patrick beckoned her closer. Jan shook her head and backed away. He picked up the riding crop, raising it as he came toward her. Jan felt her resistance melt at the threat. She stopped, and then moved toward him, slowly, never taking her eyes off the whip. When she stopped beside the worktop, Patrick laid the crop aside, but near to hand.

He picked up one of the rubber cups, holding it by the part that would cover her nipples. He applied spirit gum to the inside surface and grasped her left breast while he fitted the cup to it. As she had expected, it covered her nipple and areola. He rotated it, pressing to remove air bubbles and make firm contact with her breast. It was not unpleasant but, given the circumstances, it was threatening. She watched him prepare the second cup, and apply it. When both were in place, Jan looked down at her breasts. The nipples were now covered, but somehow they looked more erotic than when bare. She had just discovered that partially covered flesh can be incredibly provocative. She blushed, looking helplessly at her breasts. She wriggled her shoulders, but could not dislodge the cups.

'They won't come off, Jan. Never fear. You'll be modestly covered throughout the exercise.'

Jan thought that 'modestly' was not the right word. She looked at the dildo. *That* was not going to be so easy. She clamped her thighs together.

Patrick clipped the short chain to the front of her waist belt. 'Open your legs, Jan,' he said quietly.

She looked up at him, pleading. And she kept her thighs pressed tightly together. She shook her head, no, no.

Patrick dropped the chain. It hung down past her knees, silvery, like a gleaming snake. He picked up the whip and waited for a moment. When it became clear that she was not going to obey, he stepped behind her.

Jan tried to turn to face him, but the leg irons slowed her movements. He raised the whip and struck her across the bottom. It wasn't just a warning.

'Ahhhhrrgggh!' Jan screamed. He struck her several more times, making her cry out in pain. Jan stumbled under the blows, trying to escape the punishment, but Patrick was remorseless. Finally, sobbing, she spread her legs apart and stood waiting for that thing to invade her cu . . . sex. She closed her eyes, squeezing the tears from between the eyelids. She might not be able to escape, but she would not, definitely would not, look at herself as she was stuffed.

She felt Patrick reach between her legs, his hand brushing the inner surfaces of her thighs as he pulled the chain back behind her. There was a pause. She knew he was picking up the dildo, and she braced herself for the penetration. Jan had never seen anything that big, let alone imagined such a thing inside her. Other women had told her of their dreams of well-hung studs, and of the exquisite pleasure of being filled full by their cocks. Jan had squirmed and tried not to blush. Innocence was one thing. Betraying it was more serious.

When the hard rubber tip brushed her lips, Jan could no longer keep her eyes closed. She looked down past her breasts with their pert rubber caps, and saw Patrick's hand emerging between her legs from behind. The monstrous shaft was aimed at her secret centre. His other hand spread her open, and Jan shuddered at the touch. But the touch was surprisingly gentle, almost pleasant. Yet the feeling as the shaft was pushed into her was alarming. The knobs bumped her clitoris, sending stabs of electricity to her belly and sex. The shaft slid inside her easily. She was wet. So wet.

Jan sighed in pleasure, trying to resist it, to tell herself that this was just a piece of rubber. The rubber might have no feeling, but her cunt did. It was feeling stuffed full, as still more dildo was pushed in. Jan could not believe she had already accepted so much, and when she saw how much was left, and how thick it was, she moaned, no, no, once again, trying to tighten herself to prevent the invasion.

As countless other women have discovered, once the thing was inside no amount of tightening can prevent further penetration. Her hands twisted in the handcuffs as she strained to reach downward to her crotch and stop this awful thing from sliding into her body. She could not reach it. Jan thought of closing her thighs again, but the whip marks on her bottom still stung. She knew Patrick would not hesitate to use the whip again.

Finally it was all inside her. Jan was surprised that it all fitted. She felt stuffed full, and every time she made even the slightest move, she could feel the alien presence inside her as a weight and a pressure and a sliding, a rather pleasant touch against her button, as she had heard her mother call the clitoris.

Jan stood with her head down and her legs spread while Patrick pulled the chain through the ring on the outer end of her dildo. He pulled the chain tightly up into her crotch and between her arse cheeks. Jan winced as it went up into her central crack but could do nothing to prevent it. He fastened the chain to the back of her belt, and she knew that she would never be able to get the dildo out without help. At the very least she would have to have her hands free.

'Now you've got your own chastity belt,' Patrick said, standing up and resting a hand on her shoulder.

'How do you like it?' When Jan did not reply, he turned her to face a large mirror on the wall.

Jan stubbornly refused to look at herself. Nevertheless, she felt even more helpless and more provocative than before. It was the guilty knowledge of what was inside her, and of the pert rubber caps over her nipples, that made her feel suddenly more naked than before. When she saw the bulge in his trousers, Jan blushed hotly and tried to look away.

She caught sight of herself in the mirror and was transfixed by the woman who stared back at her. The handcuffs pulled her hands down and together, so that her breasts were confined between her upper arms and forced together. Her cleavage was exaggerated lewdly, and the rubber caps made her look like something out of one of the horrid magazines she knew Sam collected. The chain bisected her mons veneris, indenting the flesh before disappearing between her legs. She could see no external sign of the dildo, but she could feel every inch of it inside her.

Patrick, his trousers bulging, remarked that she looked handsome in her nakedness and her chains. Jan blushed and looked at herself again. The chains *did* make her more appealing, even in her own eyes. And they certainly made her helpless, absolving her of responsibility for what might happen. She shifted her weight from foot to foot, feeling the dildo inside her, and came perilously close to admitting that this was . . . nice.

Jan Two gave her wholehearted approval to the proceedings. Feels good, doesn't it? But wouldn't it feel better if it were the real thing inside us?

Jan did not immediately reject the idea out of hand, as she would have done only a day ago. Instead she experimented with the dildo, making it shift inside her with, she hoped, movements that were imperceptible to the eyes of others.

Patrick turned her around so she could see herself from the back, holding up a smaller mirror for her. The chain emerged from between her arse cheeks, looking exactly like one of those thong things Sam had sometimes wanted her to wear, though he had not suggested it be made of chain. Fetching, she thought in another unguarded moment, dividing her bottom neatly and making it look more naked than before. Just as the rubber caps did to her breasts. Jan clamped down on the thought, but not before Jan Two had remarked on how alive and exciting she looked.

Jan looked at herself for rather longer than she realised, secretly liking the effect. The steel bracelets on her wrists and ankles made someone else responsible for what would happen – was happening – to her. Even the red marks across her full bottom made her more appealing. If only they didn't hurt so much . . .

Every time she moved – and even when she did not – Jan was conscious of being stuffed fuller than she had ever been. The dildo reminded her constantly of its presence inside her, beyond her control or removal, something put there by her captor. But what is he doing? Oh my God, he's taking off his clothes. All of them. And he has an . . . erection, so big. When he was naked Jan still stared at his cock, standing stiffly erect. She was mesmerised. Was he going to make her suck *that*? She felt her throat close.

Robin looked hungrily at it, her wide-open mouth giving her the look of a child being offered a treat. She squirmed on the table top, spreading her legs as far as the leg irons allowed. Jan saw her pussy rings quite clearly now, bright steel against her bare, shaved cunt. (That word. Why not? So natural.) The bar that held her closed gleamed, and the silvery chain hung down between her legs. In the abstract,

Jan thought, it looked so attractive. But it was the thought of having those rings through her own labia, or her nipples, that was so frightening. Robin didn't seem to mind, though. Could it be all that bad? Jan shook her head to get rid of these subversive thoughts. But they did not go away.

The dildo heavy inside her, Jan stood rooted in the place where Patrick had left her. In truth there was nowhere to go. She could move about the room, or sit on one of the wooden chairs against the walls, or join Robin on the workbench. Patrick seemed to have forgotten about her. He turned to Robin, who squirmed. Her gaze was fixed on his cock.

Patrick unlocked her leg irons, dropping them with a clink and a thud to the floor. He stood between her legs, and once more kissed Robin on her open mouth. He rested his hands on her thighs, caressing her through the stockings. She moaned deep in her throat as the kiss drew out. Jan felt her pulses hammering in her head as she imagined receiving such a wide-open kiss as that, one she could not resist. What, she wondered, would it feel like to be kissed so deeply while one was utterly helpless, as both she and Robin were? Pink arousal greeted the thought. She felt her breasts tingling, and looking down noticed that the veins that fed her nipples were standing out once again, appearing halfway down her breasts then disappearing beneath the two neat rubber caps that covered her nipples.

Patrick was standing close to Robin, his body between her thighs. Jan guessed that his erection was lying against the younger woman's belly, its entry to her cunt blocked only by her 'chastity belt', as Patrick had described it. He bent his knees and rubbed himself against Robin.

'Ummmmmmmm,' she sighed.

Jan stood to one side, looking at Patrick and Robin entwined. Shame and fascination and, yes, a certain envy, kept her rooted to the spot. The dildo inside her shifted suggestively and her vaginal muscles tightened at the sight of their imminent coupling. But how was he going to penetrate Robin if he didn't remove the bar that held her labia closed? Where was the key? Patrick broke off the one-sided kiss as if she had spoken her thought aloud. Robin was panting heavily, her nipples erect and her breasts rising and falling within that too-tight bra from her rapid breathing. A low moan came from her wide-open mouth. Jan wondered what she would have said if she had not been gagged.

Patrick searched the pockets of his discarded trousers. Robin's face lit up when he produced the necessary key. Even Jan knew what was coming next, and she felt her internal muscles contract again involuntarily around her dildo at the thought. Patrick inserted the key in the tiny padlock and turned it. He laid the lock to one side and withdrew the bar from her labial rings. The shining chain fell to the floor.

Jan divided her attention between his erection and the opening of Robin's cunt. She squirmed closer to the edge of the table, lifting her legs and locking them around his waist as soon as he was close enough. Jan saw him reach between their bodies, and shuddered, knowing he was going to guide his cock into the eager Robin. She blushed at the thought.

Robin's loud moan signalled the moment of penetration. Her body relaxed against Patrick's and she pulled him closer with her legs. It seemed the ultimate act of welcome from a woman to a man. Jan was abashed. She had never seen that, let alone done it.

She expected him to begin, well, fucking, Robin at once. The euphemism she normally used, 'making

love to', did not seem to apply here. It was not strong
enough for what was happening, for this threatening
room, for their chains. Jan was out of her depth,
linguistically and emotionally, as she stared in fascination at the couple before her. Patrick reached to
one side, and Jan jerked as the dildo inside her came
suddenly alive, vibrating and buzzing. She let out a
yip of surprise and reddened as Patrick looked
directly at her with an impish grin. He turned back to
his partner, embracing Robin and beginning a rhyth-
mic in-and-out thrust which she matched at once,
apparently with the ease of long practice. Jan would
have been amazed at the ease with which they fitted
together if she had not been so distracted by the
dildo.

She looked away, her hands straining against the
handcuffs to reach her crotch and pluck the vibrating
plug from her cunt. This was monstrous. The thing
was going to . . . *arouse* her, and she was powerless to
stop it. It was doing so already. Her cunt was tingling
in the newly familiar way. Even as she struggled, her
gaze wandered back to the nearby couple. That sight,
and Robin's evident enjoyment of her fucking, excited Jan even more. She felt a sudden rippling of the
muscles of her vagina, and she knew that she was lost.
She was going to come.

As if to seal her fate, she felt a sudden tingling and
pricking in her nipples. With horror Jan realised that
there were some sort of needles inside the cups, and
that her stiffening nipples were in contact with them
and producing that alien sensation. The realisation
made her nipples grow even more erect, increasing the
pricking sensation and sending urgent messages to
her cunt. Which replied with its own urgency. The
combined sensations were irresistible, and Jan knew
with a dull, helpless certainty that her rebellious body

was going to make her shame herself again, before witnesses.

Robin's hollow, inarticulate, cries were now loud in her ears. Jan could not keep her gaze away from the coupled figures on the worktop. She looked aside – tore her glance away would be more a more accurate description – but couldn't stop herself from looking back again with horrified fascination. And envy. Their evident enjoyment of each other combined with the sensations from her breasts and cunt to make her frantic. Jan tried desperately to think of something else. Anything else. If only. Dear God, she couldn't help herself. She couldn't think of anything besides the couple fucking one another and the vibrating thing inside her cunt. She felt herself being pumped to the brink of orgasm. And her breasts felt as if they were being pierced by hundreds of tiny needles, and it all felt so *good*. She had never expected this. 'Oh,' she whimpered as her cunt contracted involuntarily, squeezing the thick, uncompromising dildo inside her. The ripple grew to a pulse that swept over her, threatened to sweep her away. Yet another pulse came over her, stronger, deeper. Jan tried to stifle a moan. Failed. Blushed hotly. Her body was going to shame her again. And she couldn't stop it. She tried. Fought her body for control but lost more ground with each stab from the dildo. She cried out loudly when she knew she had lost the battle. Her cries joined Robin's so that she was unable to say for sure who cried the loudest, who enjoyed their penetration most. Robin's eyes were closed in ecstasy, her body moving in time with Patrick's thrusts. Jan's eyes were open, staring at them and at their fucking.

It's a whirlpool, a trap to suck you down to their level, the old Jan warned. But Jan Two would not be denied her moment of triumph. She urged Jan to let everything go, to let the pulse sweep her away as Patrick and Robin were swept away to the land where forbidden pleasures were allowed and hidden desires gratified and mundane consequences were completely ignored.

And all the while Jan was sliding into the swirling waters, dizzy, her resistance giving way again to the insistent throbbing of the thing inside her cunt, the throbbing in her head, the beating of her pulse.

And then she was lost, suddenly, more suddenly than she would have dreamed possible, and, oh God, more thoroughly than the last time. She moaned loudly in surrender, could not fight back the next orgasm. She could feel it building up in her belly, could feel the signals racing between her tormented nipples and her engorged clitoris. Robin cried out with her next orgasm, and her cries of delight drove Jan over the edge and into her own.

She doubled at the waist, staggering with the force of it. She would have fallen if she had not backed into the wall. Her knees were weak, and she was having trouble standing. She slid down the wall until she was squatting on the floor, her ankles held close together by the leg irons but her knees and thighs spread wide. Her hips were pumping backward and forward. She bent at the waist over her captive hands, moaning and shaking as she came. Her pose, could she have seen it, was provocative in the extreme. Her bent head and widespread thighs appeared to invite penetration. The chain stretching tightly through her crotch gleamed softly, disappearing up behind her. The butt of the dildo was clearly visible in her pussy. Erotic. Exciting. A woman in helpless rut, moaning with desire and pleasure. Jan crouched, shuddering as wave after wave of hot pleasure swept through her. She crouched, in pleasure, for ages.

Only when her legs felt cramped did she slide further down until her bottom touched the floor with a bump. She straightened her legs before her and leaned back against the wall. The glorious feeling from between her thighs shook her again. Her hips jerked again swiftly, involuntarily, up and down under the power of it. The rational part of her mind, the old Jan, was shocked at the image of herself making love to the dildo so deep inside her, even as she strove to continue, to prolong, the pleasure it gave her. Her breasts stung and throbbed as the needles pricked her nipples. She moaned, closing her eyes, twisting her head from side to side as the next wave of pleasure shook her.

She had never been a screamer, but she was close to that point now, moaning loudly and continuously. Her body was beyond control, squirming on the floor and driving the dildo deeper into her cunt. She was hardly aware of Patrick and Robin. Her attention had shrunk to her pussy. Scruples and restraint were abandoned, the habits of a lifetime swept away. Her body, so long under strict control, was having its revenge. And Jan wanted more. More lust, she said later, trying to shock herself back into the old ways and failing. Jan sat against the wall, shaken by her orgasms, moaning and whimpering, struggling not to scream and betray herself to the world. An eternity later she became aware that the vibrations from the dildo had stopped, and the stinging in her nipples had lessened. She opened her eyes and saw that she was alone in the room. Robin and Patrick had gone and she was alone with her rebellious body and her tumbling thoughts. Had Robin had her nipples pierced yet? Jan wondered idly. Maybe piercing wasn't so bad after all, she thought, remembering the effect of the tiny needles on her own nipples.

The thought shocked her back to reality. The dildo was still inside her, quiet now but ready to shake her again to her foundations. Her nipples still bore the rubber caps, the needles waiting to tantalise her breasts again. She still wore the handcuffs and leg irons, and she was helpless to prevent the same thing from happening again. To prevent the other Jan taking control so easily. Would she ever be the same again?

More importantly, did she want to go back to what she had been and lose the glorious pleasure her body had given her? For the first time in her life Jan found herself questioning her own behaviour and standards.

All it had taken to change her was the glorious release of her sexual tensions, tensions she had not even known she had. Idly she looked at her chained wrists. Jan knew that the handcuffs had been crucial to her response. The handcuffs and her chained ankles meant she could not stop her body taking charge. In her chains she felt freedom, for the first time, even if she did not recognise it yet.

Four

Jan sat quietly, watching the shadows change in the long room. By turns she wondered and worried whether Patrick would switch on her dildo once more, but he seemed to have forgotten about her. She felt an increasingly urgent need to go to the toilet, but she held back, not wanting to wet herself. She wondered if he was going to force her to. Soon it was late evening and she was getting hungry. But when someone came in it wasn't Patrick. He was the face of her captors, and so far he was the only one she had seen. The stranger who came for her frightened her anew. What would this man do to her? She drew her legs as far up as she could toward her body, but she could not cover herself from his gaze, and she flushed as he studied her naked body in minute detail. Again she felt the amazement of the day before. She had been snatched from her home and plunged into this . . . whatever it was, and no one seemed to have noticed. No one knew where she was or what was happening to her. There was no one to come to her rescue. She felt terribly alone. 'Don't hurt me.' Jan was amazed to hear her voice sounding so weak.

'Relax,' he said. 'I'm not going to hurt you. It would be a terrible waste of a lovely woman. You are lovely, you know, naked or not.'

Jan did not relax, however. Words were no real assurance of safety. She tried to look unafraid, but with what results she could not say.

'I am called James,' he said.

Jan got the impression that that was not his real name. It would be foolish to believe that he would reveal that. His accent sounded South African. Definitely not English.

When she remained silent, he spoke again. 'I have come to take you to the bathroom, Jan. And afterwards to give you some dinner.'

It was such a mundane statement that relief burst through her. At the same time she incautiously relaxed the iron control over her sphincter. Jan felt a spurt of urine which she quickly checked. It would be humiliating enough to wet herself in solitude. A witness made it intolerable. She was relieved that he didn't appear to notice.

James helped her move away from the wall. Then he got behind her and put his hands under her arms, lifting her to her feet. Jan managed to stand, but he didn't let go of her. He put his arms around her from behind, trapping her against his body. Then he pinched her nipples beneath the rubber caps. The tiny needles pricked her sensitive flesh as they were forced against it. 'Oh!' she yelped, and the floodgates opened. Jan felt the warm stream running down her thighs, her legs, gathering in a puddle around her feet. She flushed in shame and tried to clamp down, but once it had started she couldn't stop it. Only when her bladder was nearly empty did the stream subside to a trickle. It felt good to piss, but the shame of doing it before this stranger who held her nipples between his fingers made her want to sink through the floor. And she felt that familiar tingle in her belly as he held her. Oh God, not that too.

'Feel better now?' he asked her. 'It's such a relief to let the body have its way, isn't it?'

Jan flushed deeply at the double entendre as he led her away from the puddle. Her feet left wet prints for several paces and her wet thighs rubbed slickly together. The dildo inside her shifted as she walked, threatening further shame in front of him. Jan couldn't possibly ask him to take it out. Maybe he didn't know it was there.

'We are going to leave the dildo in place, Jan,' he said. 'It won't stop you from going to the toilet, as we've just seen. And you may wake up in the night simply dying for an orgasm. If you do, it will only be the work of a moment to switch you on. We're going to keep your pretty nipples covered for the same reason. I watched you this afternoon. Your body responded marvellously to the stimuli. I look forward to seeing you do it again.'

He had seen her too. Was there no end to her humiliation?

Jan's alter ego chose that moment to offer encouragement. Suppose watching you turned him off? Would that make you feel any better?

In her mind, Jan felt the ghost of a smile, and the beginnings of recovery. She stood straighter, following her captor with a slight jingle of chain. It turned out that there was a bathroom just outside the long room. She stood helplessly before the toilet when James released her. She indicated her helplessness by a slight lifting of her manacled hands and a questioning look.

'Will you undo me so I can do what I have to? And please leave me in private.'

James smiled and shook his head. 'Do you want to deprive me of the pleasure of watching a beautiful woman squat on the pan? I don't get many chances to see that. You just do what you have to do. I'll help.'

Angrily, flushing again, Jan made up her mind to get on with it. She sat awkwardly on the toilet, landing with a bump because of the handcuffs. And then she couldn't go. The chain was tight in her crotch. The dildo inside her made itself felt. And he was watching intently, with a faint smile. Strain as she might, nothing happened. She spread her legs as little as possible. Still nothing.

'Go away!' she burst out. 'Please.'

Instead James knelt before her, his face close to hers. He placed his hands on her temples, holding her head steady between them, and kissed her slightly parted lips. Jan tried to twist away, but he held her. She did manage to close her lips, just before she felt his tongue brush them. 'Mmmmmmfff,' she said, struggling. Undaunted, he kissed her closed mouth, drawing it out. When the kiss finally ended, he did not let her go. He leaned forward still further to kiss her cheeks and nose. Jan shut her eyes hurriedly, knowing what was coming, and she felt his lips brush her closed eyelids, his breath soft against her skin.

'N . . . no. Please don't.' She tried to twist her face away once more. Unsuccessfully. She was flaming red with shame. But what was he doing now?

'Oh!' she cried as he pinched her nipples under their rubber caps. The tiny needles pricked her again, sending their urgent signals to her belly. The dildo began to buzz, seemingly of its own volition. Oh God, not here on the toilet. She would die of shame.

No, you won't, her alter ego said. Let me take care of it.

Jan twisted and jerked, but his fingers on her nipples were irresistible. Her body was going to do it again. The vibrations from the dildo were making themselves felt now, the ripples were starting in her belly, her internal muscles tightening with her rising excitement. Never in her wildest dreams (and they had never been this wild) would Jan have believed she could come while squatting on the pan. But unless he released her nipples and shut off that dildo, she knew that she was going to do so now.

Her hands twisted helplessly at her waist, held against her body by the tight leather belt and the short chain of her handcuffs. Jan felt her legs parting.

Suddenly they spread wide, as far as the leg irons allowed. Jan moved her feet closer together and spread her thighs, surrendering to the rising excitement. Still holding her tingling, prickling nipples with his hands, James bent down and kissed her cunt, his lips and teeth nibbling at her pussy, his tongue pushing the dildo further inside her. He didn't seem to mind that she was still wet with her own urine.

Jan clapped her thighs together but could not dislodge his lips on her lips. She succeeded only in trapping his head against her. James took the opportunity to kiss her cunt deeply, while Jan tried futilely to push him away with her manacled hands. And it was too late, too late. She felt the rising wave in her belly, and the frantic signals passing from there to her tormented nipples, and she came, moaning and twisting on the toilet seat while James kissed her labia and clitoris and the dildo buzzed inside her. Jan squeezed down on it as she came, her vaginal muscles responding even as she tried to will them not to.

Jan Two urged her to let go.

'No!' Jan said. Then 'Oh,' she moaned. Weak with pleasure, Jan felt her thighs loosening. She fought to keep them closed, clamping down hard, but the next orgasm swept away her control. James used his freedom of movement to kiss her mons veneris, his breath ruffling Jan's thick pubic hair and sending shivers of pleasure down her spine. Jan shuddered and came again, groaning in mingled shame and pleasure. The signals passing between her nipples and her cunt were irresistible, and her inability to protect herself or push him away made the sensation more intense. To her surprise, her manacled hands seemed to have become entangled in his thick curly hair, and seemed to be pulling him closer to her, holding him against her sex so that he could use his mouth to arouse and satisfy her. Her body seemed to have a will of its own, and she could no longer control herself.

Later, alone again, she remembered her earlier conclusion. Lack of responsibility made her able to come where before she had been able to avoid it, and think herself virtuous. In just the short time she had been held captive, Jan had discovered an important truth about herself and her sexual responses. She didn't know if she would ever be able to forget it. When the inner voice asked her if she wanted to forget, Jan had no reply.

She was dismayed when James drew back and switched off the dildo. As the vibrations died away Jan slowly returned to the normal world. She flushed as she remembered that a man had made her come repeatedly while she was sitting on the toilet. And added to her shame, she felt the urine flowing, as if her body was intent on showing her further how far it had escaped from her mental control. And she felt her anal sphincter open. Jan had never before gone to the toilet in the presence of a man. She was much too reserved. Had been much too reserved, she corrected herself.

Unable to clean herself, she had to endure James' wiping her cunt and bottom. Too embarrassed to

70

speak, she stood when bidden and bent over so that he could wipe away the shit. The chain between her legs was pushed into her crack as he wiped her. The chain needed a lot of wiping.

The dildo stirred threateningly as he touched it. She felt terribly grateful when he led her to the shower and turned on the water. She felt as if her shame were being partly washed away. Now, if only they would give her some clothes, she would feel like her old self. And she knew that that was why they weren't going to do it.

This time, Jan found herself enjoying the experience of being handled. James washed her body thoroughly, touching her everywhere and bringing echoes of her earlier pleasure. Finally he washed her thick chestnut hair, undoing the braid and running his fingers through the thick mane as he shampooed it. There was something incredibly pleasurable in being washed by a man while helplessly chained. Yesterday, Jan would never have believed how good it felt. She felt languorous, cared for, pampered, owned.

That last gave her pause. Yes, owned. She shivered at the thought. She was helpless in his hands, and she liked it, try as she would to fight the thought. She saw herself as a beautiful (he had called her beautiful), captive animal, handled by her keeper, at his mercy, unable to resist his attentions. She grew warm between the legs as her imagination ran away once again. Her knees threatened to give way. Jan had to make a real effort to stand and appear unmoved.

'Relax,' James said. 'The women who reach this stage have grown used to being handled. You've made remarkable progress in a short time. Most women as locked up as you were take several days, sometimes more. There's no holding you back. And you're so beautiful.'

There it was again. He thought her beautiful. He was at least ten years younger, and he thought her beautiful. James was not flattering an attractive older woman to get something from her. He had only to take her whenever he wanted. He did not need to tell her lies to seduce her. He had only to reach out and touch her body. She could do nothing to prevent him. And he thought her beautiful. Was she? Jan wanted to believe it. Sam had said the same thing to her, but she had discounted that as an attempt to get round her. But she could still turn heads in the street. Even Leslie had said so.

Where was Leslie now, she wondered, while her mother was being washed by a stranger? Did Sam have any idea that she was standing in chains in a shower having her hair shampooed? And what would he do if *he* were here? Free her or keep her captive?

The part of her newly divided personality that she called Jan Two hoped he would do the latter. And that shocked the rest of her. Sam chain her after all these years? But why not? If he knew what chains did to her, he might do it. No. Would do it. Jan imagined herself being made to sleep in chains, to live in them every day, to have dynamite sex in handcuffs and leg irons. And then she thought of her previous life, wondering how she had managed to overlook this strong compulsion to helplessness.

Showered, shampooed, clean, Jan felt more her old self. So much so, in fact, that she began to feel uncomfortable about her nakedness. Only the fact that she could do nothing about it – and that her captors would do nothing about it – kept her from asking again for her clothes. That, and a curious pride that would not let her beg. James dried her off with a large fluffy towel, disturbing the dildo inside her and the rubber caps over her nipples. But not enough to arouse her after the afternoon's and evening's exercises. Or excesses, she insisted to herself.

Three cheers for excess, Jan Two interjected. Let's do it again.

Jan supposed there was a limit to how many times she could be made to come, though the limit was far higher than she would have thought a day ago.

He dried her hair with a hair dryer and brushed it until it shone. Jan found it sensual and relaxing to have her hair brushed so lovingly. James braided it again when it was dry. 'Your hair is lovely,' he told her, leaning over her shoulder to plant a kiss behind her ear. He held the braid to prevent her from escaping, though escape had not occurred to her. Having a stranger holding her by her braided hair was illicitly exciting. She had visions of a captive maiden – well, a woman, really, one who looked uncannily like her – being dragged by her hair to the bed of her captor. She was half-sorry when he let go of it. The vision faded slowly, as if it too were reluctant to go.

James took her back u stairs, walking behind her in case she fell and, she guessed, so that he could study her movements as Patrick had done. She knew that his eyes were on her naked body as she walked before him, but she could do nothing about that either. And so she did not feel the shame she had felt earlier.

In the bedroom she made another discovery: since she could not feed herself so long as she wore the handcuffs, he had to feed her. As he showed no sign of releasing her, Jan was forced to submit to being fed by her captor. And as she ate the food he offered her, she thought about what it would be like to actually sleep in chains, with the dildo inside her and her nipples covered by those maddening rubber caps.

James had said that they might 'switch her on' at a moment's notice, at any time. How? she wondered.

When she asked him, he explained that the dildo was battery-powered and radio-controlled. 'The chain between your legs is the antenna. And here –' drawing a small black plastic box from his trousers, '– is the control. This button will switch you on. The batteries last for nearly eight hours because they only have to operate a vibrator inside the dildo.'

'Only,' Jan thought wonderingly. The effect of the dildo on her had been shattering. 'Only' didn't begin to describe that.

'We have others, more elaborate than yours. They expand and contract, and some of them can be made to thrust in and out, though that makes for a cumbersome mechanical linkage that resembles a nineteenth-century steam engine. But there are some women who like that. They say being fucked by a machine is exciting.' He shrugged at her horrified expression. 'It takes all kinds,' he said nonchalantly. 'But your reaction to our standard model was very good. I don't think we'll have to hook you up to one of our more elaborate fucking machines. We will keep you on the one you have, then gradually make the transition to the real thing.'

Jan had no trouble figuring out what the 'real thing' would be, but she wondered how they could make the transition gradual. It sounded like being a little bit pregnant. Pregnant? Might she get pregnant? Surely they wouldn't do that to her. Would they?

Reading her thoughts once again, James told her, 'We take precautions. But are you on the pill?'

Infrequent as her sexual relations with Sam were, Jan was still careful about contraception. She never knew when Sam's importunities would wear out her patience, and they would wind up in bed. Forty-two was not ancient, she reassured herself, but she did not want another child. She might soon be a grand-mother. Another child might turn out to be more of a problem than Leslie.

'Yes,' she said acidly. 'What if I weren't?'

'We keep a supply here,' he said.

'But I've missed a day, thanks to you. Your people took me away without my pills.'

James shook his head. 'They were collected while you were waiting downstairs. You will find them in the bathroom, along with some of your make-up. We want you to be as attractive and as comfortable as possible during your stay.'

'Is that why you lash women with whips?' Jan asked sarcastically.

James shrugged again. 'Some of our guests like it. Some like it so much they can't have an orgasm unless we, or someone, whips them. For some it's spontaneous. For others it's an acquired taste. How about you? Want to try it?'

'No!' she cried, shaking her head. 'Not that. Please.' Jan hated the begging tone, but she did not want to be lashed again.

'Well, never mind,' he said urbanely. 'There's still plenty of time to change your mind. I'll have Robin come talk to you about it.' He poured another glass of wine and offered it to her. ' "Come, fill the cup, and in the fires of Spring/Your winter garment of reluctance fling," ' he misquoted.

Jan rattled her chains. 'Not taking any chances on having your bird flutter away, are you?'

'A bird in handcuffs is worth two at liberty,' he retorted with another smile as he held the glass invitingly to her lips.

Jan was thirsty, but drank sparingly. The last thing she wanted was to get drunk with him, or to get

75

drunk while he remained sober. There was no telling what follies her rebellious body would lead her into if she drank too much. But she would not let him lash her if she could help it. The stripes she had already received were too painful a memory.

She ate and drank from his hands, her nakedness feeling more and more natural, or at any rate less and less embarrassing. She was a pragmatist in most things, and knew that she would have to accept what she could not change. But the habits of a lifetime are not lost in a day, or even a day and a half. She was on her guard lest he 'try something', as she put it to herself. Was the food drugged this time? Did the wine contain an aphrodisiac that would make her a helpless slave to his base desires? Jan disliked the cliché but could think of no other phrase.

And how about your own base desires? her inner voice asked. Anyway, it continued, you already contain your own aphrodisiac. The touch of a button would set you off. She did not believe that any aphrodisiac would make her 'offer herself' to him. Jan grimaced inwardly at her mother's expression. She wondered how often her mother had 'offered herself' to her father. As with most people, Jan found it hard to imagine her parents 'doing it', yet they had done it on at least two occasions. Had their mother told her sister the same things about sex as she had Jan? And did Sophia 'offer herself' very often to her husband, all those miles away in Australia? Aussie men were not renowned for their subtle seduction techniques. Perhaps Sophia was not given the chance of making the offering. Jan wondered briefly what it would be like to be married to a man who would not take no for an answer. And shivered.

'Cold?' James asked.

'Would you give me my clothes if I said yes?'

'Well, no, but I might consider wrapping you in my eager arms.' He brightened at the prospect. 'Want to try it? Several others have said it really works.'

The reference to 'several others' brought Jan back to reality. 'No, thanks. I'll just have to tough it out,' she said dryly.

'A real pioneer mother, you are,' he said as he fed her another mouthful of baked potato.

He did not show much regret at her refusal. Probably he had expected it at this stage. At this stage ... What might she do at another stage? Jan thrust the idea aside resolutely. After she had eaten and drunk she felt better, more able to face another night in captivity. Amazing what a little food and wine does for the old bod, isn't it, Jan Two suggested. You'll be fortified in no time for the next time.

Jan had no reply.

James set the tray aside. Then, to Jan's surprise and alarmed delight, he leaned forward to kiss her on the forehead, as a friend might. She tilted up her face to look at him, and he put his mouth over hers in a soft kiss. Mmmmm, she thought while trying to act affronted, while he held her long braid of hair so that she couldn't escape. She felt his breath warm on her face and smelled the faint scent of his aftershave. Piney, she thought. Fresh.

Attractive too, said her inner voice.

'Would you like to join the other two women here in the lounge, or would you rather stay in your room?'

The idea of sitting naked watching TV with two other women jolted her. Old instinct made her shake her head. She felt regret, but would not change her mind. What, she wondered, did they all do with the long hours when they were not ... having their personalities altered?

Don't you mean being fucked silly, or having their cunts or nipples pierced, her inner voice asked.

Until then she had not realised just how much time the average person spent in front of the TV, and how much time she would now have to fill without it. Jan almost said she would go, but the idea of sitting naked and in chains in front of others was too much.

At this stage anyway, Jan Two added helpfully.

James offered her his hand. She stood up, feeling foolish. Why stand? Why not simply sit? What did he intend to do with her?

'I'll get you ready for bed, then, if you like,' he told her.

Jan raised her manacled hands as far as the chain allowed, indicating that he could take off the handcuffs whenever he was ready.

He knelt to unlock her leg irons, laying them on the seat of the chair she had been sitting on. Jan stretched her leg muscles, but abruptly thought better of showing herself in front of James. She stood still, her manacled hands still raised as she waited for him to finish unlocking her. Like an animal waiting to be released, she thought with a flash of anger.

Go on, you love it, her inner voice said.

But James did not release her.

'You can sleep as you are,' he told her. 'Don't worry. You'll soon become accustomed to it. And when we wake you in the night, you'll still be unable to stop yourself from coming. Do you want to go to the toilet before I tuck you in for the night?'

Mutely, Jan nodded. 'When' they wakened her in the night. Not 'if'. She followed him into the bathroom, looking closely at herself in the mirror. The long braid was a definite improvement, she thought. Such a simple change made her look years younger, more attractive. The handcuffs and waist belt added a bizarre touch which was nevertheless attractive in its own way. When she saw James watching her looking at herself, Jan flushed and looked away.

'Admire yourself, Jan,' he advised. 'I admire you.'

Jan flushed again as he led her to the toilet. This time, when she had taken care of 'business', as she called it, he made her squat on the bidet. His hand on her shoulder, pushing her down, was strong but gentle.

Jan sat.

His fingers spread her lips and the stream of warm water flooded her centre. The soap felt good. So did his hands, washing her, caring for her. She jumped when he gave her dildo a definite push. His fingers touched her clitoris. The sensation was electric. A man, a stranger, was touching her *there*, where she scarcely ever touched herself except to wash. And she liked it. Nevertheless she strained her hands downwards, but could not reach his to push him away. She flushed more deeply, while her inner voice asked her why she wanted him to stop. There was no answer except long habit. Then she felt the newly familiar stirrings inside her, in her belly and legs. The tingles spread to her breasts, and she waited for her nipples to become engorged and touch those tiny pricking needles, and for . . .

When he turned off the water and dried her, Jan was breathing hard with excitement. She knew that she would have had real trouble stopping him . . . even if her hands had been free. There was a keen sense of disappointment as he helped her to stand. She strove to conceal her excitement as he led her back to the bedroom. What if he laid her on the bed and laid her? No. He couldn't do that so long as she was stuffed full of dildo. But what if he took it out? She would be open to him. She would not be able to stop him. Jan bit back a low moan.

James, infuriating man, acted as if there were nothing out of the ordinary, either in her reactions or in the bizarre circumstances. He stopped her beside the bed with a touch on her shoulder, kneeling to pull a chain from beneath it. It was rather a long chain, she saw, as he locked the steel cuff around her right ankle. It appeared to be fastened to the bed. He was chaining her to the bed for the night.

'It's long enough to reach the toilet if necessary,' he told her matter-of-factly. 'I'll send Robin up to keep you company in a few minutes. She will tuck you in for the night.'

James bent suddenly to plant a kiss on each of her nipples, over the black rubber caps. Jan briefly felt the caps pushed against her, the needles pricking her nipples. She felt a fresh excitement. But he straightened up, moving away from her. The door closed. This time Jan heard the lock turn. She was alone with her nakedness and her chains and desire. Not much fun, is it? her inner voice asked. And this is only your second night. Think of what it'll be like in another two nights. Call him back, why don't you?

Jan pushed aside the thought. Pride joined long habit. She would not let them see her desperation to be touched, handled, caressed. Not after two nights, not after two hundred, she decided. Her body was her own. She would do with it what she wished. Only now she couldn't reach it or free herself from the chains, or pluck the dildo from her cunt. And, oh God, what would she do if they switched it on?

You'll come like a bomb, her inner voice taunted her. Just like you already did twice today.

Jan whimpered in frustration, jerking against her handcuffs. The whimper threatened to turn into begging and sobbing, and that way lay hysterics. No. Too undignified. She would never let them see what they had been able to do to her in such a short time.

How do you know they're not looking at you now? her inner voice asked. Ever heard of video cameras and one-way mirrors?

Jan looked fearfully at the mirror across the room. She could not get out of its sight. If they were *filming* me, I'll die of shame, she thought.

No you won't, her inner voice said. No one dies of shame. They just wish they could.

Jan was tired, but not sleepy. She went to the armchair. The chain between her ankle and the bed was nearly long enough to let her reach every part of the room except the door and the large mirror. Perhaps that was because they *were* filming her through a one-way mirror, and didn't want her examining it too closely. In the end, she decided that she would have to act as if there weren't one. And as she sat down the dildo shifted, reminding her that they could make her come without even being in the room. That might be better for her because no one could watch, unless she was being filmed. The thought nagged her. Jan stared hard at the mirror, but was no wiser. She felt a familiar twinge in her pussy as she thought of her dildo, lying quietly inside her cunt, waiting for the signal to drive her wild.

Five

Jan drowsed. The sound of the door opening woke her with a jerk. She half-expected, half-feared that it was Patrick, or James, coming for her, but it was Robin. She wore a dildo strapped to her body, the shaft jutting out from the apex of her thighs. They had left her unlocked, then. With a stab of fear, Jan knew that it could only be for one person. She shrank inside. But her dildo was her protection. She could not remove it, but Robin might, unless the shaft worn by the young woman was intended for the only other place it could go. No, Jan almost shouted. The stifled scream was loud in her mind as the young woman closed the door and crossed to her armchair.

Robin smiled, and Jan noticed that she was no longer gagged or in handcuffs. She carried a familiar black box. A wild, uncontrolled orgasm was just a button-push away. Jan swallowed a lump in her throat and tore her eyes away from the thing in the younger woman's hand, while her thoughts flew to the other thing inside her that could be stirred to such devastating effect by the button under Robin's thumb. But Robin didn't push it.

'How are you enjoying things so far, Jan?' she asked.

'Not very much,' she retorted. 'How do you think

I like being abducted and subjected to these indignities? How would anyone like it?'

'You could have fooled me this afternoon, then. It seemed that you were having a good time from my vantage point, though I admit I lost concentration towards the end.'

Jan flushed with shame. So Robin had been watching her involuntary performance, even as Patrick was screwing her. Jan felt another stab of envy, quickly stifled, when she recalled that Robin had had the real thing stuffed inside her, while she had been forced to make do with the dildo. Jan tried to push aside the thought and the envy. Her other self reminded her that she didn't really have much to complain about in any case.

She tried another tack. 'How can you go on luring women into this place? Aren't you ashamed?'

Robin seemed unfazed. 'Not especially,' she retorted. 'Anyway, they all seem to like it well enough once they get over the initial shock. It didn't take you long to get into the spirit, did it?'

Jan flushed again as the accuracy of Robin's assessment sank in. She could not take the moral high ground very easily any more, not since those first fearful, delightful moments in her kitchen. But she was not ready to admit her new stance to a stranger.

'James suggested I keep you company for a while.'

'With that?' Jan indicated the dildo sticking out in front of her.

Robin grinned. 'If you want it. Do you?'

'No,' Jan replied, with what she hoped was the requisite firmness. She was no longer sure of what she wanted or what her body wanted, she corrected herself. They were not always the same, though they had been in the past. Hadn't they? Jan was having trouble remembering her motives of just a few days ago. Even her voice was not to be trusted. She had a tendency to squeak where before she had spoken boldly. Her reply to Robin's outrageous offer had very nearly emerged as a squeak of alarm. Mature women do not squeak, she told herself.

'Well, it's not wholly a selfless offer,' Robin explained. Indicating the dildo that jutted rudely from her crotch, Robin continued, 'There is another bit, about as big as yours, stuck up inside me. When the visible end gets moved – as when stuffing it up your backside – I get a nice bonus at my end. Sure you don't want to have a go?' she asked hopefully. 'Or I could unlock your waist belt and unplug you. Then we could do it the natural way, face to face. The men thought you might want to try something new, but I won't tell them if you don't want me to. It'll just be between us girls.'

Jan was horrified, but not as horrified as she would have been before her abduction. 'NO!' she shouted. 'I don't want to talk about it.' Face to face was not what she considered natural, any more than the other way. She hated the thin edge of hysteria in her voice.

'Well, I'll see if one of the others would like it. In the meantime, we'll have to do something else to pass the time,' Robin said cheerfully. 'Anyone for bridge or Monopoly?' As she spoke she moved closer to Jan.

She felt trapped by her armchair. She struggled to stand, but Robin was too quick for her. She sat astride the arms of the chair, her thighs in the long sheer stockings spread widely and her breasts in Jan's face. She still wore that too-tight satin bra, and Jan noticed that her nipples were as yet unpierced. Struggling for something to say, she could only manage, 'Didn't you get pierced today? Patrick said . . .' She broke off in confusion as she heard herself.

'I got pierced, but not that way,' Robin grinned. 'We kind of forgot to do it. Anyway, there's always tomorrow.' She laid the black control box in Jan's lap, just out of her fingers' reach.

All Jan could think of was how close it was. Only a little stretch, she thought, and I could . . . She stifled the thought, blushing.

Robin's erect nipples were inches from Jan's eyes. She could see those veins pulsing beneath the fine skin, beating in time with her heart. She could not tear her eyes away. Robin seemed excited by something. Could it be me?

'Go on, kiss them,' Robin urged the older woman, pushing closer and offering her breasts. 'I'd like that.'

Jan turned her face away, but she could not escape the presence of this immodest outrageous young woman. She was trapped in the chair, her hands chained at her belly and those nipples close to her face, the dildo brushing against her stomach. And Robin . . . Robin was encouraging that contact, thrusting with her hips against her helpless companion. With or without her help, Robin was going to make her . . . Jan was at a loss for words.

Robin picked up the plastic box, and Jan knew that she was a moment away from . . . But no. Robin was offering the box to her.

'Go on, take it. Take control of your sex life. Just push the button, sit back and enjoy the ride. I'll just lean against you and we can come together.' She was pressing the box into Jan's limp fingers.

Instinctively she grasped it, then let go of it as if it had burned her hand. It slipped between her thighs, and as luck would have it, landed on the button. Jan felt the dildo begin buzzing inside her. With a loud cry she tried frantically to reach the box, but the chain brought her up. 'Turn it off, turn it off, please!' she shrieked, her voice cracking.

Robin shook her head and moved closer, spreading her thighs more widely and rubbing her own dildo against the older woman. She again offered her breasts, holding Jan's head between her two hands and forcibly turning her to face them. Jan closed her eyes and mouth, but she could not close herself off from what her dildo was doing to her. 'Nooooo, please,' she whimpered as the first twinge passed through her belly. Her hands strained against the handcuffs, trying to reach the control box before it was too late.

Jan squirmed and strained to reach the control box, trying to ignore the insistent vibrations inside her. And Robin was busily rubbing the dildo against her stomach, which actually did nothing for Jan but certainly seemed to please Robin. Jan risked a look at the young woman sitting astride her, and saw that Robin was becoming aroused. Her breath was rapid and her nipples were taut and crinkly, almost in Jan's face. They really did look delicious, Jan thought, pale strawberries set in her dark areolae. Darker than mine, Jan thought fleetingly. More sensitive as well? Certainly more experienced.

Robin's hands were now clasped behind Jan's neck as she thrust herself against the older woman. Jan looked down and saw the shaft inside her moving in and out as she moved. The labial rings gleamed against her shaven patch, looking more decorative than Jan had earlier thought. Would they really be so bad as she thought? She tried to imagine herself pierced like Robin. What would Sam think if she did it? She thrust the thought aside.

At that moment Robin leaned forward, crushing Jan's breasts and nipples against her chest, just below her own breasts. At once the tiny needles inside the rubber caps pricked Jan's nipples, and she gasped at the sensation. The twinges from her cunt were growing stronger, and this new stimulus took her breath away. She was going to come, and soon. She couldn't stop.

Robin beat her to the climax, moaning and thrashing as she came. Jan, looking at the younger woman's nipples at close range, suddenly found them irresistible. It would be churlish, she thought, to deny Robin the pleasure she sought. Jan opened her mouth and drew one of them in, sucking at it. Robin opened her eyes and smiled encouragingly at Jan. She nodded enthusiastically as she came, pressing herself against Jan's breasts.

Jan's own climax overtook her without warning. The wrenching spasm in her belly spread suddenly through her body as the dildo vibrated against her clitoris and the needles pricked her nipples. Her hands moved restlessly, pulling against the handcuffs and the waist belt, but she was not aware of it. She abruptly bit Robin, surprising them both. Robin didn't seem to mind. She had another long, moaning climax as Jan rolled the nipple between her teeth. Jan too was moaning, her mouth full of Robin's nipple. The two women were past the point of no return.

Jan felt Robin's hands on her own breasts. Robin must have known about the tiny needles in the rubber caps, for she was pinching Jan's nipples and making them prick her. Jan gasped at the touch, losing control once again, moaning and shuddering with the strength of her release. The last vestiges of restraint vanished as her clitoris and nipples were stimulated unbearably. Without quite knowing what she was doing, Jan managed to grasp the end of Robin's dildo between her manacled hands. She pushed and pulled on it, and Robin gasped and shuddered as she felt the new stimulus to her clitoris.

The old Jan would never have dreamed of making another woman come. Now it seemed not only fair, in the light of what Robin was doing to her, but also necessary. Robin felt no compunction at making Jan come, and oh it was wonderful. It must have been the same for Robin, for she suddenly shuddered against the older woman, pinching her nipples under their maddening caps. She screamed at her climax, drowning out Jan's loud moans entirely with her cries.

Robin leaned forward, her chin on the top of Jan's head. Jan also leaned against the young woman who straddled her. She kept her grasp on the protruding end of Robin's dildo, occasionally moving it and bringing a groan from her as she lay against Jan.

Jan looked down into Robin's crotch, wondering once again how it would feel to be pierced there. The dildo inside her was still active, threatening her, she would have said earlier, with yet another of those wrenching spasms she had grown to like so quickly since her abduction. She was in two minds, to endure the next orgasm in relative silence, or to ask Robin to switch her off. And suddenly it was too late. 'Ohh,' she moaned, 'ohgodohgodohgod.' They had done it to her again, and once again she had been powerless to resist. She had surrendered once again to her body's rebellious urges, and once again she was exhausted from the delicious sensations.

Robin roused herself enough to switch Jan off before once more succumbing to her own post-coital languor. The two women remained locked together, Robin's eyes open but unfocused, Jan idly studying the younger woman's wide spread thighs sheathed in those red stockings. Yes, she decided, before she could stop herself, they looked nice. She might even buy something like that for herself. The old Jan rebuked her for her lapse, but the thought had already formed.

At last Robin stirred and slid off the chair. Jan missed the touch of her hands on her sensitive nipples, but she had to acknowledge that she was almost worn out by the sexual marathon she had run in the hours since dawn. Never in her wildest dreams would she have believed herself capable of such exquisite pleasure. No going back, she thought. She was no longer sure she wanted to. The changes in her personality, those frightening changes she had tried to resist, were already taking place. Jan could already feel a weakening in her resolve to resist. The things they had made her body do were having the desired effect.

Robin stood looking at Jan, her breasts confined and emphasised by that too-tight red satin bra, her nipples poking impudently through the holes, her areolae clearly visible. The matching suspenders and long sheer red stockings emphasised her nudity in a way that Jan had already noticed, and she felt another stab of envy. Robin wore high-heeled red shoes, definitely not the kind worn by Judy Garland in *The Wizard of Oz*. Her eroticism shrieked out loud. Jan, completely naked save for the handcuff belt and the shackle around her ankle, reflected on the erotic effect of partial and provocative nudity, and felt her envy grow even stronger. How nice it would be to look like that, to have men wanting her as she knew Robin was wanted. She gave herself a mental shake, horrified anew at the way her mind casually contemplated those new lewd thoughts. But the image of herself clad in a similarly revealing fashion would not go away. When she added handcuffs and leg irons to her mental image of herself, she flushed hotly, not wholly with shame or horror.

'God, I needed that,' Robin said in a voice that still shook slightly with the after-effects of orgasm.

Jan looked sharply at her face. Had she been able to please this sophisticated and worldly young woman, and herself old enough to be her mother? She felt a stir of pride. Would she be able to stir Patrick as well? Confusion overcame her. How had that idea popped up when she had been dodging it consciously and unconsciously for almost all her adult life?

Robin's next words made Jan blush anew.

'You must have needed it too. I'm glad you felt good.'

Jan wondered if she were that obvious. Obviously so.

Robin extended her hands to Jan and helped her to stand. She led Jan to the bed, the ankle chain dragging behind her, and indicated that she was to lie down. Jan was more tired than she could remember ever being. She lay down, and the young woman tucked her in, pulling the covers up, as Jan was unable to do for herself.

As Robin turned to go, Jan thought wildly, I'm going to be here all night.

Chained to the bed by her ankle, her hands held close to her waist by the handcuffs and belt, she would be helpless to resist anything or anyone that came to her in the darkness. Jan's vaginal muscles tightened involuntarily around the dildo as she tried to imagine what would happen tomorrow. It was certain to be something new and bizarre. Beyond that she could not guess.

Robin crossed to the door and knocked in a complicated pattern. When they both heard footsteps approaching, Robin came back to the bed, kissed her forehead and bade her a good night. The door opened and Robin left. The door closed and locked behind her.

Eventually Jan did sleep, but she was restless. Her dreams were filled with images of piercing and penetration and delicious sensations in all those newly awakened parts of her body. She tossed and turned, moaning, waking often to find herself indeed a captive in chains waiting for her captors' pleasure.

And your own, the new part of her thought.

She wondered how Robin would pass the night. Not alone, she guessed, and felt another stab of envy. And each time her nipples beneath their rubber caps made contact with the bedclothes, she felt another stab of a different sort.

Six

Jan woke slowly, with an unwelcome grogginess and lassitude. The night's broken sleep, coming on top of the previous day's gymnastics, caused her to wonder how she would feel after two weeks of this, the time threatened by Patrick. The day was grey and rainy. The English spring was a treacherous time, as T. S. Eliot and others had observed, promising and denying by turns.

With difficulty she disentangled herself from the bedclothes, hampered as usual by not being able to use her hands. Jan made her way to the bathroom, the dildo heavy inside her, her nipples erect and prickling. She sat on the toilet and did her 'business', but was unable to wipe herself because of her handcuffs. Annoyed and ashamed, feeling dirty, she wondered how she would manage. The bidet caught her eye, and she flushed as she remembered James' hands on her body, washing her, touching her intimately, arousing her. She stood and crossed to it, managing to turn the water on by kneeling beside the basin and straining against the chain. She struggled to her feet and squatted on the seat, letting the water wash her clean. She remained a good deal longer than necessary, luxuriating in the sensation of warm water caressing her hidden parts. Finally, she shook herself from the spell and stood again with difficulty. She used one foot to turn the water off.

You're learning, the new part of her personality added encouragingly. Soon you won't even miss your hands.

As she imagined herself wearing chains for days, even weeks, Jan flushed. Her image in the mirror made her blush as well. A handsome mature woman in chains, her nipples covered by pert rubber caps, stared back at her. A wanton, she thought, half-angry, half-pleased, and wholly unsettled.

She tore her gaze away and went back into the bedroom, but there was nothing there to distract her thoughts. The mirror showed her the same image she had seen in the bathroom. There was no escaping her new self. Jan sat in the armchair, not wanting them to find her lying in bed.

She was still sitting there as the day grew outside her window. In the rain-misted distance, across the fields, a wood appeared stark and black. Jan could see nothing outside that would allow her to guess the location of her prison. Having arrived blindfolded, she could not even guess its general position in relation to her home. With a stab of dismay she imagined herself there, safe, secure, her own self (though uptight, Jan Two added), instead of here, naked and in chains, and stuffed full with an enormous dildo she was powerless to remove.

The image of herself lying on the bed in her chains, her legs spread apart and fastened to the bedposts, arose again. She tried to banish it from her mind. But her nipples had noticed. A sharp prick disconcerted her, destroying her attempt to appear unmoved.

The opening door startled her. Jan struggled to her feet, unwilling to be caught even sitting down by her captor, lest he think her loose.

Which you're becoming, her alter ego added.

Jan was flustered when Patrick entered bearing breakfast. It seemed such a prosaic thing after her restless night and lurid dreams. He set the tray down on the serving table and sat down. He invited Jan to sit beside him. She shook her head stubbornly. With a shock she noticed that the riding crop lay on the tray alongside the food, a reminder of the consequences of disobedience.

'Don't be a goose, Jan,' he said with a chuckle. 'This is not the prelude to rape. It's breakfast. All civilised people eat before sex. And don't look so disappointed. You can have sex – or rape – anytime you want.'

His reading of her confused thoughts was accurate enough to make Jan blush again.

You're spending a lot of time looking pink, her alter ego said sardonically. You ought to get an all-over tan so no one would notice. Think of lying nude in the sun, chained and helpless, while scores of admiring men . . .

Slowly, Jan sat down. She did not want to appear too compliant, but she was hungry, and there was the whip . . .

The wild animal tamed by hunger, Jan Two suggested.

And, not wholly disliking the metaphor, Jan waited to be fed like any animal.

And fed she was, mouthful by mouthful, a bite of egg, a piece of bacon, a sip of coffee or orange juice. Patrick was careful to wipe her lips between bites or sips. Jan began to like the idea of being waited on, of having everything done for her by a handsome man.

He'll be able to do anything *to* you as well, her alter ego added, bringing another flush to her skin and raising goose bumps all over her arms and body.

This was the gentler side of bondage, she realised. Someone else would have to help her to do everything (*everything*, her alter ego repeated) while she was unable to help herself. It was the ultimate in personal service, if she looked at it like that. The captive beauty was fed by her handsome captor, she thought. She felt a shiver begin in her cunt and travel all over her body.

Jan was keenly aware of the man sitting beside her. She had watched him yesterday as he fucked Robin, and she remembered how the sight of his erect cock, thick and dark red, had kindled a new fire in her own belly. He smelled good. She was also keenly aware of her own nakedness, and of her inability to cover herself. She felt his glance, assessing her body, and hoped that he would find her attractive. The abrupt change in her viewpoint startled her.

Breakfast over, Patrick rose and unlocked the manacle from Jan's ankle. He retrieved the leg irons from the floor and replaced them. Jan did not resist as the manacles closed once more around her ankles. Without being told, she struggled to her feet and waited for his instructions.

Patrick nodded approvingly, whether at her obedience or at her naked body Jan could not be sure. He picked up the riding crop and led the way to the door. Surely he wasn't going to lash her again. She felt her stomach knot in fear while her body seemed to shrink and grow cold.

As she had done the day before, she walked ahead of him, feeling his eyes on her body almost as palpable as the touch of his hands. The stairs looked as daunting as ever, and she grasped the handrail as she descended. At the bottom she looked questioningly back at Patrick. He gestured her toward the long room she had seen the day before.

Jan wondered if she was going to be switched on once again. She shivered, feeling the dildo's weight inside her as she walked before him.

This morning the room was empty. The worktop to which Robin had been chained by her labial rings was clear. Patrick went to the drawer as he had done before, taking from it a small bottle containing a clear fluid. It had an eyedropper cap.

'A tested aphrodisiac, Jan,' he told her with a straight face. 'One drop of this on your tongue and you will want to have wild, abandoned sex with the nearest male. Lucky fellow. You won't be able to stop yourself.' He unscrewed the top and drew a small amount of the fluid into the eyedropper. He set the dropper down on the worktop and began to undress.

Jan did not believe that this was happening to her. She could see the bulge in his trousers, and when he dropped them the whole thing sprang into view. Rampant sex was staring her in the face. 'N . . . no. Don't. Stay away.' Her voice shook uncontrollably. She was not ready for the 'real thing'.

Will you ever be? asked her alter ego. Cut the shrinking violet act and behave like a real woman.

Patrick stared boldly at her. Hungrily, she thought. Jan was not accustomed to the blatant lust she now saw in that erect cock. She shrank away. At the same time she thought, he wants me. She was pleased, awestruck and terrified at the same time. This doesn't happen to ordinary people, she thought. And then she remembered having the same thought as the two men had abducted her from her own house and brought her here.

Naked like her now, he picked up the eyedropper and advanced. He looked terrifying. Well, his cock did. It stood out like a rod. He was going to shove that thing into her, and . . . She retreated a step at a time as he came on. When the wall stopped her, she stood at bay, shaking her head, struggling against her handcuffs, looking around wildly for escape, for rescue, for a miracle.

Patrick came on, the eyedropper in his right hand. 'Open your mouth, Jan,' he said.

She clamped her lips shut.

He stood before her, his cock rudely poking her belly. 'Open your mouth,' he repeated. His voice sounded menacing.

When she still refused, he used his free hand to pinch her nostrils shut. Jan struggled to escape, her hands twisting and tugging against the handcuffs. She tried to melt into the wall. She couldn't breathe. Her stomach was knotted, her chest tight. The room began to go dark as she held her breath while her lungs screamed for air. Jan whimpered, 'No.'

He was implacable. Jan tried to breathe through her closed lips, between her clenched teeth. Her breath whistled as she struggled.

Patrick brought the eyedropper toward her mouth. She stared at it, feeling herself about to black out. The eyedropper came closer.

And then suddenly it disappeared. He released her nostrils and Jan drew in great grateful breaths. Air had never seemed so sweet as now. Her vision cleared and she could see Patrick clearly once again. He still stood before her. His cock poked her, as if seeking entry. Jan closed her thighs, the movement making her keenly aware of the dildo deep inside her.

He looked amused as he dripped the clear liquid onto the top of her left breast, just above the rubber cap. It felt cool and pleasant, trickling down her skin. He laid aside the eyedropper and grasped the rubber cap.

Instantly Jan felt the pricking of the needles on her nipples and areolae. He twisted the cap, sending electric tingles and twinges to her cunt. She felt herself tightening down there in the new familiar way. And then the cap came off, revealing her reddened nipple. Jan looked at it in surprise. She had not seen it for over twenty-four hours. But there was no time for contemplation. He was applying more of the liquid to her right breast, grasping the cap and twisting it too. Again the tingles and twinges, and her right nipple came into view. Only then did she recognise the smell of the solvent used to remove false moustaches and beards at the amateur dramatics group back home. Suddenly she was angry at being teased. She became still angrier when she saw the amusement in Patrick's eyes.

He used cotton wool to dry her skin. She relaxed slowly. Her nipples slowly returned to normal, and she was surprised at the sense of let-down. On the whole, she realised, she preferred the caps with the needles to this bland touch, but she couldn't bring herself to say so.

'I know you'd rather wear the rubber caps,' he said, reading her thoughts again.

Jan gasped at the accuracy of his assessment.

'But we have to let your nipples come up for air every so often. Otherwise the skin breaks out in an ugly rash. Besides, I prefer them this way. Much nicer to lick and bite,' he said, suiting the action to the words so swiftly that Jan had no time to react.

'Oh,' she gasped as he bit her nipple. Then as her vaginal muscles tightened around the dildo, she felt her stomach and belly tighten in sympathy. She knew another orgasm was not so very far away. 'Oh my,' she groaned.

'But there's no time for that now,' he said.

Jan could hardly believe he was not going to make her come. She had been expecting it. Wanting it, even, in that dark place where her subconscious lived and gave its orders to her newly rebellious body. She was relieved and disappointed at the same time, but she could not very well ask him to continue. Too much loss of face was involved.

Patrick was unfastening the chain between her legs, the chain that held the dildo inside her. Were they going to take that away as well? Dear God, was she going to be deprived of – would she finally be free of, she corrected herself – that vile thing inside her?

It seemed so. Patrick pulled the dildo out of her, and Jan felt empty for the first time in nearly twenty-four hours. It was a strange sensation. Before her abduction she had been empty there almost all the time. It hadn't taken her very long to become accustomed to being full, and to miss the feeling when the thick intrusive shaft was taken away. She gazed at it, fascinated anew by its length and girth. It glistened with her own secretions. I had all that inside me, she thought with a sort of awed pride. And in the next instant was assuring herself that she was glad to be rid of it.

Patrick held the dildo under her nose, and Jan smelled herself for the first time. A clean, salty smell, she thought, not at all disgusting as she had expected. She took a deeper breath, and then flushed as she realised that she was inhaling the scent of her own rut. She looked at Patrick, but he was impassive, as if this were an everyday occurrence. Jan tried to be as matter-of-fact as he was. It wasn't easy.

'Today we will do something different, lest one good custom should corrupt the world.' Patrick smiled at her.

'What do you mean?' It was out before Jan could stop herself. She had been counting on more of yesterday's pleasure, more than she cared to admit.

'Nothing too strenuous,' he told her. He told her he thought she needed a rest and a bit of time to think things over. He was going to take her back to her room in a few minutes. 'Then another of our many satisfied customers will come and have a talk with you. It will be an easy day.'

Jan watched as he tidied away the solvent and the rubber caps. Her breasts felt naked without them now. They don't feel as exciting either, do they? Her alter ego articulated what Jan didn't want to say.

Patrick led her back up the stairs to her room, where he removed her leg irons and handcuffs. He chained her to the bed by her ankle and left with a promise to see her again soon. After Patrick left her, Jan couldn't settle. Her conscience, the old pre-abduction Jan, woke up. The insouciant alter ego went into exile while she reviewed the events of the past day. She gave herself a strong dose of the how-could-you's, and her rebellious body reacted to her mental self-contempt as to a dash of cold water. She grew ashamed once more, old habits reasserting themselves after their banishment (no, their defeat) by the body's revolt. Never again, she promised herself. I won't let them do that to me again.

Sure of that, are you? The small voice sounded doubtful.

Jan tried to silence it. Yes. Tomorrow I will escape. I must. I won't endure any more humiliation. There was a small chuckle from the back of her mind, from the corner where she imagined the devil-figure dwelling.

Jan made her way into the bathroom, and ran a tub of hot water and added Radox. She pinned up her hair, got into the water and lay back. The chain from her manacle rose out of the water and lay across the side of the bathtub. Her sense of having fallen into a nightmare was acute as she stared at it. The house was quiet. Jan relaxed slowly, but couldn't shake off the sense of having a bad dream. The chain that fastened her to the bed lay heavily on her mind.

Jan dried herself again in the blasts of warm air, and then brushed her hair and looked at herself in the mirror. Back in the bedroom, she examined her chain and manacle closely but could not see how to open it without the key. A file or a hacksaw would do the job, she thought, but she had neither. Plan A wasn't going to work. Plan B was wait for the moment of unlocking and make a beeline for the door.

The devil-figure snickered. What will you do for clothes, even if you do get past Patrick?

Jan had no answer to that vital question, and the image of herself running naked through the country-side was not appealing. Think of something else, she said.

She was no closer to a solution when the door opened, and in came an unknown woman in a maid's outfit bearing a tea tray. Jan thought of knocking her out, taking her clothes and running for it. In the movies it took only one punch, but Jan had no idea how to go about it in real life. And there was still the small matter of the chain. Instead, Jan thought, I'll get information from her. Knowledge is power.

Yes, but is it enough to get you out of here? And do you really want to go? The small voice was getting louder again.

'Yes, I do, so shut up,' Jan said.

The maid looked queerly at her.

Jan smiled and pretended that there was nothing unusual in people talking to themselves. 'What's your name?' she asked. Not the most brilliant of openings, but she had to start somewhere.

'Antoinette,' the maid said, matter-of-factly.

She was in her thirties, Jan guessed, attractive, though dressed immodestly in a short tight black satin dress with black tights and high heels.

It's more than you have, dearie, the small voice said loudly.

'Do you work here regularly?' Jan asked.

'I don't even know where here is,' Antoinette replied. 'I'm one of the guests, like you. I arrived here as I imagine you did.'

'Tied up in the back of a van?'

'Yes,' Antoinette said.

'Don't you want to escape?'

'Not particularly,' Antoinette said.

'Why ever not? Surely you don't want these men, if that's the word for them, using you and torturing you.'

'Of course I do. That's what I signed up for. Didn't you?'

Jan couldn't believe her ears. Had the whole world gone mad? 'Signing up' for sexual abuse was crazy.

Careful about the abuse, the little voice said. Were you abused? Or did you love it?

Jan blushed at her thoughts, but ploughed on. 'What do you mean?' she demanded. 'Surely you were abducted?'

'Oh, I see,' Antoinette replied. 'This must be your first time. I got abducted the first time too. This time I called for them to come and get me. I have an emergency number to call when I really need a bit of sex with B & D.'

'B & B?' Jan asked.

Antoinette smiled pityingly and said, 'No. B & D. Bondage and domination, as they call it in the trade. With a bit of humiliation and sexual torture, and some dynamite orgasms thrown in to make it interesting. When I get too horny from not getting enough of what I fancy, I call the emergency number and they come take me away in a van. It's convenient, because I can arrange things before the call so I won't be missed, and then there's the uncertainty about when they'll come for me, and the anticipation of coming to whatever place they're using at the time. It makes the wait really nice. I get hornier just knowing they're coming soon.'

Yes, the world *had* gone mad, Jan decided. At least Antoinette's world had.

What about Robin's? the voice asked. And what about your own?

Jan ignored the voice. 'Why?' She demanded.

'Why not?' the maid retorted. 'We all try to do what we like – what pleases us – whenever we can, don't we?'

'And you like *this*?'

'Sure. Don't you?'

Jan was taken aback by the conviction in her voice. If Antoinette was so sure of her own likes and pleasures, maybe her own reaction was the odd one. No, that's crazy. This can't be happening, she told herself again.

Careful how you answer, the voice in her head warned.

'Look,' Antoinette said, not unkindly, 'Patrick said you might need to get a few things straight. If you'd like, I'll join you for tea and biscuits and tell you about what happens here, and we'll see if that will help you get over the first surprise. I was surprised too the first time.'

Jan nodded abstractedly. 'Yes, I think I'd like some company if you can stay. But ... the first time, you said. How many times have you been here?'

Antoinette set the tray down on the table and gestured for Jan to take one of the chairs. She sat down herself. Jan noticed how the short skirt rode up her legs, showing nearly everything. She flushed at the idea of dressing like that, although she was sure that Sam would approve. She sat hesitantly, as if sharing tea and conversation with this surprising woman would somehow implicate her more deeply in the plans of the men who had abducted her.

More than you're already implicated, you mean? Jan Two was back at work. Don't be so holier-than-thou, she advised Jan.

Still embarrassed, Jan sat down stark naked and with an all-over blush which she strove to ignore with little success. She longed for her candlewick dressing gown. She shook herself mentally and set about making conversation. 'So, how any times have you been here?'

'This is my first time here,' Antoinette said.

Jan looked questioningly at her.

'In this particular house, I mean. On the other two visits they used different houses. I don't know where they are, any more than I know where this one is. I think the men involved are doing something like house-sitting for absent owners, and then abusing the privilege, as it were, by inviting along guests of their own. Of course, they could also be here quite illegally, breaking into vacant houses here and there, I mean. I don't know the exact situation, but it's more exciting to think of them as housebreakers, so I do. I asked James once, but he wouldn't say.'

Jan did not find the idea of their captors as housebreakers very exciting. The police didn't take kindly to housebreaking. It wouldn't do for the boys in blue to show up while she was chained up, naked. There would be a scandal at the very least. Jan squirmed when she thought of herself as headline news in Godalming. A story like that was sure to make the tabloids. Lurid headlines, embarrassing pictures, journalists dogging her footsteps asking for a statement. No, it was too much.

But Antoinette continued as if there were nothing to worry about. 'The first place was somewhere in the West Country. I could tell by the accents on the local news, but I never tried to find it again. For the first few days I thought about escaping and reporting it all to the police. Like you're probably doing, I expect. But I didn't. By the time they let me go, I had lost all interest in telling the police anything. I wanted to stay there forever, but I had to get back to work. They seemed to know a lot about me before they grabbed me. They knew when I would show up at work, and made sure I was delivered home in time.'

'And you came back again?' Jan was incredulous.

Antoinette nodded.

'How did you find them again?'

How come you want to know? asked Jan Two.

'They gave me an emergency telephone number. Last week I just had to come, as it were.'

'You could trace the number,' Jan said. 'Or the police could.'

'I don't want to,' Antoinette replied. 'Anyway, I don't think the number is all that easy to trace. It was a different number from the last one. A mobile phone number with voice mail. I expect they change it fairly regularly, so make sure you get the latest one when they let you go.'

'Why?' Jan asked.

'Ask me that question again after you've been here a week, if you still don't know the answer, that is. By then you'll know, and you'll be just as reluctant to talk to the police or trace the number.' Antoinette smiled knowingly at Jan. She crossed her legs with a whisper of nylon on nylon, showing everything this time and seeming not to care in the least.

Jan looked away, studying the nearly untouched biscuits on her plate. She ate one, and then another. Eating allowed her time to digest what Antoinette was saying. When she looked at Antoinette again, Jan noticed that she wore a steel collar around her graceful neck.

'So, tell me how they came to abduct you,' Antoinette said.

Jan poured a second cup of tea to gather her thoughts before relating the details of her abduction. Antoinette nodded knowingly at several points in the story. When Jan reached the point of her arrival she looked at her companion. She was too embarrassed to tell Antoinette anything about what had happened to her since then.

Nor did Antoinette press her for more details. There was a long silence before she spoke again. 'That's about what happened the first time they grabbed me. I kicked and struggled and went all indignant, but they didn't pay any attention. They just gagged me and bundled me into the van. It took me nearly a week before I responded properly to being there, but after that it was heavenly. After I stopped fighting, I mean.'

Jan wondered if Antoinette had felt about sex as she did, but she couldn't ask her that. Not yet, anyway, said her alter ego.

Instead, she asked, 'Why did they take you? And why me, instead of any of thousands of other women?'

'I really don't know,' Antoinette replied. 'Harold sort of let slip that they . . .'

'Harold?' Jan asked.

'He's one of the men here. Or rather, not here. Not now, I mean. You may meet him. He likes to look over the new intake, he says. They aren't involved all the time with all the women who come here. But luckily for me James is here now, and James *is* involved with me.'

Antoinette smiled broadly, and Jan wondered how any one could take pleasure in abduction and forced sex, no matter how attractive the partner.

Oh, the inner voice interjected, you mean you don't understand how you reacted so positively, shall we say, to your own abduction and sexual arousal?

Jan was saved from further attempts to quell internal mutiny when Antoinette continued. 'Harold let slip that they do some rather extensive research into the women they take on. I mean, it's not just a matter of grabbing the first one that takes their fancy. I suppose that the first step in the process is seeing someone they fancy. But they go on to find out if that woman is likely to respond positively, as they say in management circles, to the kind of program they run. I don't know how they go about it, but I guess they do something like follow the women about and collect information before making a final decision.'

Jan wondered whose fancy she had taken, simultaneously affronted and pleased by the idea. Someone had fancied her enough to take this big step. Who, she wondered?

Patrick, said the inner voice. I'll bet it's Patrick. I fancy him. Don't you?

'If they weren't careful,' Antoinette was saying, 'they might take the wrong woman: one who's angry and persistent enough to cause a lot of trouble.'

'I don't remember being followed,' Jan said, wondering if she was going to make trouble when she was released.

'Neither do I, but then I wasn't looking for anyone following me. Were you?'

Jan shook her head. She still couldn't imagine why

they had chosen her. She had never dreamed of anything like what had happened to her.

Enjoying it? her inner voice asked.

Jan shook her head again, this time in an attempt to deny her own disturbing thoughts. How could they know that she might respond 'positively' when she herself hadn't known? But someone had fancied her, she thought, enough to take the trouble to look closely at her life. The thought was both disturbing and pleasing.

'In my case,' Antoinette was saying, 'they struck lucky. I love what they do to me. I won't do anything to stop them.'

Jan was on the verge of saying that these perverts couldn't be allowed to go about abducting women and 'transforming their personalities', as Patrick had put it. But Antoinette was quite content to let them do it to her. Jan, more pragmatically, thought about the publicity that was sure to follow any police involvement. It would do the discloser no good to claim that she was forced into captivity. Even if people took her at her word (and most of them wouldn't), the press would make her infamous in less than a day. And when the national furore died down, as it always did, there was still the local reaction, which was likely to be much, much longer lasting. For Jan that was the most powerful argument against trying to bring her captors to 'justice'.

Anyway, the dark inner voice said, you can't really say that much more than dignity has been offended, if it has been. Think about it.

Jan didn't care to think about it. If she had been set free at that moment she would have fled back to her familiar life.

And then you'd be forever wondering what you were missing, the troublesome voice said. For my money, I'd prefer something like this.

Jan knew that she would have to make up her mind sometime, but just now the chain on her ankle would keep her here.

She changed the subject. 'Do you like playing maid, Antoinette?'

'Not especially, but someone's got to do it now and again. Your turn will come the next time you come back.'

Jan resolved that there would be no 'next time', once she had managed to get through this one. She changed the subject again.

'And you really don't want to escape? I mean, you've got clothes. And you're not chained to anything like me.'

Antoinette touched the steel collar around her neck. 'This is a specially adapted electronic dog training collar. If I tried to run, it would bring me down with an electric shock. I know, because I've seen it used on big dogs by a friend who trains them. It tells me to stay around. But I don't mind because it also reminds me that someone *wants* me to stay here, and has taken the trouble to have this made for me.'

Antoinette stood up, the short skirt sliding down so that she looked more decent (by Jan's standards) and began clearing the table. 'Got to run,' she said. 'I'm on in a little while. I enjoyed the chat. We'll talk again later.' She appeared eager to be 'on'.

Jan remembered that Robin had said something like that on the first day, and had obviously enjoyed being 'on' when she and Patrick were, well, screwing. Jan used the coarse word deliberately, trying to shock herself. It didn't work. The effect was to recall a vivid image of the young, red-headed woman in flagrante enjoying every moment.

Alone once more, Jan thought about Antoinette and Robin. They were obviously happy to be here.

Well, I'm not sure I am, she thought, but couldn't think of anything to do about it. In the end there was nothing to do but wait for her captors to make the next move. She took a blanket from the bed and draped it around her shoulders before sitting down in the armchair. The sleepless night caught up with her and she slept.

Seven

Patrick roused her with a touch on her shoulder. Jan woke with a start. He had come into the room without waking her. Heaven knew how long he had been there with her, watching her sleep. She was alarmed by his presence, but this time the inner voice offered some helpful advice.

He's not going to hurt you, the small devilish figure said. If he were going to, he'd have done so by now. Relax.

Jan couldn't relax totally. Who could? she asked herself. But her panic subsided.

'Slept well?' he asked with a smile.

Jan thought he was particularly nice looking when he smiled. But she was not going to let him know that. It didn't fit with her resolve to get away, or at least to resist further co-operation. 'Not all that well,' she retorted.

'Try the bed next time. I'm told it's more comfortable than an armchair. But now it's time to get on with today's program.'

Jan didn't like the sound of that.

Jan Two reminded her that she hadn't liked the last day either, not to begin with. But you sure enjoyed it when you got going, she added.

Jan blushed guiltily at her thoughts.

111

Patrick unlocked the manacle from her ankle and lifted the blanket away from her with a theatrical flourish.

Jan's first instinct was to cover herself with her hands, but she thought better of it. It hadn't done any good the last time, and she didn't want to let him know that she was fearful. She stood up and looked him in the eye. 'I want to leave,' she said. 'Now. May I please have my clothes?'

Jan Two made panicky dissenting noises.

Patrick shook his head, and Jan felt her heart sink. She hadn't really expected to be set free. The talk with Antoinette had revealed that such things didn't happen, but she felt as if she had to try. Self-respect satisfied, she would have to face whatever else they could do.

Jan Two applauded her attitude.

Instead of yesterday's handcuffs and waist belt and leg irons, Patrick had brought rope. Aside from that, today was beginning like the day before.

And look how that ended, said a familiar voice.

Jan knew that resistance would do no good. And as she waited for Patrick to tie her up, she felt her heart thudding in her chest with excitement. The last time, at this point, she had felt fear and indignation. Jan was not stupid. She couldn't deny that a part of her now welcomed the opportunity to experience the pleasure of being made to come while being helpless to prevent it. She couldn't deny any longer that she had enjoyed yesterday after the initial resistance, as Jan Two had noted. And if she were helpless, she wouldn't be responsible for what they did to her.

Nor for how good it feels, added the voice of her darker self.

Patrick chose a short length of rope from the lot he had brought. 'I know this is not an everyday

112

experience, but if you just relax you'll see that there's nothing to be afraid of.'

Except my own reactions, Jan thought. Why didn't she bolt for the door? She was free of the chain. The door was open. Because I'm naked, she told herself. And because Patrick could no doubt catch me with little effort. And he might not be so gentle then.

Go on, Jan Two urged. Try it. You might like being man-handled.

Jan shook her head angrily to silence the impish voice. She watched with bated breath as Patrick approached her with the rope in his hands, standing very still, all her senses alert in the face of this new, unsettling experience.

He moved behind her, and Jan knew that he was going to tie her hands behind her. She felt the impulse to bring her arms behind her ready for tying, and at the same time the opposite urge. I can't allow myself to show any eagerness, she told herself, while the devilish figure in the back of her mind sneered.

He resolved her dilemma by taking her hands behind her back. He held them together, palm to palm, and Jan shivered in combined dread and anticipation. When she felt the rope encircle her wrists she almost tore herself from his loose grip and ran for the door. But in the end, crucially, she didn't. And then it was too late. The rope tightened and her hands were beyond her control. She stood still as he finished tying her. Only when it was done did Jan test the ropes. They were tight, and she was once more captive. She let out a deep breath. Well, that's that, she said to herself resignedly but with an edge of excitement.

But Patrick was not done with her. On the previous day, he had simply locked the handcuffs and leg irons abound her wrists and ankles, and driven her before him down the stairs and into the 'demonstration' room. It had all been very quick. And frightening. Today he went more slowly. Jan was acutely aware of his nearness. He placed his hands on her hips and held her.

Jan gave a nervous shudder, as she had seen her horse do when startled, but she was otherwise still. His breath was soft on the back of her neck as he lifted her long hair to one side and his lips touched her skin. Jan felt her scalp prickle as she flushed with embarrassment and pleasure. His lips felt scalding to her aroused senses. She bent her head down. She was unsure whether she did so in order to give him better access or simply because she did not trust herself to look into the mirror opposite for fear of seeing herself being man-handled, as her alter ego had put it.

At length the soft kiss ended. Patrick stroked her hips with his hands and stepped away from her. Jan felt a stab of disappointment but remained silent, head bent and eyes on the floor.

Patrick pulled her elbows together and tied them, forcing her shoulders back and her breasts out. Jan gasped as the rope bit into the skin of her arms, but continued to gaze at the floor. She thought he was finished when he knotted the rope between her upper arms. She tried the ropes once again, and found that she couldn't move her hands or her arms. Her breasts bobbed as she moved her shoulders and upper body. Flushing, Jan felt and saw that her nipples had begun to tighten in excitement. She wished he would touch them, tease them as he had yesterday.

Yes, breathed her alter ego. Yes!

Jan breathed shakily, feeling warm and tingly.

Patrick came to stand in front of her, more rope in his hands and still more draped over his shoulder. Jan had no idea how she could be tied more securely than

114

she already was. She looked at him questioningly. But Patrick wasn't interested in more security. He was intent on the more erotic aspects of bondage, as Jan discovered when he wrapped a length around the base of her left breast, against her chest, and pulled it tight. Her breast tightened, the nipple looking, she thought, like the nose cone of a rocket as the rope grew tight.

Jan gasped at the sight of her bound breast, shivering as he did the other one in the same way. Now her breasts stood out tight and stiff from her body, the ropes biting into her skin. Her nipples were hard and tight as well, crinkly with excitement. Jan's breath was loud in her ears, and when Patrick stepped aside she glimpsed herself in the mirror.

A woman without arms stared back at her, face flushed, nostrils flaring, undeniably excited. The exaggerated thrust of her breasts accentuated the narrowness of her waist and the flare of her hips. Her long legs and full, ripe thighs looked Rubenesque. That's me, Jan thought with a thrill.

Even her alter ego was impressed. Wow! Nice tits.

This was a hundred times more sensual than yesterday's almost perfunctory handcuffs and leg irons. The tightness of the rope against her sensitive skin and the lingering touches as he tied her up were far outside her own narrow sexual horizons. Just being bound like this made her feel like a different woman.

You are, Jan Two asserted. Try to enjoy the new you.

Bound, Jan again felt free of all responsibility. Someone else had transformed her body into this vision of captive woman. Someone else would make her shudder with delight and release.

Yes, but *you'll* be doing the shuddering, the small voice reminded her.

Jan tried to quell these riotous thoughts, to control the body that was growing rebellious again.

Her darker self asked, why bother? You know how it's going to end. You just don't know how or when he'll make you come. But it'll be dynamite. Think of yesterday.

Jan thought of yesterday and admitted the truth of it to herself with a guilty start. The guilt was followed by the thrill of knowing that the miracle was going to happen again. Fascinated, she and the bound woman in the mirror gazed at one another.

Patrick allowed Jan to grow accustomed to her new image before he stepped behind her once again. Jan didn't register his movement until two hands appeared from behind her to cup her taut breasts.

'Oh!' she gasped as she felt herself held. The hands stroked her gently, sliding smoothly over her sensitive flesh and making her shudder. She gasped again, more deeply, when he pinched her nipples between thumbs and forefingers. Jan rolled her shoulders and arched her back, pressing her breasts into his hands. Her head went back to lie against his shoulder. She closed her eyes, allowing herself to drift in waves of sensuous pleasure. She felt warm and safe and free from guilt if she kept her eyes closed. And the sensations from her breasts were divine.

Oh God, Jan Two said. Why ever did you wait so long?

I don't know, Jan responded. Her thighs parted and her knees loosened as the caress went on and on. His breath was warm on the side of her neck as he planted small kisses on her hair and earlobe. Seduction. This was seduction. And Jan loved it.

But the dream was shattered as she felt his stiff cock pressing rudely against her bottom. Jan opened her eyes and saw herself being held by the stranger who had abducted her. His cock prodded her, seeking entrance to her body. She stiffened and pulled away, long habit reasserting control over her body. She felt that she was doing the right thing, resisting her base urges, but why, she wondered, was it so hard?

Patrick released her and stepped back. In the mirror Jan saw him standing behind her smiling ironically. Furious with herself and with him, she turned to face him.

Patrick regarded her levelly.

'Let me go!' she demanded, pulling against the ropes that held her hands and arms behind her. 'Please, let me go,' she wailed, feeling foolish and confused and angry at herself.

You're just saying that because you know it's too late, her alter ego mocked. You should have spoken sooner.

Patrick shook his head again. 'We must keep on trying, so you can see a bit more of what your body can do. Seeing is not as convincing as doing the real thing, but I guess you're not ready for that yet. We have plenty of time to let you convince yourself.'

Jan would have cried, 'Never!' if she hadn't been so conscious of sounding like the damsel-in-distress figure in a bad movie. With a curious detachment she regarded herself and decided that she didn't want to appear that way.

Jan Two approved.

Patrick produced a leather collar which he buckled around Jan's neck. It fit snugly. There was a small but decisive click behind her head as he locked the collar on her. He snapped a dog lead to the ring of her collar and tugged Jan toward the door.

For a moment she resisted but in the end she had no choice. If she resisted too strongly, the riding crop, never far away, would soon break her will.

They made the same trip down the stairs as they had done the day before. This time, with her hands and arms immobilised, she was extra careful. Jan was fearful again, wanting to know what was going to happen to her, but she fought the urge. Dignity, she reminded herself. Don't beg.

Not much dignity in being led like an animal, Jan Two said happily.

Better than letting him think I'm available, Jan thought back.

And you're not? You could have fooled me yesterday.

That was yesterday. Today is a new day, she insisted, straightening her back.

Patrick led Jan into the long room. He tethered her to one of the posts that supported the floor above. There was no one else in the room, and Jan feared that she was about to become the subject of a demonstration rather than a spectator at one. Patrick said nothing as he left her there. Alone, Jan struggled without success to free her hands and arms of the ropes she had found so exciting a short time ago. Her bound breasts felt so damnably vulnerable and exciting. She bounced on her feet, making them bounce but failing to dislodge the ropes that were tied so tightly around them. Jan gave up after a long struggle.

She was alone in a room that held nothing but two straight-backed chairs and those storage cabinets from which Patrick had extracted her dildo the day before. She wondered if it was still there. Stop that, she told herself. But she could not. The strong sunlight came in through two windows on what had to be the south wall, the bright band inching toward her as time passed and nobody came for her. Jan tormented herself by wondering if they had forgotten her. Being helpless in a strange house made her sweat in dismay and perverse excitement. She tugged again at the ropes that bound her.

When Patrick came back Jan was becoming frantic, but she would never have admitted to anyone the relief she felt when the door opened. He's come for me, Jan thought with relief and a new dread.

But he had not. He led Robin into the room on a chain. The chain emerged from between her legs. Jan pictured again those neat rings that pierced the young woman's labia, and the bar and tiny padlock that locked her cunt closed. Like Jan, she had no choice but to follow where she was led, although Jan thought herself lucky that she was merely being led by a collar and chain. She did not want to imagine how it must feel to be led irresistibly by those rings. She felt new and different sensations between her legs just thinking about it. And she shivered with a strange excitement.

Robin's hands and arms were tied behind her back, but unlike Jan she was not completely naked. She wore that too-tight bra again, forcing her breasts and nipples up and out, and stockings and suspenders again, long black ones today, reaching to her crotch. The chain of her lead provided a striking contrast to the sheer nylon of her stockings. Stiletto-heeled shoes complemented her long legs.

Quite erotic, Jan thought, before she could stop herself. She felt relief at Robin's appearance. At least she would be spared from participating in the perverted games the men played here. Well, for today, she reminded herself.

Wait until tomorrow, her inner voice remarked with growing enthusiasm.

Patrick tethered Robin to the same post. Jan felt embarrassed again. What does one say to one's fellow captive? Hello? Nice to see you again? Lovely weather? Wasn't last night nice? Jan was at a complete loss for words.

Not so Robin. 'OK today?' she asked brightly.

Jan nodded faintly. She was not feeling OK, but it seemed both impolite and weak to say so.

'We're finally getting around to piercing me. We got sidetracked last time, didn't we? So, today it is! I think you'll enjoy watching, and I don't mind, if that worries you.'

Jan was not enthusiastic. She was quite sure that she *would* mind watching, but she knew she had no choice. And it would be impossible to tear her gaze away. She had learned that much about herself the day before.

Robin's breasts were engorged, Jan saw. And Robin was clearly, enthusiastic, obviously looking forward to her new . . . adornments? Accessories? Acquisitions?

Jan felt slightly ill as she looked at the breasts thrust virtually into her face. She imagined them pierced and with the rings in place. She felt even more ill as she looked down at her own bound breasts. She imagined them with rings, and shuddered. Maybe they wouldn't insist, she hoped. After all, Robin was doing this voluntarily.

Patrick was laying out the things he needed in the background while Robin made bright conversation. Jan eyed him uneasily as he laid out needles, a syringe, surgical spirit and the rings themselves.

'. . . it's just like having your ears pierced,' Robin was saying. 'Doesn't hurt a bit. You ought to think about getting your tits done. They'd look ever so nice with rings. Not that they don't look nice enough now, but still . . . It'd be a real surprise for your husband.'

Yes, Jan thought, it would.

Patrick approached them. They fell silent, but Robin winked at her. 'Here goes,' she mouthed to Jan as he unclipped her lead from the post. He led Robin to one of the chairs by the worktop. When she sat down, he tied her arms behind the chair. Robin sat contentedly while he selected more rope from another cabinet. With it he tied Robin's ankles and knees together and pulled her feet beneath the chair. The chain led from her crotch over her thigh and down to the floor, the silvery links contrasting excitingly with the black stockings she wore. Patrick tied her hands to her ankles. Her breasts looked terribly vulnerable.

Robin drew a deep breath, but to Jan it looked more like excitement than fear. I'd be scared stiff if it was me, she thought. How can she be so calm?

Patrick tied the young woman to the chair with rope around her chest, below her prominently presented breasts, and around her waist. Robin tugged experimentally at her bonds but made no real attempt to escape.

She smiled at Jan. The return smile was more of a grimace. Even Jan Two was silent. Jan guessed that the tying of Robin was more a ritual than a necessity. It did not seem that she was going to bolt for the wide open spaces. Suddenly Jan realised that what counted was the ritual. And the feelings that went with being tied up.

Like now? Jan Two asked.

Jan didn't reply. She was remembering what had nearly happened upstairs. If she hadn't been tied, would it have gone as far as it had? She doubted it, and thought she understood why.

Patrick, meanwhile, was coming for her. Her heart leaped and she drew in a deep breath. But he was only coming to lead Jan to where she could watch

Robin being fitted, as he called it, with the nipple rings.

I won't look, Jan promised herself.

Want to bet? Jan Two asked.

He led Jan to the worktop, where he fastened her lead to one of the drawer handles. She had an unobstructed view and wished she hadn't.

Want a blindfold? Jan Two taunted.

Patrick put on a pair of surgeon's latex gloves and picked up a swab and the bottle of surgical spirit. Jan looked away. When she looked back he had begun dabbing Robin's nipples and areolae with the surgical spirit. The nipples tightened as the alcohol evaporated. Robin sighed and shivered. Jan stared.

'The syringe contains a local anaesthetic,' Patrick told them. 'Robin's a real trouper,' he smiled, 'and she says she could go cold turkey without any help, but I prefer it this way. Besides,' he went on, 'she'll get an extra thrill when she can't feel her nipples. Won't you, Robin?'

The young woman smiled and nodded, watching closely as he injected the anaesthetic around her areolae. She shuddered as he moved the needle.

'Now we'll wait for her to go numb,' Patrick announced. He looked at Jan, and was amused to see that she was staring intently at Robin's nipples.

Jan tore her gaze away, and was disconcerted to know that he had seen her staring. Minutes passed, and she was congratulating herself on being tough with herself, when her eyes were jerked back by the sound of a loud plop. Patrick had flicked one of Robin's erect nipples with his forefinger.

'Feel anything?' he asked.

Robin shook her head. Patrick picked up the piercing needle, cleaned it with alcohol and showed it to Jan. Her stomach felt queer.

He was using a needle like those used by jewellers before the invention of the modern punch. 'Erotic piercing is mainly done with these,' he explained, 'because punches aren't very good for it.' He held a block of wax against one side of Robin's nipple. 'A backstop,' he explained.

Jan swallowed a tight lump in her throat but couldn't stop looking. She would never again look at beeswax or needles without thinking of this. The needle touched Robin's flesh and she went still. Jan felt a sympathetic twinge in her own nipples.

Patrick pressed harder, the skin indented, and then the needle was passing through and into the block of wax. He waited a moment, and Jan was mesmerised by the spectacle of Robin's nipple transfixed by the bright needle. Patrick waited a moment. Robin too was looking down at her pierced nipple.

'Doesn't that hurt?' Jan asked.

Patrick looked inquiringly at Robin, who shook her head. He looked at Jan as if to say, see, nothing to worry about.

Jan was not sure.

Patrick finally withdrew the needle and did the same thing to Robin's other nipple. He cleaned both piercings with surgical spirit. Robin did not protest, so Jan guessed that she still felt nothing.

Now it was time for the insertion of the rings, the one irreversible step. Left alone, the holes would close, just like those made for earrings, Patrick explained. The rings would pass through and the halves would lock together. Thereafter they could only be removed with surgical cutters.

Jan's stomach tightened as Patrick pressed the half-ring through Robin's nipple. He left it while he did the same to her other side. Then he fitted the other halves of the rings and pressed them together. Jan heard the faint double snick as they closed and locked. She thought she might faint if he did that to her. Robin looked down at her new accoutrements and up at Patrick. She smiled and nodded.

Patrick leaned closer to inspect his handiwork, and looked up again to see Jan's eyes locked on the stainless steel rings. Jan blushed when she knew that he had seen her. He turned the rings in Robin's nipples so that the joint was concealed. They looked as if they had been there forever.

Jan admitted to herself that the rings did look decorative. Erotic too. She imagined Robin being led about by them in a few days' time. She felt suddenly warm in face and cunt.

How about being led around that way? her alter ego asked.

Patrick untied Robin from the chair and led her away, leaving Jan at a loss for words. She had watched, and had not fainted. She had seen Robin pierced without any apparent ill effects. And she wondered why the idea of piercing her nipples still worried her. It's just that I don't fancy it, she told herself. I could stand it, but I don't want it. As for having rings in the other place, well, definitely not. She twisted her shoulders to relieve her cramped muscles and waited for him to come back for her.

And what are you hoping he'll do when he does come? Her alter ego was back. Feeling horny?

Jan shook her head angrily but the mental image and voice wouldn't go away.

Eight

As it happened, she had plenty of time to think. The sunlight coming from the windows turned more golden with the afternoon. After what felt like hours of standing while absolutely nothing happened, Jan sat down on the worktop. Once again she toyed with the idea that she had been abandoned, but she knew better. And it wouldn't help, she knew. It would only make her look foolish. A quick tug at her ropes convinced her that she was not going to get free unaided.

Patrick was probably seeing to Robin in the way the horny young woman liked best. Jan felt a stab of jealousy at the idea of him and Robin screwing again while she waited helplessly in solitude. And bored. The admission surprised her. She was in the most bizarre situation of her life, and she was bored. Jan was learning something else about bondage. If one went in for it, one had to be prepared to spend long periods doing nothing but waiting for someone else. She didn't think much of that.

Would you rather Patrick were touching you? her alter ego asked, surfacing once more.

Jan almost said yes. She shook herself mentally, but the thought persisted. Standing (or sitting) around in enforced idleness was not much fun.

Yesterday, though frightening, had certainly not been boring.

Jan Two snickered.

Jan imagined Patrick approaching her with his rude red cock sticking out, ready to stick it into her. That broke the spell. Never, she said silently.

Well, how about a nice dildo then? suggested her alter ego. Get warmed up with that as we did the last time. Then you'll want the real thing.

Never, Jan repeated, but with less determination. She hadn't managed to hold herself in check yesterday, and she suspected that self-restraint wouldn't be any easier today. Uneasily, she remembered that the hard rubber shaft was probably in one of the drawers. Maybe in the very one she was sitting on. Jan slid off the worktop as if it had suddenly grown hot, standing nervously as far away from it as her tether permitted. Nevertheless she felt a nagging urge to open the drawer and look. Looking won't hurt, she told herself.

Go on then, the inner voice urged her. Turn around, grab the handle with both hands and pull.

Jan edged toward the drawer. She turned her back to the worktop and had actually grasped the drawer pull in her bound hands before the spell broke. The idea of being caught fumbling with the dildo was too awful to bear. Besides, she told herself, I couldn't do anything useful with it if no one came.

No, but Patrick could certainly do something with it when he comes back. Go on, her darker self urged.

Jan stood with her hands on the drawer handle and fought the internal battle. She pulled tentatively and felt the drawer slide partway open. As she was fumbling in the drawer, the door opened. Jan let go of the handle as if it had burned her. She blushed in confusion as she saw Patrick. He wore only his shorts, as if he had just come from doing Robin. He looked . . .

Eager for you? her alter ego suggested.

She was certain he had guessed her intent. As unobtrusively as she could she let go of the handle behind her, striving to appear neither confused nor glad to see him, nor ready to co-operate. In her startled embarrassment she almost spoke. Just in time she remembered that there was nothing she could say that wouldn't sound either silly or provocative. Etiquette books were of no help in this situation.

Patrick crossed the room. Jan felt her heart flutter.

Be still, my beating heart, Jan Two mocked.

Jan nearly smiled at the quote before she realised that a smile might give Patrick the wrong idea. Damn, she thought, this is awkward.

Wordlessly, Patrick unclipped her lead from the drawer handle and slid the drawer shut. 'Find what you were looking for?'

Jan wished vainly for invisibility, to be anywhere but here. For anything that would hide her flaming pink blush.

'How maidenly,' Patrick remarked. 'Not many women blush so prettily.'

'Damn you!' Jan burst out.

His smile made her blush more strongly. She was unable to control her body or her emotions, and she hated that. Silence was her only refuge.

Laughing, he bent to kiss her lips. Jan turned her head away angrily. Patrick held her chin in one hand and turned it back. Unable to resist, Jan glowered instead.

'You're beautiful when you're angry,' Patrick said.

The cliché made Jan even angrier, but she was unsure whether she was more angry with him or with herself. Both, probably. She clamped her lips closed, fearing another outburst as much as her own response if he kissed her.

Patrick released her chin and bent suddenly to kiss her nipples. He did so quickly, one after the other.

Jan was taken by surprise, and with her hands and elbows tied behind her back she could do nothing to stop him. Her bound breasts looked as if she were offering them to him. There was nothing she could do about that either. And her nipples, damn them, sprang erect as he licked and teased them. Jan backed away, but came up against the edge of the worktop.

Patrick followed her, kissing her breasts and nipples, not touching her or trapping her with his hands.

Jan bent backwards over the worktop but he merely leaned forward, frustrating her attempt to escape. He placed his hands on the worktop on either side of her to support himself and continued to kiss her breasts. Jan's back was bowed. She supported herself with her bound hands against the worktop, but she could retreat no further. The further she leaned backwards the more her breasts thrust upward. She felt the familiar tightening in her stomach and belly.

'Don't!' she cried, intending to sound firm and angry, in control, firmly resistant, arousal-proof. It came out as a despairing wail, and her anger was redirected toward herself. She knew that she was wetting herself. This was intolerable. In a moment she was going to . . .

Get hot? the inner voice suggested. Come? Spread your legs and beg him to fuck you?

'No,' she whimpered, answering herself.

His cock was erect, pressing against her belly as she leaned away from him. Her hips were thrust forward by the worktop behind her. Jan felt trapped. No matter what she did she felt as if she were offering

128

some part of herself to him, while the insidious inner voice urged her to open her thighs and let him shove it inside her.

'Jan, Jan, what are we to do with you?' Patrick said ruefully, drawing back slightly and looking into her upturned face.

Jan had no answer, too busy fighting her own internal battles.

Patrick stepped back.

Damn it! You were nearly there, her alter ego raged. Jan herself nearly agreed. She was panting and aghast at her state of arousal. It didn't take much, she thought. And, what's happening to me?

Patrick nearly happened to you, the inner voice declared, and echoed his own rueful appraisal. Get yourself together, girl. Get fucked and stop dithering.

It occurred in a flash to Jan that she was enjoying the dithering. It was a form of extended foreplay. But that implied that she was going to go the whole way at some point. She was not ready for that, but couldn't say any longer that she would never be. Let's see what happens next, she extemporised. She already knew that they were not going to let her go. Now she guessed that she would yield at some point. It had been so long that she didn't remember what the 'real thing' felt like.

Relax and find out, Jan Two suggested.

I can't. Not . . . yet.

Jan Two groaned in despair.

Patrick moved Jan away from the worktop so that he could get at the drawer she had been trying to open. The dildo – her dildo, or its twin – was inside. Jan flushed anew but could not take her eyes off it as Patrick laid it on the worktop and rummaged in the drawer for further necessities.

Jan tried not to cry out in relief as she watched the preparations for her penetration. Yesterday was about to happen again. And she would not be responsible or have to face the real thing just yet. A part of her realised that she was being manipulated into a position where she would have to ask for the real thing, but she pushed the thought aside. I'll worry about that later. Perhaps I'll have the courage by then. And she realised that that was a further admission that the changes they had threatened her with were already occurring.

Patrick turned to her with the dildo in his hand, and Jan felt her stomach knot up with anticipation while her older self tried to induce panicked flight. The deciding factor was her helplessness to prevent what was going to happen, and she took refuge in that, tugging at the ropes that held her wrists and elbows behind her back to reassure herself that she was indeed helpless.

He looped another piece of rope around her waist and knotted it tightly in front. Another piece went between her bound wrists, over the rope. This trailed down behind her as he approached with the dildo. Jan didn't shrink from it as she had done the first time. It still looked huge, but she knew now that she could take it, and what it would do to her when she had.

Nevertheless her own code of personal conduct prevented her from co-operating openly. She shivered but stood still as he knelt before her and parted her labia with his fingers. She looked down at the hard black rubber shaft as he guided it into her, watching it disappear and savouring the feel of being stuffed as it slid home. Patrick reached between her knees for the rope trailing down behind from her bound wrists. He settled it into the crack of her bottom cheeks and pulled it through her crotch. Jan felt the rope pass through her divided labia and into her pussy.

Patrick pulled the rope tighter, and Jan gasped as it pressed against her clitoris.

At least you know where your clit is and what it does, Jan Two said brightly. Well, if this is what it takes to break your will, we'd best get on with it.

Yes, Jan agreed silently. Let's get on with it.

Patrick looped the ends over the rope that circled Jan's waist. And pulled it tight.

Jan gasped and stood on tiptoe as she tried to escape that pressure on her most sensitive parts. Patrick waited until she was up as high as she could go without levitating, and then pulled the rope even tighter. Jan felt her hands being drawn down behind her back until her wrists were nearly level with the base of her bottom. The rope held her hands and arms down, and every time she tried to move she felt the rope between her legs press against her spot.

'Oh!' Jan gasped. 'It's cutting me. Don't.'

Patrick knotted the crotch rope and stood back to observe. Jan had to come down eventually. She did, wincing at the pressure against her crotch and clitoris.

'It's cutting me in two,' she hissed in dismay, even as she felt the first of those twinges she had come to relish. She was doing this to herself. Jan the autoerotic madwoman is going on autopilot, she thought as she struggled against the rope. The dildo inside her shifted as she moved. 'Ohhh!' she gasped.

Things were moving too fast for her. 'Take it out,' she pleaded. 'I can't do this.'

Want to bet? Jan Two snickered.

'Do what?' Patrick asked innocently.

The rope between her legs sawed at her, and Jan gasped in surprise as she felt the approach of pleasure. I can't escape, she told herself. I can't stop myself from coming. I can't do anything. She recited the phrases over and over, a mantra to mesmerise herself, as she wriggled and pulled at her bonds.

'If you're all ready, we'll have a tour of the place. I can show you some of the other features before you become too aroused to appreciate them.' Patrick grasped her lead and led her toward the door she had not been through yet.

Jan resisted at first, but the pull was irresistible. She stumbled after him, across the room, aware at each step of the dildo inside and of the rope tight in her crotch. The dildo shifted with each step, the rope rubbed against her clitoris. Jan strove to ignore the sensations as she followed him into a glassed room with a large swimming pool. By that alone she knew that the house was very big. She had had no real idea of its scale before this.

'Our isolation tank,' Patrick told her. 'Also for relaxation, of course. You can try it later.' He led her around the pool close to the glass wall. The day was fine and clear, and Jan saw in the distance the dark wood she had seen earlier. In the middle distance a man and a woman strolled in the grounds of the house. Seeing them, Jan felt even more naked. She shrank from the glass, not wanting to be seen in this state. Patrick noticed, and halted the procession.

'Please, go on!' Jan said tensely. 'They'll see me!'

'And why shouldn't they?' He pulled her closer to the transparent wall, Jan fighting as hard as she could. He pulled her close and turned her so that she faced the outside. From behind he reached round to cup her heavy bound breasts, pinching her nipples while he kissed her behind the ear.

Earlier, Jan had found that quite pleasant. Now, afraid of being seen by strangers, she struggled to break free and get out of sight. 'No! Please! Take me away from here.'

Instead he pushed her forward, closer to the glass. Jan was inches from it when the sun emerged from behind a cloud, bathing the room and her in light. She felt as if she were standing nude on a stage before an audience consisting of most of the rest of the world. As she struggled to push herself back from the glass, the man raised his hand and waved to her. Oh God, he's seen me. She struggled even harder.

Patrick removed one hand from her breasts and waved back. Jan wished he hadn't chosen that moment to be civilised. At least his hands had covered her. The man and woman turned toward the house.

'Oh God! They're coming this way. Please take me away!' She almost added, 'and hide me,' but it was too late. The couple approached while Patrick held his struggling captive in full view of the rest of the world. The rest of the world, on closer approach, turned out to be James and Antoinette. Today she was wearing an all-over body-stocking of sheer black nylon. From a distance it had looked like a black jump suit, but now Jan could see the woman's body fully revealed. She couldn't believe that any woman would choose to go about in public like that.

Then she realised that she had no choice. Antoinette's hands were bound behind her back, and she wore the leather training collar. James held her lead slackly. She followed him as he looked steadily at Jan. He studied her for an eternity before smiling and nodding at them.

Jan blushed hotly, still struggling in Patrick's arms.

'Relax, Jan,' he told her. 'They're ours.'

'I know,' she retorted faintly. 'But what difference does that make? I don't want to be ogled by anyone.'

'Well, one immediate difference is that they won't be reporting you for public indecency and lewd

133

display. And you really should try to distinguish between an ogling and an admiring glance.'

Jan was not mollified. 'Damn you! I hate you! How could you humiliate me like that?' Even to her that sounded like a line from a melodrama, but she could think of nothing else.

Jan Two chose that moment to resurface. Oh, be quiet, she rasped. Don't be a goose.

Jan relaxed slightly, almost smiling at that one. No one had called her a goose since her school days. But she was still embarrassed.

Patrick's next words did nothing to lessen her discomfiture. 'We'll run into them later. They started outside while we began in here. Our paths are sure to cross. Afterwards,' he added as an afterthought, 'we'll look around the grounds – just like the nice people at the sanatorium suggested to Mrs Robinson.'

Jan could not believe her ears. She felt as if she had been doused with icy water. Surely he wasn't going to . . . But she had said that before, and been dismayed to see just what he would do. 'No!' she shouted, 'No! No! I won't go!'

Patrick took his hands from her breasts and covered his ears in mock horror. 'Such a noise about such a tiny thing,' he admonished her smilingly.

Freed from his grip, Jan turned and ran blindly, oblivious of the lead trailing from her collar and of the thing inside her. The pool lay directly in her path. She plunged into the cool water. As the water closed over her head she panicked, struggling wildly to get back to the surface and the air, tugging madly at the unyielding ropes on her elbows and wrists as she felt herself sinking. Jan's long hair floated free around her head, blinding and disorientating her. Up and down were matters of opinion. I'm going to drown, she thought despairingly. Her lungs felt as if they were on

fire, and she fought her panic and the nearly overwhelming urge to inhale as she struggled.

And then, perversely, she was aware of the dildo
inside her, and of the tight rope in her crotch. An
electric tingle of excitement shot through her. The
sensation was so intense that she nearly came, even as
she struggled to save herself. She nearly inhaled water
as the dildo stabbed her again.

Then someone was beside her, righting her, guiding
her back to light and air and life. As her head broke
the surface, she took a huge breath, still struggling
wildly, expecting to sink again. Her long chestnut
hair was wrapped around her head and face. She still
couldn't see anything; had no idea where safety lay.
And from between her straining thighs the signals
continued.

An arm under her chin supported her and a voice
in her ear told her to stop struggling. She took
another breath, and another. She didn't sink, and
gradually it dawned on her that Patrick was towing
her through the water. Jan went limp, so grateful for
his presence that she would have hugged him. And as
she went limp she felt her body begin to float. Her
legs and feet broke the surface. So did her bound
breasts, taut and wet and slick, thrusting up toward
the sky. And her mons veneris, with the rope tight
against her clitoris and the dildo forced up inside her.

'Next time you fall into water with your hands
tied,' Patrick told her calmly, 'don't panic. You'll
float. Everybody does.'

He doesn't know what's happening, Jan thought,
but she could not tell him. Something hard bumped
into Jan's shoulder. Tiles. The edge of the pool.
Patrick towed her a bit further, and then took his arm
away. Jan forgot his advice and panicked again,
thrashing and sinking. This time a tug on her lead

brought her back to the surface. Fingers parted the hair across her eyes, and she saw a ladder in front of her. Her feet found a rung below the water. Patrick reached from behind her and grasped the sides of the ladder. His feet found the rung below hers, and his body was against her back, holding her to the ladder. Jan shuddered against him.

'Climb,' he commanded her.

And she did, weakly, lifting her feet from rung to rung and feeling him doing the same, his body supporting hers from behind as they ascended. As she emerged dripping onto the top rung of the ladder Jan shuddered again as the rope and the dildo made themselves felt. She felt his cock pressing against her bottom as he climbed behind her.

Back to the real world at last, her alter ego said approvingly. You're noticing the important things again.

Jan lacked the energy to frame a reply. The dildo and crotch rope were still sending the most extraordinary signals to the rest of her body. Even the cock against her bottom felt good. Reassuring. Warm. Exciting. Just a little shift, and it would slip into her bottom. Jan yelped and jumped onto the tiles, her wet feet skidding from under her. She landed on her bottom, knocking the breath from her lungs. Gasping and struggling to rise, she became aware of laughter behind her.

'Anyone would think you'd backed into a red-hot poker,' Patrick said.

Well, you nearly did, her inner devil said, smirking. Why'd you jump away?

He knelt behind her, his arms encircling her shoulders and chest as he lifted Jan to her feet. His hands cupped her breasts, and once again she felt an electric tingle go from her nipples to her cunt. The other bits made themselves felt at the same time. 'Ohhhh!' Jan sighed. And then 'Oh!' as she felt his cock against her bottom again.

Don't be such a goose, she told herself.

No, her alter ego replied. Just hold still and be goosed.

Patrick fondled her breasts, and Jan knew where that would lead.

Unless you act silly again, said the familiar inner voice.

As she teetered on the brink of surrender, a mental image of her mother formed in Jan's mind. Mrs Graham was aghast, as she had been on the day when she caught Jan and Donny from around the corner playing doctors and nurses. What are you doing she had shrieked, though she knew perfectly well what was going on. The lecture that time had been aimed at frightening her. Men put that thing into you, her mother told her, obviously opposed to the whole idea. And then you have a baby.

The shame, embarrassment and fear she had been made to feel then had been with her ever since, reinforced by as many matriarchal sermons as her mother could find occasion for. And there had been a remarkable number of occasions. But why? Jan wondered. If all this felt so good, why did her mother think it so bad? And the answer struck her with great force: *because* it all felt so good. The pleasure equals sin argument had echoed through most of her young life, reinforced by religious education and by what then passed for sex education.

If what they told you was all so wrong, her alter ego asked pointedly, why are you still fighting it?

Because, Jan thought. Because I am what I am and can't change.

Try, suggested the inner voice.

Give me time, she replied.

How bloody much time do you need? demanded her other half. You're forty-two now.

Just a little more *time*.

Her other half sneered but kept silent.

The inner debate was broken by another urgent signal from her tits to her cunt. And indeed the alarm bells were ringing throughout Jan's nervous system. While she had been debating internally, Patrick had continued to tease her nipples. The crotch rope and the shaft inside her were working their magic too. Now Patrick released her nipples and bent over her shoulder to kiss them. Jan's attention snapped back to present matters with an obvious jerk as her body quickly responded.

Jan felt one of those twinges in her belly that had, ever since her abduction, signalled the onset of sexual arousal. It passed like a wave through her body, and she shivered again with the anticipation of approaching release. The sun had gone behind a cloud and the glass enclosing the pool allowed her to see herself and Patrick as in a cloudy mirror. She saw a bound woman sitting on the tiled floor while a man bent over her breasts, kissing and teasing them while the woman shuddered with pleasure. This time the reflection of her arousal excited the woman – me, Jan thought – whereas before it had frightened and even repelled her.

Watching their reflections on the darkening glass, Jan felt detached from them. She sank into unselfconsciousness as into a warm bath, allowing her mind to grow fuzzy and her body to respond as it had recently learned to do. It felt so good to be held, sheltered and aroused. So natural. 'Ahhhh,' she sighed as the next ripple of the coming storm spread down her legs and through her belly and was met by the wave from her bound and throbbing breasts. Jan tensed to meet the next wave, stronger than the first, felt more keenly because she was bracing herself for it.

The storm broke upon her suddenly, as it had before. As she relaxed from that wave of pleasure, the next one shook her. Her back arched and her hips thrust upward with the strength of it. She offered her bound breasts to Patrick's tongue and lips and teeth, her legs and body open to his touch, and he brought her to another peak of ecstasy. Behind her back, her bound hands flexed and clawed. She shuddered in his arms.

Jan was vaguely aware of Patrick shifting until he sat beside her, facing her with one arm supporting her shoulders while his mouth roamed over her breasts and his other hand found its way to her crotch to press the dildo deeper into her and to stroke her sensitive, swollen clitoris.

She drew her legs up, bent her knees and spread her thighs more widely for him, her body doing automatically what her mind would have prevented. The reproving figure of her mother was rushed away. Jan leaned her body against him, warmed by the touch, made reckless by the sensations flooding through her. Thought fled before the storm, and when it was over Jan felt as if she had been washed up on the beach of a tropical island with only one other inhabitant. He who held her while the shudders passed, diminishing to shivers and finally down to stillness.

Jan felt him stand, felt his arms go under her shoulders and knees, felt him straighten as he cradled her weakened body against his chest and bore her away. She felt him plant a long kiss on each of her upthrust nipples. She murmured sleepily as he carried her through the big house and up the stairs and laid her down on her bed and lay down beside her. Felt him draw the blankets over their bodies and take her in his arms before she drifted into exhausted sleep. The last image she remembered was of a tiny, reddish devil-figure sprawled on her back with her legs wide open and a smile on her Jan-face.

Nine

Jan woke in the morning when she felt Patrick get out of bed. I've done it at last, she told herself in wonder. I've spent the night naked in a stranger's arms.

Jan Two woke up at the same time. She seemed to have recovered her energy and her hornier-than-thou stance. That wasn't anything to write home about, she said scornfully. You spent the night tied up with a dildo up your cunt. That ain't the real thing. Grow up.

Not yet, Jan said, alarmed again. She felt all the courage of the day before drain away as she looked at Patrick's ... *thing* hanging down. And looked hurriedly away.

Her alter ego looked disgusted. What happened to you? Yesterday you were halfway to calling things by their right names. Now you're back to euphemisms and blushes. A man can take only so much.

Jan struggled to a sitting position and swung her feet onto the floor. Her bound breasts were an embarrassment now, seeming to offer themselves to Patrick when she couldn't even bring herself to look at his ...

Cock? her inner devil suggested helpfully. Prick? Shaft? Schlong?

Face, I was going to say, before you opened your foul mouth.

Hah! said the inner voice derisively.

Patrick came to stand before her, and suddenly it was in Jan's face.

Go on, kiss it! the little devil urged her. I'll take the blame, though why anyone should need to blame anyone I can't say. Go on!

Jan opened her mouth halfway before closing it again decisively. She looked up instead at Patrick's face. He seemed in good humour. Not put out by Jan's reticence. She was thankful for his forbearance. She was beginning to think that she would go the whole distance with him in the end, but she needed more time.

Her inner voice maintained a scornful silence.

Patrick knelt to untie the ropes around her breasts. Jan relaxed as they regained their normal shape. There were deep red lines in the skin where the ropes had been. He helped Jan to her feet and untied her wrists and elbows.

Jan gratefully moved her arms to get rid of the cramps from nearly eight hours in bondage. She carefully avoided looking at Patrick or his schlong. Now where did I hear that one? It sounded comical when she considered it. The rope between her legs reminded her of its presence, but she lacked the courage to ask him to loosen it.

With his uncanny skill in reading her mood, Patrick untied it and pulled the dildo out.

Jan looked at it again. Outside, it seemed huge. Inside, it had felt wonderful.

'Did you know,' he asked Jan, 'that it was customary among many of the American Indian tribes for unmarried women to wear just such a crotch rope? It was supposed to remind anyone who happened upon a naked woman that she was untouchable. After the marriage ceremony the groom untied it and performed the customary defloration.'

142

Was that an indecent proposal, or merely conversation? Jan chose to take it as the latter. Her alter ego continued to look disgusted.

'I wonder,' Patrick went on, 'just how many Indian women used it as a convenient means of masturbation, undetectable by others unless she became too demonstrative. It seemed to serve you pretty well yesterday.'

Jan blushed and looked away. 'My hair is a mess,' she said, inanely. It had dried itself overnight without benefit of brush or comb. Jan remembered with a smile her mother saying that she looked as if she had been pulled backwards through a hedge.

Patrick parted the hair before her face and smiled down at her. 'Beautiful smile from a beautiful woman,' he said as he kissed her. 'Good morning.'

Jan was both surprised and pleased at the compliment. Her smile turned shy. 'Good morning.'

'You have the bathroom first if you like,' he told her.

Jan noticed that the door to her room was open. Had been open all night. I could have escaped, she thought. Then she remembered how she had spent the night. I could bolt now, she thought then. But she didn't. I'm still naked, she rationalised.

Patrick closed the door as he left, and the chance, such as it was, had gone. Jan went into the bathroom and ran the tub full of hot water and added scented bath salts instead of her usual Radox.

Jan Two noticed the alteration in routine. Going to smell nice for Patrick when he comes back?

Jan climbed into the water and sank down gratefully. The hot bath felt good. The cramps and stiffness from a night in bondage gradually soaked away. She washed her hair with shampoo and added conditioner.

Patrick will like that, Jan Two said.

Jan made no reply. She dried herself and her hair with the hot air dryers, and took her time brushing it out. Two hundred strokes, she had learned as a schoolgirl. Why two hundred, and not three, or only one? Jan lost count as she thought of Patrick and what she had done and felt the day before. Sleeping with him beside her had been nice too, even with her hands tied behind her back.

Could do better, said her other half.

Patrick was back when she emerged smelling fresh and feeling shy. He was dressed but there was no breakfast tray, as Jan had expected.

'You look good enough to eat, Jan.'

More maidenly blushes, which didn't escape the scorn of her inner devil.

'Sorry I can't stay to eat with you, but something's come up. I've got to leave now but I'll see you this evening. Antoinette will be up in a few minutes to help you, but in the meantime you need to put these on.'

'These' turned out to be the familiar leg irons and handcuffs and belt. Jan was disappointed (because he was going) and relieved (because she would not now be called on to make the decision she half-feared and half-welcomed). So, in two minds, Jan stood quietly while he locked the leg irons onto her ankles and fitted the belt to her waist. The handcuffs were to the front, and she locked them around her own wrists without waiting to be told.

Patrick nodded approvingly.

Jan Two approved. You're learning.

Patrick kissed Jan on the lips. She didn't draw away, but she didn't open her lips either. Then he left, closing the door after him. Jan sat on the side of the bed to await developments. She hoped that Antoinette wouldn't be too long. She was hungry.

Antoinette came about a half hour later to take her down to breakfast. Yesterday's revealing body-stocking had disappeared. She was dressed as before in the 'immodest' maid's uniform. Today Jan thought the outfit less immodest that she had the day before. Today she wore leg irons like Jan's. The contrast between her sheer black tights (or were they stockings?) and the hard steel was (Jan thought suddenly) erotic. More so than her own. Jan noticed that Antoinette still wore her collar.

Antoinette smiled and seemed glad to see Jan again. 'I wondered if you had escaped,' she joked. 'You were talking about it the last time we met. I'm glad you're still with us.'

'I haven't much choice, have I?' Jan replied, suddenly half-pleased to be included in the rather obscure group inhabiting this unknown house in the middle of she knew not where.

'I suppose not,' Antoinette said. Changing the subject, she asked if Jan was hungry.

Jan was.

'Come with me then. The others are just sitting down to breakfast.'

'Others?' The idea of eating with other people, naked and in chains, suddenly made her less hungry. 'No,' she said sharply. 'I mean, I'm not hungry. I'll be all right.'

'Or do you mean you'd rather not face strangers dressed as you are?' Antoinette asked.

It seemed to Jan that everyone here could read her mind. She felt even more naked than before, if that was possible.

'I felt the same way,' Antoinette said. 'But you'll get used to it. It only took one hungry day to convert me. And since your keeper isn't here to look after you, you're sure to get hungry soon. Only Robin and another woman are there, anyway. It'll be all girls together this time. I think the other keepers arranged it that way for your benefit.'

'No. I'll be all right,' Jan insisted, to the disgust of her other half. 'I can't eat anyway when I'm like this.' She indicated her handcuffs, which kept her hands close against her belly. That should excuse me, she thought.

You're just afraid, her other half said scornfully.

And, Jan had to admit, she was.

Antoinette looked at Jan again and changed her mind. 'If you really would rather not go down just yet, I'll come back for you after the others are finished. I don't think our keepers would have too much trouble with that.

That word again. 'Keepers'. Jan was not sure she liked it. It sounded as if they were animals at a zoo. 'How many keepers are there?' she asked.

'Between four and five that I know of, but there may be more. There may be others that come when I'm not here, I mean. Patrick is yours, and he shares Robin with James, who also looks after me.' Antoinette smiled when she mentioned James, but she seemed perfectly serious about the 'sharing' arrangement and not obviously jealous.

Jan wondered if there was an understanding between her and Patrick too. She didn't like sharing him even with Robin.

Getting jealous of your almost-lover? Her inner voice asked.

Jan shook her head angrily to banish the thought, but it stuck. How ridiculous – being jealous of the man who kept her captive. But she remembered reading somewhere that kidnap victims often formed bonds with their abductors. No. Out of the question.

Antoinette left the room, leaving the door open. 'Back in a few minutes,' she said as she disappeared.

This is my chance, Jan thought. All I have to do is walk out of here. She started for the door. Both her inner voice and her common sense came to her rescue. She looked at her handcuffs and leg irons, and at the naked woman who stared back at her from the mirror, and she thought of the excruciating embarrassment she would feel if she were found wandering in the countryside in that state, even if she claimed to be a kidnap victim. Jan stopped half-way, undecided. Her old habits told her to run while she had the chance. Run and escape.

It hasn't been all *that* bad, has it? the familiar voice asked.

Her darker self was opposed to flight. And she herself had to admit both the justice of its observation, and of the foolishness of wandering around naked and in chains. She might fall into worse hands than Patrick's.

Or better, her new self said.

Jan thought, run, you fool. This is the chance you've been waiting for. But she didn't. I'll wait for a better chance, she decided.

When Antoinette returned Jan was sitting on the bed looking at the distant wood.

'They're just going now. Come with me.'

Antoinette took the opposite direction to the one she and Patrick had taken the day before on the way to Robin's piercing.

'Will you be able to manage the stairs without hands?' Antoinette asked.

'I've had some practice,' Jan replied dryly.

'So you have.' Antoinette led her down another set of stairs and into the dining area, which Jan had not yet seen. She might have seen it yesterday if the scheduled tour had not been cut short.

There was a long refectory table, seating nearly twenty people. Jan imagined ranks of nude women seated down one side faced by their 'keepers', all making small talk as if it were the most natural thing in the world. Then she remembered the 'sharing'. Probably each keeper dealt with several women. The idea made her frown.

Only one end of the table, nearest the kitchen, was set this morning. Antoinette helped Jan to seat herself and began to clear the remains of the meal left by the other two women. Jan felt awkward, but relieved not to have to face anyone else just then. 'I see you didn't run when the chance came,' Antoinette remarked as she set out fresh coffee and fetched a platter of scrambled eggs and bacon from the microwave.

Jan shrugged, managing to indicate her chains, her nudity, and her reluctance to abandon the adventure all at once.

'A woman who really hated it would have run, even naked. But I don't know of anyone who has.' She sat next to Jan and poured two cups of coffee.

Jan felt uncomfortable, sitting naked so close to the other woman, but Antoinette only asked prosaically if she took milk and sugar. She buttered toast and served the eggs and bacon. Marmalade and strawberry jam, honey, salt and pepper were all to hand. An ordinary English breakfast. Jan remembered her last breakfast and her tidy kitchen, and the two men bursting into her ordered world to drag her away to this other ordinary breakfast.

Well, not that ordinary, her darker self remarked. Fortunately.

Antoinette fed them both, dividing her efforts between Jan and her own breakfast. By the end of the meal Jan had relaxed somewhat. She no longer felt as if she were sitting mentally on the edge of her chair. She even began to feel that the silence was getting awkward. 'Who are you?' she asked Antoinette, 'and how did you get into this?' There her courage failed her and she reddened with embarrassment.

Antoinette didn't seem offended. 'We don't use last names here, so I am just Antoinette, and I work in a merchant bank as a currency trader. I've got both males and females, under me, but mostly men, above me.' She shrugged to indicate that that was the way of the world. 'Some of the men, as you can imagine, see me as a threat or an interloper, or both. It's a boys' club.'

Jan nodded.

'And I'm a closet submissive,' Antoinette continued, 'or slave, if you prefer, who secretly longs to be owned and dominated by a man. You can imagine what that knowledge would do to my career if it became public.'

Antoinette smiled at Jan, and she relaxed, nodding her understanding.

'I suppose you too have your own secret agenda.'

Jan reddened and tensed up again. She didn't know what she wanted anymore.

'That's all right. If it embarrasses you to talk about yourself, or if you don't know yet what you want, don't worry. It takes a while to sort yourself out no matter where you are. But you will know before you leave.'

Antoinette smiled and poured a glass of orange juice for herself. 'Want some?'

Jan nodded, and Antoinette held the glass for her to drink.

'Strange,' she said. 'I'm the one serving you when I would rather be tied up and helpless, or even better, tied up being fucked stupid by my keeper James. But I'll have to be patient. They say that patience is its own reward, but they're wrong. The reward for patience, for postponing the big moment, is an even bigger moment when it comes. The trick is not to postpone it for too long. There is a tide in the affairs of men, and women, which taken at the flood, leads on to monster screaming orgasms.' Antoinette smiled at her misquotation. 'Someone more famous than I said something like that.'

Jan smiled too.

Getting easier, the red devil said. Way to go!

'I suppose it will be my turn soon,' Jan said. As soon as the words were out Jan wished she hadn't spoken. She hadn't known she was going to say that.

'I should hope so!' Antoinette took another sip of her juice and offered Jan some more. 'I know!' she said, standing up. 'Wait here. I'll be right back.'

She left the room through another door which led to a room unknown to Jan. Jan admired once again the contrast between Antoinette's leg irons and the sheer stockings. Alone, she looked idly out of the kitchen window. The day was dry but cloudy, with a wind that tossed the branches of the distant wood and bent the flowers in the garden. She saw Patrick emerge from another door, dressed in jeans and a sweatshirt. Something squeezed her stomach at the sight of the man who was her 'keeper', and was perilously close to becoming her lover. That idea caused another tightening in the stomach and belly. He went to a saloon car parked at right angles to the window, got in and started the motor. When he turned to drive off, Jan saw the number plate clearly. She quickly averted her gaze before she could memorise even part of the number. No names, no pack drill, she repeated the childhood mantra to herself.

Antoinette returned with a bottle of champagne and a corkscrew. 'They made the mistake of letting me see where the liquor is kept,' she said with a grin.

150

'Let me liven up your orange juice a bit.' Antoinette opened the bottle with the customary pop and spray of bubbles, pouring their glasses full.

She offered the glass to Jan, who thought that drinking in their situation might not be wise. It might loosen your tongue, she warned herself.

With any luck it won't only be your tongue that gets loosened, said her red devil. She drank anyway, feeling both decadent and adventurous. It was surprisingly good champagne.

Antoinette drank her buck's fizz and crossed her legs. A lot of leg got shown in the process. Jan envied her and even her 'immodest' dress.

'I'm here because I asked them to collect me, just as I told you. I needed a spot of ownership in the worst way. When I'm at work it's all pinstripe business suits and white blouses and opaque black tights. It's all quite modestly provocative. But I long for some immodest provocative stuff too, like this little number. I suppose it's descended from Chanel's "little black dress," but there must have been a sharp pair of scissors somewhere in the descent from decency. I love to imagine what my business colleagues would think of this outfit. And of the other things I get up to when they can't see the rising career girl. There'd be heart attacks all round, and I'd be sending my CV round again. But they don't know. And that's another pleasure.'

Jan was beginning to understand the forbidden fruit effect more fully. She drank again when the glass was offered, and felt more relaxed than she had since her abduction. Ogden Nash's line about the relative efficacy of chocolate and alcohol with women ran through her mind, and she almost giggled. There was something decidedly wicked about sitting late at the breakfast table in the nude and drinking champagne.

Her mother would have been horrified. So would her daughter have been, only a few days ago.

'I guess it won't do any harm to tell you that James and I are about to become an item. Not married, God no. Anything but that. Who wants children and a mortgage? But a little living in sin, that's what we're after. Too bad it really isn't sinful anymore. Anyway, I had this littler number fitted just three days ago, and there's a party planned for a few days from now, when I unveil myself, though you may not think I'm so well veiled just now.'

Antoinette stood up, pulling the short tight skirt to her waist. She was wearing stockings and suspenders, as Jan had guessed. This apparently wasn't the place for tights. Or pants.

Jan looked away hurriedly, wishing she had drunk more before this display. Could Antoinette be planning to seduce her too? No, of course not, she insisted. She's just finished talking about James, her intended. I wonder if she knows he nearly had me not too long ago.

Antoinette sat down again and spread her legs. She reached down to her cunt and fiddled about.

With a start Jan realised that the other woman was spreading her labia and exposing her clitoris. I suppose I should use the right names for things, she told herself.

Antoinette used her fingers to expose her clitoris, and Jan was shaken when she saw the stainless steel ring that pierced it. It was bizarre, that steel there, of all places. She had imagined that she was well acquainted with erotic piercing after seeing Robin's adornments. The world was still full of surprises, not all of them soothing.

'Patrick did this for me,' Antoinette was saying.

Jan was shaken again. How could he, when he was *her* keeper?!

'This will be all healed in a day or two, long before the party. Then James and I will walk down the aisle, as it were, with him leading me on a chain attached just there. And you will all wish us well. It'll be super! I can't wait. And afterward, when he comes to stay with me, I will get him to chain me to the dinner table when we eat, or to the coffee table when we watch TV. It's not what the average upwardly mobile career woman comes home to, is it?'

Jan used the time while Antoinette was delivering this extraordinary pronouncement to recover her poise (which she partly did) before she was required to express an opinion. The old Jan would have been tongue tied and horrified. The present Jan, after several days of 'personality transformation,' and with most of a large glass of champagne inside her, was less shocked. She felt a strange compulsion to reach out and touch Antoinette's ring, to feel for herself the hard bright steel against this, Antoinette's softest and most sensitive place. She found herself regretting the handcuffs.

Antoinette stood and moved closer so that Jan could see more clearly. And while she still couldn't touch Antoinette, she did see her pierced clitoris and the shadowed passage leading into her cunt. Pink and gleaming slickly, right in front of her. Jan had never tried, even with mirrors, to see her own body this closely. She swallowed hard, wanting to avert her gaze as she would have done a few days ago. But now she couldn't tear her eyes away to save her soul. If I've still got one, she thought.

Hey, the inner voice said, so this is what the fuss is all about! Looks pretty nice.

Jan's hands stirred restlessly in the handcuffs as she gazed at Antoinette.

The small rattle of chain broke the tableau.

Antoinette grinned guiltily and lowered her skirt. 'It's a surprise. Don't tell James,' she said with a wink.

'I don't know James that well,' Jan replied, with the strongest sense of having fallen through the looking glass.

'Well, now you know the career girl's darkest secret. If they knew about this at the bank I'd never be able to control the people in my section. And it would get me run out of the bank like that.' Antoinette took another drink from her glass and offered the other to Jan.

The champagne made her feel better. I must be getting drunk, Jan thought, gulping it down. I think I like being drunk, once in a while.

Progress, remarked her red devil.

Jan mused about being chained to something immovable at home (though not necessarily by my cunt, or tits, she hastily averred). Would Sam do it? Would he enjoy it? Jan was nearly certain that *she* would. Being owned, as Antoinette put it, had its attractions. It would all have to be secret, of course. It would be too embarrassing if her friends or acquaintances ever found out.

Her fantasy grew. She imagined herself beavering away at her gardening book while chained to her desk in the study. She thought about cooking, imagining herself in the kitchen at home, dressed 'immodestly' (or even nude) and chained to the table. Jan decided that she would have to be secured by her ankle, with a manacle like the one that fastened her to the bed here. In that way her hands would be free to attend to her work. And then there was the bed. An arrangement like the one she had here. Perhaps Sam would consider altering the locking arrangements on their bedroom door.

Or, if Sam was not interested, or if he preferred his paramour to her, would Patrick . . . Jan shook off the fantasy. Whatever had made her think of Patrick like that?

Antoinette was refilling their glasses. Outside it had begun to rain. No, she decided, it would not do to escape from this warm comfortable house to make her way across country on a rainy day wearing nothing. On the other hand, there was a lot to be said for sitting here with an interesting companion getting sloshed on champagne.

Jan heard footsteps approaching, male from the sound of them. Her reflexes took over and she tried, unsuccessfully, to cover herself while wishing once again for invisibility. Instead, she had to be content with the pink blush that covered her. James came into the kitchen, greeted them both with a 'good morning' and bent to kiss Antoinette on the lips. With a slight hesitation he turned to Jan, and when she did not actively warn him away, he did the same to her. 'Good to see you up and about and getting the insider's picture from Antoinette.' He put a dog lead down on the table and turned back to Antoinette. 'Is there anything left in that bottle?'

'Not much,' Antoinette replied with a slightly guilty look.

'I'll just get another one, then.' He fetched a second bottle and sat down opposite Jan with a smile. James poured for them all and lifted his glass in salute before drinking. Antoinette held the glass for Jan as before, and then drank from her own.

Jan felt both flustered and embarrassed to be drinking in these circumstances. Her mother would have been horror stricken. Phrases like 'drunken Bacchanale' came to her, but without any great force. She was, she realised with a thrill of pleasure, just drunk enough to be pliable. She giggled and blushed.

'Has Antoinette been entertaining you?'

Jan nodded, not trusting herself to speak.

'I told him about my work and a bit about this place, sort of putting her in the picture. You know.'

'And do you like the picture she's been putting you into?' he asked Jan.

She didn't know what to say, so she remained silent.

'She's still getting used to our ways,' Antoinette replied for her. 'She'll settle in.'

He turned to Antoinette, but spoke to Jan, 'Has the silly cow been mooing about wanting to be owned and dominated? She's always going on about that to me. I don't know where she gets these ideas. Do you?'

It was Antoinette's turn to colour slightly. Jan was still tongue tied.

'She has fantasies about coming home from work and lounging around in sexy underwear and chains. Spending her evenings chained or tied to bits of furniture. Being fed by hand and bathed and dried and tucked up at night.' He shook his head in wonderment, but with a smile that took the sting from his words.

'You left out the bit about wanting to be . . . fucked stupid.' The words were out before Jan could check them.

'Have you no shame?' he asked Antoinette.

'Not much,' she replied.

'But I won't permit that. She'll have to keep her office gear on. Her uniform, as she calls it. I have a thing about women in uniforms.' James leered at Jan. 'You don't happen to have a nurse's uniform, do you?' he asked. 'Or a nun's habit?'

Jan could think of no reply that wouldn't sound silly. Nor did she know if he was being serious with her. Silence once more came to the rescue.

James refilled their glasses while Jan thought about spending the days and evenings as Patrick's captive.

His property. She wasn't sure she'd like being 'owned', but the idea of being on temporary loan was beginning to look attractive. Her aversion to sexual arousal was going rapidly. Was it because these men gave her no choice, or merely because they all seemed to take for granted her acquiescence? No one here seemed in the least embarrassed to discuss or do any of the things she had avoided even thinking about.

James was speaking again. 'I am here to take Antoinette to the next session, but there's no hurry. It's a bonus to be able to drink champagne with such lovely companions.'

Antoinette smiled. Jan blushed. The collar around her neck seemed heavier. Her head felt lighter, as much from the champagne as from the knowledge that she was not to be the next victim just then.

Ten

That night Jan was left in her bedroom once more with her hands cuffed to the waist belt and her ankle chained to the bed. The dildo was in place, and her nipples were covered by the rubber caps. But this time Patrick had left the control box on her nightstand. 'In case you wake up and feel the need for a bit of diversion,' he told her with a smile.

Wake up? Jan thought. I don't know how I'll sleep. 'Please take it away,' she asked him, not trusting herself alone with the means to control her orgasm. 'I don't want it.'

Liar, her alter ego said. You're afraid you'll use it. And why not? That's what it's for.

Not for me, Jan retorted as she debated the matter with her second self. I can't do it to myself.

Why not? her alter ego asked again.

Patrick did not take away the tempting black box. Obviously he intended to make Jan decide what to do, and she sensed that her decision would be an important one. If she switched on the dildo stuffed inside her cunt, from weakness or from need (both seemed the same at that point), she would never be able to pretend that she hated what was happening to her here.

In the silent room her alter ego asked her why would she want to go back to what she was, and Jan had no answer. She lay awake staring at the control box, just visible in the glow of the bathroom light through the half-open door.

In her imagination she saw herself thrashing about in the bed on her own, still a captive but not forced by anyone to do this. She tried not to think about the box lying so handily on the night stand. Think of her daughters, Jan told herself, grasping at the thought.

Sophia, her eldest, had begun to make settling-down noises fairly early. She had married an Australian straight out of university and had emigrated with him. Leslie, the youngest, was the result of giving in again to Sam's pleas for a bit of 'the other'. Not that she regretted her youngest daughter. She tried to love them both equally, but inevitably showed favouritism to Sophia. She was self-sufficient, while Leslie was just plain wild. The difference between mother and daughter on too many things (especially sexual mores) was wide.

Leslie was often embarrassing, Jan thought, always going on about sex and orgasms and things that no one should speak of in public, or at least not to one's parents. Sam often held Leslie up as an example of what he would like Jan to be, for she talked as frankly with him as she did with her mother. Jan hated being compared unfavourably with her daughter, but she was not going to change her own outlook.

Are you sure? her alter ego asked. You could have fooled me.

Jan wrenched her thoughts back on track.

Leslie needs to settle down with a nice man and produce children of her own. Maybe then she would shut up about sex. Getting up at three in the morning to deal with a crying infant would keep her too busy for anything else, Jan thought almost vindictively.

Leslie, for her part, had never expressed any desire to have children. 'I'm having too much fun to get tangled up with kids,' she said whenever Jan brought up the subject. Sex and marriage, sex and marriage/ They both go together like a cat and carriage. Dad was told by mother/I want the one but not the other. So Leslie had parodied her mother's attitude in a cheeky e-mail verse several weeks ago. What would she think if she could see her mother now?

She'd probably approve, Jan Two said.

Merely being seen by either of her daughters in her present state was too embarrassing to contemplate.

Forget your daughters, her alter ego commanded. Don't even think about England. Think instead about getting to that little black box and about what will happen when you push the button. Go on.

She resisted the blandishments of her other self for what seemed like hours before she finally admitted that there was no ignoring them. Jan slowly got out of bed and went to the nightstand. She stared at the control box for a long time before she noticed that her hands were straining against the short chain that connected them to her waist belt. With a despairing groan Jan stooped, bending her knees and straining against the handcuffs, before she had the thing in her hand. And still she hesitated, debating within herself what to do. She was conscious of holding a good part of her destiny in her hands.

Go on, her alter ego said. No one's watching.

I'm watching, Jan replied. The urge to use the thing grew moment by moment, until she felt she couldn't stop herself, couldn't simply put it down.

Atta girl, Jan Two urged as her finger caressed the button.

The habits of her long years of abstinence came to her rescue. She rose abruptly and flung the control box as far away as she could with the limited use she had of her hands. No. I won't let them make me do this, she thought fiercely.

Jan Two was dismayed. In her imagination Jan saw the tiny devilish figure looking disappointed. She could imagine it stamping a foot in exasperation, and smiled at the picture. Jan got back into bed, feeling the dildo inside her shift as she moved. With difficulty, unable to use her hands to any real extent, she managed to slide her legs under the coverlet. Such a simple task seemed to take ages, and when her naked body was at last covered, she discovered a new source of worry. The quilt pressed down on her breasts. She felt her nipples growing tight and erect, and she felt the pricking from the tiny needles inside the rubber caps. Jan tried to rub them off on the quilt, but succeeded only in making her nipples more erect as the needles pricked them.

She tried lying on her side, but found that the most comfortable position was on her back. On her side, her hands hung awkwardly on the short chain that connected them to her waist belt. The circulation was cut off, and they began to feel numb. Jan heaved herself onto her back and allowed her hands to lie on her belly. They felt better, but her nipples stayed erect and in contact with the needles.

She guessed that there would not be much sleep that night. Her imagination had presented sleeping in bondage as an attractive proposition, and in other circumstances she might have come to enjoy it, but the sensations from her nipples were causing alarming feelings further south. Jan drowsed, but woke when her vaginal muscles clenched around the thick shaft inside her. She groaned and tried to ignore the signals flashing between her sensitised nipples and her full cunt. She drowsed, woke, and drowsed again.

Finally, she could lie still no longer. With a mental

groan, Jan got out of bed again and went in search of the control box. It was nowhere in sight. Where had it landed? She made her way to the bathroom door, opened it fully for more light, and resumed her search.

The voice in her mind urged her on.

After what seemed like hours she found it beneath the armchair. But she couldn't reach it, strain as she might. There was not enough slack in the chain that held her hands against her belly. Laboriously she struggled to her feet, brushing her nipples against the chair. The signal that flashed to her cunt made her stagger. Oh God, why had she flung the thing away? And how was she going to get it back? Jan moaned in frustration as her internal muscles squeezed the dildo.

She leaned her hip against the armchair and pushed. It slid a few inches. Jan shifted her feet, braced herself and pushed again. Inch by inch the chair moved across the thick carpet. It felt as if she were pushing it through treacle. Finally Jan looked down to see the control box lying at her feet. Gratefully she sank to her knees and reached for it. Her hands strained toward it, but the belt held them tightly against her body. Damn! She swore as she realised that she would have to lie on the floor and worm her way over to the thing. But she had to have the control box. There would be no rest until she had let her body have its way.

Her alter ego asked her why she wanted rest anyway when the alternative was so delightful.

She sank back on her heels and allowed herself to fall to one side. Unable to break her fall with her hands, Jan landed on the carpet with a thump. She pushed with her feet and lifted her hips, sliding a few inches at a time towards the goal. Inside her cunt the weight of the dildo shifted and Jan groaned softly.

The chain between her ankle and the bed slithered across the floor as she moved. The old familiar Jan was appalled as she struggled to reach the thing that would only make the new Jan much stronger, much harder to resist. But the old Jan was no match for the desire that had been growing in her for the last several hours as she lay alone in the dark.

At last she had it in her hands. And Jan hesitated. One part of her mind urged her to throw it further away, out of reach entirely. The other part of her urged her to take it straight back to the bed and get on with the main attraction of the night. The tension was well-nigh unbearable. Her hand shook as she tensed herself to throw. If she flung the box across the room from her present position it would be out of reach, beyond the scope allowed by the chain on her ankle. Go on, her older self urged.

Don't you dare, her alter ego said firmly. Push the button.

Jan did neither. Instead she wormed her way toward the armchair. She leaned a shoulder against it and managed to sit up. Turning to face it, she put her head against the seat cushion and with the leverage of her neck muscles she turned so that she could get to her knees. Kneeling, she could lean forward until the upper part of her body fell forward onto the seat of the chair. From there she intended to get to her feet. Standing, she could either walk to the bed, or to the limit of her chain if she decided to put temptation behind her and throw the box away.

The bed, the bed! said her alter ego.

No, said her older self. Get rid of it.

The instant her breasts contacted the chair Jan knew she had made a mistake. The needles in the rubber caps pricked her nipples and her body jerked as they sent an urgent signal to her cunt. Her grip on the box tightened convulsively. Later she couldn't be sure whether she had pushed the button by accident. With a startled cry she felt the dildo inside her begin to vibrate, and she was lost. Nothing on earth could make her turn it off again.

'Oh God,' Jan moaned.

Way to go! her alter ego exulted. Irresistible.

Jan rubbed her breasts against the seat cushion, forcing the needles into her nipples. 'Ohhhhhhh,' she moaned softly as the dildo buzzed against her clitoris. Don't, said the fading voice of Sam's wife. Jan thought of Patrick, his hands on her body, and knew she couldn't go back. Didn't want to go back. It was a conscious choice, pushing the old self back and allowing her alter ego to take charge. As she rubbed her breasts against the cushion and ground her hips against the front of the chair, Jan knew she was denying her past. And as she became more and more aroused, she kept having alternating images of Sam and of Patrick. Which one did she want to take charge of the emerging new woman?

Patrick, her alter ego said, and it was with his image in mind that Jan went over the brink of her first orgasm. The twinges grew and spread in her belly and cunt and thighs and breasts. Electric tingles drove her onward, becoming surges of electric pleasure as she came, moaning, grinding herself against the chair, surrendering her body to pleasure.

This was what she wanted. Wanted now more than anything else except maybe Patrick. He had led her to this, forced her to accept her body as an instrument of pleasure. She wanted him to be there to make her take the next step. Make her come as he thrust into her. The image of Patrick between her thighs drove her to the next peak. She nearly dropped the control box as she came.

Jan's hips moved backward and forward as she drove herself against the front of the chair. The dildo inside her buzzed and vibrated, driving her to ever greater frenzy. There was a buzzing in her head too. She thought she would black out. Still she kept on, unable to deny herself the pleasure her rebellious body gave her. Her old self was banished to the corner of her mind where her alter ego had lived until only a day or so ago. Her cries of dismay were weak indeed compared to the pleasure of sexual release. And Jan realised that the dismay her old self felt made her present enjoyment all the greater.

She buried her face in the back of the chair, biting the fabric to stifle her moans. The old Jan had not yet reached the screaming orgasm stage, but she was not very far from it. This act of restraint was all that remained of her former reticence. Jan guessed that it, too, would be lost if she stayed here. And she would stay. There was no escape.

As she came yet again, Jan felt her resolve to demand they release her weaken still further. The thought of leaving here now dismayed her, a further measure of the change she was undergoing. On the verge of blacking out, dizzied by her ecstasy, Jan only just managed to press the button on the control box. The vibrations stopped as she slumped forward onto the chair. The box fell from her nerveless fingers to the floor.

Jan had no idea how long she half-lay on the armchair. When she again took stock of herself, she felt worn out but exultant. She had managed to make herself come. Masturbated, she corrected herself, with the help of her new equipment and her new attitude. It would have been better if she had had someone – Patrick, say – to help her, but she had begun to overcome her aversion. Indeed she was beginning to forget how she had felt before her abduction. If Patrick, or even Sam, had come upon her just then, she imagined she would roll over onto her back and spread her legs.

Finally she knew she needed to get into bed. Lie down, at any rate, and try to rest. She knew that she would wake up needing more of that gut-wrenching pleasure before the night was over. With a stab of dismay Jan realised that she had dropped the control box, and would have to repeat her earlier contortions to get it back. This she did, conscious of the dildo inside her and of the pricking at her nipples as she wormed her way across the floor. When she had it once more in her hands, she struggled to her knees and made her way to the bed.

Jan managed to slide beneath the covers and roll onto her side. She fell asleep almost at once and woke sometime in the night with the control box in her hand. She pushed the button without hesitation or internal debate, and felt the dildo come alive inside her cunt with a terrible anticipation. Oh God, how had she ever done without this? Her body took charge almost immediately. Jan moaned and writhed in the bed as the familiar electric currents passed between her cunt and her breasts. Once more she found herself revelling in release, her own cries of pleasure loud in her ears. Still not a scream, but nearer to it, nearer than ever to telling the world that Jan Norris was becoming a different woman.

Jan slept, and woke to pleasure yet again. It wasn't until the sky outside her prison window was turning grey with the new day that she finally slept. Even in sleep she clutched the black plastic box that was the key to delight. The old Jan might have made the effort to put it back on the nightstand, to conceal her use of it from whoever came to her in the morning.

But the old Jan was defeated, banished to a far corner of the mind. The tiny devil-figure that Jan thought of as her new self grinned with satiation. It urged no further sexual callisthenics upon her. And it was this devil-figure that made her forget to feel embarrassment when she was found with the tell-tale box.

That is how Patrick found her when he came with breakfast, curled up in bed and clutching the control box. Smiling to himself, he opened the curtains and bent to kiss Jan awake.

She awoke suddenly, but made no attempt to draw back. Jan opened her mouth to his kiss as if she had been doing it all her life. It went on for a long time, and when it ended she opened her eyes to smile at him.

'Good night?' he asked without irony. Jan was grateful for his matter-of-fact tone.

He helped her to sit up, taking the control box from her hand and ignoring her embarrassment. Morning had driven the new Jan back into exile, strengthening her old feelings of guilt. Patrick didn't allow her to dwell on them. He had brought breakfast for them both. He set the table and helped Jan into the bathroom. With his help Jan made her toilette, feeling only slightly embarrassed this time at having to be helped with this intimate task. You're learning, she told herself with some satisfaction. Since Patrick didn't offer to free her hands, Jan didn't ask. Asking for something that one knew was going to be denied seemed undignified. And she had learned to enjoy the helplessness. And it's more feminine, she thought.

And more erotic, the tiny devil-figure added silently.

Breakfast, Jan said silently, striving for matter-of-factness.

Eleven

This time it was James who took her to the 'demonstration' room. As was by now customary she shuffled ahead of him in her handcuffs and leg irons. By this time Jan knew enough of the routine to anticipate more in the way of sexual arousal, and was looking forward to it in her by-now customary half-fearful way. Her fear this time, however, was more about exactly what would happen to her, rather than about having anything at all happen. Patrick had promised to give her another chance with the whip, not too long ago. Perhaps, she thought, James had been delegated to break her in. And maybe this was the time. That was fear-making. Jan was relieved to see that there was no sign of the whip in the long room. But there was no telling what might be kept in the storage cabinets.

She did not want to ask what he was going to do. The answer might not be pleasant to hear, and asking the question might betray her own ambivalence. Or make her sound too eager.

'Today we will try you out with a bit of sensory deprivation. It's a devilishly effective way of breaking the will of even the most stubborn woman. You will do anything we ask of you after a bit of isolation. And anyway, you probably need some rest after all the things you've been experiencing.'

Jan coloured. She had heard of sensory deprivation, as had everyone who had seen the advert in which the confused man from the building society ends up in the 'isolation tank' of the angry young woman, but she didn't really understand the process. It sounded terribly negative, she thought, but not as threatening as being whipped or pierced, or meeting what Patrick kept calling the 'real thing'. The real thing, James' thing, as she called it, was still standing at attention, as if he found her attractive. Did he? Jan hoped so, as all women would, but the handcuffs, and her now-empty cunt made his admiration a bit more than casual.

'What are you going to do to me?' she asked.

'Nothing too bad. First I'll get you ready for the pool, and then I'll take you to watch another demonstration. After that I'll throw you into the isolation tank. Well, the swimming pool really. You can soak for a few hours and contemplate inner realities. Patrick will be back to fish you out before too long.'

'But I'll drown,' Jan exclaimed. 'I can't swim, if I'm tied up . . .'

'No you won't. That would be a terrible waste of a beautiful woman. But just be patient and all will be revealed.'

There was that 'beautiful woman' phrase again. Did James too think she was beautiful? Did he really? Did he want her body? Dear God, did he want to fuck her? His erect cock suggested he did. Jan felt faint, well, vapourish, her mother would have said, having lewd fantasies about men's things. She remembered James and Robin the other day, doing 'it' right before her eyes, and Robin's cries of ecstasy. Well, there was no other word for it, was there? And would she feel the same ecstasy, if James shoved that thing into her? Shivers and hot and cold flashes. Was she menopausal or merely virginal? Jan found herself wishing that Patrick had not had to go away. He would understand. Wouldn't he?

But James was taking more things from the cabinets and cupboards which lined one side of the room. There seemed to be an awful lot of equipment there for educating women like herself. Much more than she could have guessed. Much more than was strictly necessary, she imagined. Jan stood helplessly in her chains while he produced what looked like a dancer's leotard. Only this one had no arms, and was made of leather, with a zipper up the back, and laces and straps. There was a wide waist belt to go with it, also of leather.

Almost any sort of bondage gear would be new to her, but this looked to be a good deal more confining than her present equipment. Well, Jan thought resignedly, at least it will cover me in all the right places. And there's no danger of him shoving *his* thing into me while I'm wearing that.

Too bad, her alter ego added.

But he was not finished. He produced a pair of tights, still in their pack. 'Marks & Sparks' best heavy support tights for the enhancement of your lovely legs.'

'I'm not going to be seen in public, am I?' she asked in alarm. But he had called her legs lovely. Were they? Really? She looked at herself in the mirror. Passable, she thought, not wanting to flatter herself. But Sam too had admired them. He had often said so, usually with a note of regret when she put him off yet again. And now James was saying the same. She revised her opinion of her legs favourably, more from the latter endorsement than from the former.

'I like the look of a woman's legs in tights or

stockings,' James continued. 'Call me a pervert if you like, but there it is.'

Jan thought that 'pervert' was not quite the right word, but she let it pass. She knew that she was going to be forced to wear the things he selected for her, if forced was the right word. James collected several lengths of rope as well. She shivered in anticipation and dread as he beckoned her over to the worktop.

He knelt to remove her leg irons. For one wild moment Jan thought of running away. But where could she go? The old dilemma restrained her. She stood still as James opened the pack and shook out the tights. Dark grey, she saw, with a sheen to them that looked fashionable. The kind of tights a career woman who spent long days on her feet would choose. She imagined Antoinette would wear something similar at her bank.

James rolled the tights just like she always did when she was dressing. He lifted her foot and worked the tights up to her ankle. He did the same to the other foot. Then he pulled them up her legs, smoothing the sheer nylon against her skin and pulling the gusset into her crotch. It was an intimate service from a stranger and she felt oddly cherished as he performed this task she had always done herself. Jan looked at herself in the mirror and saw a mature woman, nude, her long hair braided and hanging down her back, and her lovely legs (his word for them) sheathed in smooth, shiny, clingy nylon. The support tights seemed, by their elasticity, somehow to caress her from toes to waist in a way that normal tights never did, and she wore tights almost every day. On this day she wore handcuffs as well, and was being attended to, handled, by this man who found her attractive (else why had he called her beautiful?).

Her train of thought was interrupted as James eased first one foot and then the other through the leg openings of the leather leotard-like garment. He worked it up to her thighs and then paused to replace her leg irons.

Jan thought this thoroughness about keeping her helpless was overdone, but then she realised that it was a ritual, a way of reminding the captive at every turn that she *was* a captive, someone owned, however temporarily, by another. By a man who found her attractive, and who chose this way to let her know that he wouldn't let her escape.

Then he was removing her handcuffs, unlocking the steel bands she had worn on her wrists for so long. She raised her hands above her waist for the first time since they had been fastened to the leather belt. Jan felt somehow more naked without the handcuffs. It was disconcerting. All of this was so alien. So exciting, her alter ego suggested, and Jan realised that she was correct. But it shouldn't be. She should be frightened, seeking escape, not conspiring with her captors in her further captivity. Not allowing herself to be handled. She should be rebelling, fighting them.

Jan quieted her misgivings by reflecting that her docility was enforced by her bondage. It was this that made her accept, and enjoy, the things that had happened to her. It was why he had replaced her leg irons before removing her handcuffs.

James allowed her to exercise her cramped muscles for a few minutes. She was grateful for even this.

Then it was time to be confined again. James pulled the leather garment above her waist, and Jan saw that in the front there was a kind of bra. Stiff leather cups, at any rate, obviously intended for a woman's breasts. She wondered idly if there was a male version

172

without the bra, and with special provision for the penis.

'We call this a sweat suit, when it's made of rubber instead of leather. Though leather can be pretty sweaty on a hot day, it does at least breathe.' James was explaining even as he was working the upper part of the garment onto her body, fitting her breasts into the bra section. She co-operated, enjoying the touch of his hands on her naked flesh even when her old self was screaming at her to resist.

'Your arms go inside the suit,' he said, crossing them behind her back and threading her hands through loops sewn to the inside of the garment on either side of the back opening. Then he was zipping her up, the leather enclosing and confining her.

Jan tried to move her arms. She couldn't. They were held behind her back, pressed indeed against her spine, by the tight leather garment. Even when she was zipped up, he wasn't finished with her. Helpless as she was, he went on to make her more so. There was a lacing arrangement that allowed him to adjust the garment even more snugly to her body. She felt it tighten around her waist, her arms and hands, felt her breasts forced into the cups. In the mirror Jan caught a glimpse of an armless woman in a tight leather suit, wearing dark grey tights, her ankles locked into leg irons. Me, she thought, with a certain awe. A 'me' she would never have dreamed of. Her long legs were emphasised by the tights and by the high cut of the garment at the hips, revealing even more leg. The tight garment hugged her figure, emphasising her narrow waist, her full breasts, her flaring hips. Her arms were conspicuous by their absence. She could not move them, and she felt off balance. Even the handcuffs had allowed her a certain amount of movement. But not this garment.

James closed a flap over the zipper and laces, buckling it shut, and locking the buckles with small padlocks.

Overkill, Jan thought, but she shivered at the extent of her present helplessness.

The wide leather belt was buckled snugly around her waist, below her imprisoned arms, and locked with still more padlocks. Jan could not have imagined this degree of helplessness. She shivered at the tight embrace of the leather.

James surprised her by producing a pair of her own shoes. More of her things that the abductors had gathered from her house. She recognised them as an older pair which she had been meaning to get rid of. In her opinion they were not appropriate for a woman of her age. She thought the heels too high and the toes too pointed now, but she remembered when she had thought them very nice shoes. James seemed to believe that they were appropriate, because he was urging her to put them on, holding them one at a time while she did. Another glance in the mirror showed the same armless woman in tights and leather, but now wearing a pair of stiletto high heels that exaggerated her legs, showing them off as an asset she had not fully appreciated.

Jan found it difficult to walk in the shoes, lacking her arms to use for balance, and wearing the leg irons with the short chain joining her ankles. Nice ankles, she thought, looking at herself again. Enhanced by the hard, bright manacles locked around them.

With a tug on the lead he forced Jan to follow him toward whatever fate he had planned for her.

Jan shivered in anticipation as she was led helplessly across the room and through another door at the far end. She followed her captor with difficulty, hampered by her leg irons. He carried the rope in his

174

free hand, his erect cock still signalling his interest but it could only be academic now. There was no way he could shove it into her without undoing her tight and elaborate bondage. Yet she was aroused by her bondage and she knew, from Sam's books, that some men certainly were. She also knew of at least one woman who was.

That woman followed James into the room with the swimming pool she had fallen into earlier. As she had done before, Jan shrank away from the glass wall. She tried to retreat, but the lead prevented her. 'Please, no. Everyone will be able to see me.'

'Share the wealth, Jan,' he said, pulling her forward. 'If you've got it, flaunt it.'

'Noooooo, please don't,' she moaned. Vainly. She was forced to follow him.

But this time James didn't linger, leading her through the pool room and into a conservatory at one end.

That was much worse, from Jan's point of view. Instead of having only one wall made of glass, she was surrounded by it, plainly visible to anyone who happened by. She imagined once again that the whole world was outside looking in at her.

James led his unwilling victim near to the glass wall. He fastened her lead to a hook above her head while Jan tried unsuccessfully to become invisible. Wildly, she looked around, expecting jeering crowds. Her agitation increased when James left her there.

'Come back,' she begged. 'Don't leave me here.'

James paid no attention.

He was gone and Jan was alone in her glass cage. She jerked at the lead, at the tight leather garment, the unyielding leg irons. 'No,' she moaned. From the corner of her eye Jan saw a movement at the corner of the house. Someone was coming. They would see her. She fought yet harder to escape.

James waved cheerfully at her as he walked back to the main part of the house.

Relief washed over her, leaving her weak kneed and shaken. But it was short-lived. Where James had passed, anyone else might pass too. Jan looked agitatedly around, but saw no one. She felt embarrassed, as if she had asked to be bound and put on display in a glass room. Exhibited for the entire world to see. Had she asked for that? Well, no, but she had not made much of an attempt to escape, and she had enjoyed yesterday and last night.

Jan turned her thoughts to other things. Where was Robin this morning? she wondered. What did she think of the new rings through her nipples? Was she being beaten, or fucked stupid, as Antoinette had put it, at this moment? The house was very large, from what Jan had seen of it. Robin, or a whole flock of Robins, could be enduring unspeakable tortures or relishing exquisite pleasures and she would not be any the wiser. Just as anything could be done to her without the knowledge of anyone else. Jan felt a return of dismay with the realisation of her isolation. No one who could help even knew she was in need of help.

Her alter ego asked tauntingly if she really wanted to be rescued from this and returned to her everyday existence, never to feel the keen delight of orgasm.

Jan came very close to shouting 'Yes!' It wasn't the actual sexual arousal that made her cringe, she realised suddenly, it was her embarrassment. The moment passed. Jan knew that she could never go back to what she was, even if she somehow found herself back in her own kitchen. She would be forever looking at the back door, expecting, half-hoping that two men in balaclavas would burst in and make her captive, bearing her away to a place like this.

Thus her thoughts came full circle, and she relished once more the feel of the tight leather garment hugging her figure like a second skin, confining her upper body and arms, holding her helpless. She spread her legs, feeling the chain come taut between her ankles. The leg irons, biting into her flesh, reminded her of her helplessness and made her shiver deliciously. Her embarrassment lessened.

Another movement outside the glass wall caught her eye, made her breathing tight, brought a flush of embarrassment to her face. The blackbird fluttered out of sight, and she breathed again. She couldn't be nonchalant, as James suggested. She hadn't the experience.

Well not yet, her alter ego said.

Jan tried to think of Patrick. Where was he now? What was he doing? With whom? She felt jealous of him. Ridiculous, she told herself, but that changed nothing. I'm older than he is, she reminded herself.

So what? her alter ego asked. He's really good looking.

She shook herself mentally. That way led to infatuation, older woman taking younger lover. Whispers and sniggers from friends and acquaintances. Yet it was all right if Sam did the same thing.

Unfair, her alter ego said. Wasn't she entitled to some fun of her own?

Fun wasn't the right word for what had happened to her.

How about ecstasy then, her alter ego suggested. Passion? A real orgasm? With a real man?

Jan shied away from that thought as well, but not as thoroughly as she had done before.

Noises off brought her back to the present.

James came back into view from the house, leading a vaguely familiar woman by a collar and chain like

Jan's. Her hands were tied together in front of her body, pulled down tightly to her belly by what Jan now knew as a crotch rope. Her breasts, as Jan's had been, were squeezed up and out between her upper arms. That's what I looked like, Jan thought. It was even more erotic than she had imagined. James was leading her to the conservatory. Jan felt embarrassed again to be seen as she was, as if it were all her own doing, despite trying to tell herself that they were both in the same situation, both captive.

And of course you had nothing to do with it, did you? The voice of her darker self sounded sarcastic.

The other woman was taller than Jan, with short dark red hair and the fair complexion that usually went with it. She appeared to be of Jan's own age, which was oddly comforting. So I'm evidently not the only mature woman in need of a 'personality change', she thought.

Jan felt an immediate bond with her on the basis of their age. But the other woman seemed completely at ease, whereas Jan had been afraid and ashamed. She must be a lot further along the road than I am, Jan guessed. She made up her mind to ask about her, to talk to her if possible. But not just then. The other woman was gagged, her mouth stuffed full of some packing held in place by a scarf folded and tied behind her head. The scarf was green, evidently a fashion accessory. It complemented her red hair and, Jan saw, matched her green eyes.

'Jan, meet Barbara,' James said as they entered the conservatory. Like Antoinette, he avoided using last names.

Bizarre, Jan thought, introductions in a situation like theirs. She nodded to Barbara but didn't speak, struck once again by her familiarity.

Barbara evidently knew Jan. She seemed embarrassed by the knowledge.

Her embarrassment was contagious. Jan flushed. She knew that she was recognised even though Barbara's identity still eluded her.

James, watching the interplay, went on, 'Barbara is from your own town, and you seem to know one another. Have you two met before? I do hope I haven't committed a faux pas by introducing two friends.' James smiled insincerely.

Jan thought that such social niceties were wildly out of place here, and that James had deliberately brought Barbara here to embarrass her. Or both of them. Her guilty secret was no longer secret. If she too lived in Godalming, Barbara would spread the word about Jan's presence here, and she would be unable to go anywhere without being pointed out. The neighbours would know. And Sam and Leslie. And everybody would be sniggering at her. It would be awful. Everyone would believe that she had come here freely. It wouldn't help to say that she had been abducted. Why didn't you go to the police then, they would ask. She turned a brighter shade of pink with embarrassment.

Unable to speak, Barbara was nevertheless looking at her with a touch of panic too. Jan smiled weakly back at her.

As the tableau drew out, Jan felt some of her panic fade when she saw that the possibility of exposure worried the other woman much as it did her. She realised that by exposing her, Barbara would likewise expose herself. So she might well keep quiet. Nevertheless they would have to talk later, agree to keep one another's secrets. A secret shared was infinitely harder to keep than one known only to oneself. Still, the damage was already done. The only thing was to sweep up the pieces and go on as best one could. Yes, she thought, they would definitely have to talk.

'Barbara has come to be beaten, and she has graciously invited you to watch. We both thought it might be educational. Watch her reactions as she is whipped,' James said. 'She loves it. It makes her horny.' As he spoke he was untying Barbara's crotch rope.

Barbara stood quietly while he brought over a chair and stood on it to thread the end of the rope binding her wrists through an eye in the ceiling. He pulled Barbara's arms up over her head until she was stretched tautly. Her arms rose above her head and were pulled together by the tension. She hung her head forward between her upper arms. When she looked up at Jan, she had to strain her neck to see her.

Jan stared incredulously at them both, but particularly at Barbara. How could being beaten with a whip make anyone ... horny? Her alter ego reminded her that only a few days ago she hadn't realised that being tied up could arouse anyone sexually. The world was full of strange people with even stranger needs and desires. Then she felt a stab of fear. Were they going to string her up and beat her too?

Jan had to admit that Barbara made a stirring sight as she was strung up to the ceiling. Would I be as stirring, she thought suddenly. The comparison made her blush, but she couldn't help making it, nor hoping that the answer was yes.

As she looked at Barbara again, Jan saw with surprise that the other woman was showing all the signs of sexual arousal, at least insofar as she was familiar with them. Barbara was flushed and breathing rapidly, her firm breasts rising and falling interestingly. If Jan had been worried about being seen by strangers, Barbara should have been much more so. At least, Jan thought, I've got this leather body-suit. Absolutely every part of her companion was exposed.

Barbara was not daunted by her nakedness. Jan wished that she could be as cool about her own. Barbara was plainly thinking about what her nakedness portended. She knew what was coming, and was looking forward to it in a way that mystified the uninitiated. Better her than me, Jan thought, so long as she likes it.

James got down from the chair when he had finished tying Barbara. To Jan's surprise he also removed the gag, untying the scarf and extracting a wad of cloth from Barbara's mouth. Then he left the conservatory again, and once again Jan began to worry about being seen. It didn't help much to have a companion.

'Don't worry,' Barbara said. 'No one is going to see us. This house is nearly a mile from the nearest road, and the grounds are private. James took me on a tour the other day, and we saw no one.'

'Are you sure that no one will come?'

'I'm sure.'

Jan relaxed somewhat at the assurance. 'I think I'd die of embarrassment if anyone saw me like this.'

'I can see you, and you don't look like dying just yet,' Barbara observed dryly.

Jan marvelled anew at her coolness: strung up waiting for the whip, she could still make jokes. Barbara's coolness made Jan feel better. 'But you're . . .' The thought was unfinished.

'Used to it? Is that what you were going to say? I didn't realise it showed. But you're right. I'm used to it. I'm one of the regulars, you might say. I guess this is your first time.'

Jan nodded.

'It gets easier each time. The next time you'll wonder what made you so embarrassed.'

Jan didn't automatically deny that there would be

a next time, as she would have done earlier. I'm changing, she said silently.

About time, added the little devil figure.

'We know what's going to happen to me,' Barbara said. 'What about you?'

'I don't know how you can – how anybody can – look forward to being whipped. It terrifies me every time they mention it.'

'Just between you and me,' Barbara said, 'I don't think you have anything to worry about. They aren't going to do anything that hurts you. But don't tell them I said that. They like to imagine that the women who come here all fear them a little bit.' She looked closely at Jan, arching her back in order to raise her eyes far enough. 'Look, we'll have a talk after this. James intends to let you see me being whipped, and afterwards he'll leave us together. We can get acquainted.'

'Do I know you?' Jan asked. 'I think I should, but I don't think we've met.'

'No we haven't met exactly, but I do know you. When James is done with me I'll tell you a story about mutual acquaintances.'

Jan was not sure she wanted to know about mutual acquaintances, but she was curious about her companion.

James chose that moment to return. He brought a cane and a riding crop with him. 'One for each of you,' he said with a smile. 'Jan can choose first.'

Jan shot a frightened glance from him to Barbara, who winked at her and mouthed, 'don't worry.'

'Stop teasing Jan and get on with it,' she said to James.

'Can't you wait a bit?' he asked her.

'Can you?' Barbara retorted.

'Touché,' he said, beginning to undress. To Jan he

remarked, 'It's not polite for me to be dressed when she is naked.'

Jan stared at his cock as he dropped his trousers. It stood out stiffly, bobbing as he moved. She forgot to look at the whips, so absorbing was the sight of James nonchalantly shedding his clothes before them. Barbara watched too.

When James was naked he picked up the cane. Barbara watched with bated breath as he flexed the long whippy instrument. Jan watched with fear. Unconsciously she tried to move away but was stopped by her lead. She thought there would be some preliminary talk, but James got right down to business, standing behind Barbara and letting the cane touch her bottom.

Barbara gasped at the touch and began to breathe rapidly, her breasts rising and falling quickly. She tensed herself and waited with every sign of anticipation for the first blow. It landed on her bottom, leaving a red line in her flesh. The sound of cane meeting woman sounded loud to Jan. Barbara grunted and jerked. But she didn't scream.

As far as Jan could tell the blow had been quite hard though she was no judge. Probably it had been, she decided, trying to detach herself from what was happening.

James drew back his arm and struck again, a bit lower but still on Barbara's bottom. This time the smack sounded louder. Barbara yipped and shifted her feet. The next blow landed across the backs of her thighs. 'Ah!' she said.

James allowed the cane to trail down her legs, caressing her. Barbara moaned softly as it moved over her limbs. When he raised it she tensed in anticipation of the next blow. She yelped when it came. Even Jan could tell that it had been harder than the earlier ones. The red line across her thighs looked redder and angrier than the others, the smack of wood on flesh louder in her ears. Not me, she thought with a shudder.

James increased the pace of the beating, moving up her bottom and onto her back. The swish of the cane in the air and the dull smack as it found its mark became a steady background. Soon Barbara's self-control cracked. First she moaned, then the moans turned to gasps and finally to screams. To Jan they were ear-splitting. It all looked terribly painful. She could see no sign of the pleasure Barbara had claimed she'd get. When James moved around in front of her to lash her breasts and stomach the screams became still louder. The cane made the full globes bounce with each blow, leaving red lines in its wake. Barbara's scream when he struck her nipples was shattering. Similar red lines marked her stomach and belly, perilously close to her cunt. Jan cringed as she imagined her own breasts being struck like that. She struggled inside the tight leather body-suit, instinctively seeking to escape even though she was not the one taking the punishment. By watching she imagined that she would be implicated in Barbara's beating, and might attract the same treatment herself. It was dangerous to stand too close to the target.

James broke off once again, but this time he took Barbara's tortured breasts in his hands, caressing the striped, reddened flesh and planting kisses all over them. At first Barbara was moaning in pain. Gradually her moans changed in character, seeming to come from deeper within her as James stroked where before he had punished. Even Jan was aware of the change in Barbara. She was moving from torture to arousal before her eyes, even as Jan was moving from fear to wonder.

When James took a reddened nipple in his mouth Barbara groaned loudly and arched her back, offering her breasts and nipples to her tormentor. Plainly, she was excited, but Jan couldn't tell how much of it was due to the beating.

To Barbara it made no difference. 'Oh!' she cried, sharply, when he nipped her with his teeth.

Sounds like pleasure to me, the inner voice said. Want to try it? I'm game.

Jan shivered at the thought of her own flesh marked with those red weals.

James continued to arouse Barbara. And Jan watched them as she had watched James and Robin on her first day. Her old habits urged her to turn her eyes away, but they weren't strong enough anymore to compel her. She remembered, without any prompting from her alter ego, that she hadn't been able to look away even on the first occasion.

Barbara's moans of pleasure made Jan wish she were being aroused, but not at the price her companion had paid. The reddened weals on Barbara's back and thighs and breasts looked very painful, and if one were to judge from her screams she had found them so. But the pain was all forgotten. Jan didn't think she could do that.

Jan tensed herself inside the tight leather body-suit when Barbara suddenly screamed again. It wasn't a scream of pain. She felt envious.

James released Barbara and picked up the whip again. The bound woman tensed herself again, obviously knowing what was coming next. Jan remembered her description of herself as an old hand at this. Yet as Barbara waited for the beating to resume Jan could see no evidence on her body that she had ever been beaten before. Apparently the weals that now showed would fade and there would be no outward sign of her strange predilection. Barbara would look like any of thousands of women. Only Jan would know that she had been here and been whipped and made to come.

And don't forget, the inner voice reminded her, you're here too. And enjoying the stay. Jan felt the inner split healing. The promptings of the inner voice she had thought of as separate from herself now felt more like a new aspect of her personality. She no longer thought of the devilish figure as the enemy within whose subversive urging had to be resisted.

James stood behind Barbara once again. The limber cane swished through the air and landed on her bottom. The red marks were renewed as he lashed Barbara again, and again she was screaming, but to Jan the screams sounded different from the first ones. These were more like the necessary precursors to the next arousal. Barbara seemed to forget the pain as soon as she became aroused. Did the pain make her arousal more intense, providing a counterpoint to the pleasure, so that each sensation contributed to her excitement? Jan shivered as she imagined herself subjected to those opposite sensations. Would I scream and scream and come and come? No, of course not, she decided. But still . . .

James held the rod nearly vertical and allowed it to slide between Barbara's bottom cheeks, running it backward and forward and obviously, even from Jan's limited point of view, sliding it over her anus. And Barbara was now thrusting her bottom out as the whip caressed her. James pulled the cane away and struck her once again across her full buttocks. Barbara moaned this time. Then he suddenly struck upwards between her legs. Even Jan needed no help to guess where that blow landed. Barbara screamed so loudly that Jan thought her vocal cords would snap. But they didn't. The scream went on, growing even louder as James struck her again in the same place.

Jan knew she couldn't stand that. She clenched her thighs tightly together, feeling the smooth nylon of her tights rubbing between her legs.

James struck her between the legs a third time. Barbara screamed, her throat taut and her head back.

James dropped the cane once again, and moved around to stand before Barbara. She was whimpering and clenching her thighs together as if to defend herself from being struck there again. James knelt and grasped Barbara's hips with both hands, stilling her shuddering body. He bent forward and kissed Barbara's mons veneris and belly. And Barbara grew still as once again her body told her what was coming next. Her thighs parted and her hips thrust forward.

James bent his head between her parted thighs and Barbara sighed with anticipation. Jan knew where he would kiss the bound woman next, and she felt a tingle between her own clenched thighs as she imagined being kissed there as Patrick had done to her on her very first day. It had been electrifying. Barbara, far more accustomed to the intimate kiss, closed her eyes and offered herself to James. There was no sign of reluctance or reserve. Wanton, Jan's older self said despairingly from a distance. But Jan knew what the kiss could do.

And James was doing it to Barbara before her eyes. Barbara spread her legs as widely as she could and James buried his face between them. Her head hung downward between her stretched arms and her eyes were closed as she concentrated on what was happening between her legs. 'Ahhhh!' she sighed. James continued to arouse her, and Jan watched the shudders grow in intensity. Barbara grew tense as her climax approached. She had forgotten again about the torture and was poised for the ecstasy.

Suddenly she screamed, her body shaking and her hips thrusting backward and forward. To Jan the scream seemed even louder than when she had been struck on her cunt. It went on and on, filling the room and Jan's ears. And she knew at last that there was no chance of anyone coming to investigate the goings-on in this secluded house. Those screams would have brought someone at the run if they had been heard. And Barbara went on, oblivious of the sounds she was making, obviously intent only on her own release.

Abruptly the scream cut off. In the sudden silence Jan saw Barbara slump as her knees gave way. She hung by her bound wrists, her arms stretched tautly above her. As far as Jan could tell, the redheaded woman with the red weals covering her back and thighs had fainted from the intensity of her orgasm.

Wow! Jan said silently. Approvingly. A bit enviously, but not enviously enough to want to trade places just yet.

James stood and threw a smile at Jan before once again getting onto the chair and loosening the rope that held Barbara upright. The other woman slumped as he lowered her to the floor, where she lay limply until James could lift her body onto one of the chaise longues. There he raised her bound wrists once again above her head and secured them to the back of the seat. With great care he straightened her legs and bound her ankles together, tying them to the foot of the seat.

Only then did he approach Jan, who cringed with anticipation of the whip.

But he only unfastened her lead from the hook that secured her and led Jan to another chaise longue, facing Barbara. He seated her and raised the reclining back until it supported her before he removed her leg irons and bound her ankles together. He tied them to the foot of her chaise. The lead was drawn tightly from her neck to the back of the seat and snapped onto it.

'She'll be waking up soon,' he said, nodding toward Barbara. 'I think you two should have a talk. I'll be back for you afterward.' He left the two bound women alone, going out toward the pool naked as they were.

Jan sat very still in her tight leather body-suit. Her ankles were bound very tightly, and she knew that she could not free them. She struggled a bit for form's sake, and then sat quietly. There was nothing else to do. She looked at her nylon-sheathed legs, visible from hip to toe, with a critical rather than a disapproving eye. James and Patrick had both said that they were beautiful, and she admitted now that they were, at least, striking. The contrast between the smooth nylon of her tights and the tight ropes around her ankles pleased her. It was . . . erotic, she decided, relishing the word this time. Yes. They were nice legs. She was glad that she had them. Glad that the two men had admired them. Glad, too, she realised with a thrill of excitement, to be bound and on display. The paradox pleased her. Wanton, she thought, applying the word to herself at last without shame.

Like Barbara. And Robin. And like Antoinette. And the other women who had come here to be re-educated. I wonder what Leslie would think of her mother now, she thought. Perhaps she would be less patronising if she knew. And what would Sam make of her?

Barbara shifted on the chaise across from Jan. She moaned and tried to roll over, but her bonds prevented it. Jan looked again at the red marks on her breasts, and remembered how Barbara had first screamed, and then surrendered to pleasure as James had fondled and teased her nipples. Jan's own breasts felt neglected. She allowed herself to imagine Patrick fondling them, bending to kiss her engorged nipples, caressing, driving her wild . . .

Barbara opened her eyes. They were focused on Jan with no sense of shame or embarrassment. Jan tried to look as frankly at her but she felt the flush rising up to colour her cheeks. Her ears burned.

'Mmmmm,' she sighed. 'That was good. Did you notice?'

'Did you really enjoy that?' Jan asked.

'Either I did, or I'm a very good actress. Which do you think it is? You're with the Little Theatre in Godalming. You must have some idea about acting.'

Jan looked at Barbara sharply. 'How did you know that?'

'I know a great deal about you. I know where you live, and what you do, and I know Leslie and Sam.' Seeing Jan's embarrassment and alarm, Barbara added, 'You needn't worry. I'm not going to tell anyone about you. I'd be putting myself in an awkward spot as well. Your guilty secret's safe with me.'

Jan couldn't decide whether to believe Barbara, but there was nothing she could do about the situation short of murdering her. She returned to the easier question: 'How do you know all this?'

'I'm Sam's mistress,' Barbara said. 'Or one of them, at any rate. He may have others, but I'm not worried about that. More important, are *you* worried about him shagging me? Or them?' Barbara was matter-of-fact in her admission.

Jan was silent for long moments, adapting to what she had heard. She had believed for a long time that

Sam was seeing someone else, as she had put it at the time. Knowing for certain was another thing. She supposed she understood his actions. If you can't get what you want at home, she reasoned, it wasn't unreasonable to look for it elsewhere. And Sam hadn't been getting what he wanted at home. But meeting his mistress, or one of them, was unsettling. Barbara didn't seem embarrassed by the situation, so Jan decided that she would have to look the same.

'I suppose I shouldn't be surprised.' That sounded indecisive. 'No,' she said. 'I'm not worried. And I'm not angry. Not at you nor at him. I haven't been very . . . accommodating.'

'Why not?' Barbara wanted to know. She seemed to be genuinely puzzled by Jan's attitude. 'Didn't you think your refusal to have sex would drive Sam to someone like me?'

Jan had no ready reply. A few days ago she would have refused to consider her reasons for keeping her legs crossed. Now they seemed absurd. After what had happened to her here, it would be foolish to try to justify her earlier behaviour. Frankness and self-honesty made her decide not to try. 'I don't know,' she said. 'These last few days have been a revelation.'

Jan was silent for long moments. With the revelation came the knowledge that she was going to have to revise her whole attitude toward sex, and to Sam. And toward Barbara and any other women involved. It wasn't easy.

'So, what are you going to do?' Barbara asked.

'About you and Sam? Nothing. I guess that you give one another pleasure. I shouldn't begrudge that.'

'No, not about Sam and me. I meant, what about yourself? Are you going to leave him, divorce him, throw him out, whatever the wronged wife does?'

'No . . . I think not. I'll let him decide.'

'You're still evading the real question, if you don't mind me saying so,' Barbara told her. 'Are you still going to keep those nice legs crossed?'

'I don't know yet,' Jan said. She wasn't sure she liked the two of them discussing her legs, or anything else about her, but she knew that when two people are intimate, as she and Sam hadn't been for a long time, they will share intimate secrets. A sudden thought made her smile. 'Does Sam tell you his wife doesn't understand him?'

'No, he doesn't say that. I asked him if that was why he was seeing me. He said that you both understood one another, but that that didn't solve the problem.'

Jan was on the verge of asking how she and Sam had 'solved the problem,' but decided not to. If Barbara wanted her to know all the details, she would tell her. Or Sam would. Or not.

Meanwhile, Barbara had another question. 'Are you going to tell Sam you've been here and what you've done?'

This one was harder than the last. After another long considering silence, Jan said she probably would. 'Why not?' she asked. 'If there is going to be a change in things at home, he'll want to know why.'

Barbara smiled. 'Why not, indeed? If you'll let him, I'm sure he would keep on with what you've learned here.'

Jan was not completely surprised. After all, she had seen Sam's collection of books and magazines. And she suddenly remembered where she had seen Barbara before. Sam had a photo of her among the things he kept (mainly) private. I wasn't prying, Jan told herself. Merely cleaning and tidying. 'Your photo doesn't do you justice,' she told Barbara. 'You're really much nicer in person. Don't stop seeing him because of me.'

192

'Just as it takes two to tango, it requires the same number to stop dancing. But don't let what you've learned today stop you from dancing with him either. Let him screw you. Things will work out somehow.'

There was one thing, however, which Jan had to know. 'Does Sam whip you?'

'I think you mean, does he take pleasure in whipping me, don't you? I really don't know how much pleasure he takes. I suppose there is some. After all it's the ultimate male power trip in many ways. But mainly he does it because he knows I like it. I told him so early on. He never brought up the subject on his own. Nor did he ask to tie me up. But once I indicated which way my interests lay, he did whatever he could to please me. I am certain that he enjoys bondage. He might have asked me to let him tie me up if I hadn't spoken first. He is thoughtful, and he likes to please a woman. Give him a chance to please you. I know he wants to.'

Jan felt shame at her long denial of Sam's desires, but she couldn't admit that yet. 'I know he's interested in bondage,' Jan said instead. 'I've seen some of the magazines he keeps around the house.'

'You just didn't know you were interested in it, did you?'

'No,' Jan replied. 'These last few days have been . . . interesting.'

'So how do you feel right now?' Barbara asked.

After a long silence, Jan finally said, 'Excited. Aroused, I suppose you'd say. I feel helpless but not afraid. Or at any rate not really frightened. It's more a tingly anticipation every time I try to move and find out I can't. And having to wait for the next thing to happen is exciting. Having to rely totally on someone else for even the smallest thing is exciting. I feel as if I have been freed from responsibility for myself, so I can enjoy what happens without the guilt I've always felt about sex.'

Barbara smiled. 'Are you going to let Sam tie you up, then?'

Jan didn't know. 'I don't think I could ask him,' she said finally.

Why ever not? asked the inner voice in exasperation. Barbara asked essentially the same question audibly, adding that Sam knew where his wife was spending her free time this week.

Jan was shocked. 'Sam set this up?'

Barbara nodded.

'Now I really feel embarrassed. Sam told you he was going to do this?

Barbara nodded again. 'He says he wants you. This was going to be his last attempt to change your mind.'

Jan flushed as she thought about what Barbara knew about her and Sam. And she knew virtually nothing about Barbara except what she had seen. Then her sense of fairness reasserted itself. If she had let Sam have her, she might have found what she wanted right at home. She need not have come here. And not met Patrick. Jan was by now thoroughly confused. What did she really want?

How about both of them? her alter ego suggested. At once. Maybe with Barbara, make it a foursome. Or ask Robin. What would Sam make of that young woman?

'You want them both,' Barbara said, smiling at Jan. In her mind's eye Jan saw the red devil doing the same.

'Why do you let Patrick do this to you and not Sam?' she asked.

'I don't ask Patrick to do it. He just does whatever he wants. Sam never asked,' Jan replied evasively.

Liar, said the voice in her head. If he had, you'd have run a mile. You needed this softening up. It's much too late to deny you love it now. And Patrick.

Jan flushed and looked away.

Barbara's voice cut across Jan's confusion. 'It looks as if you aren't ready yet. You'll know you're ready when you can ask a man for what you want. I suppose it's just as well Patrick or someone like him has you in his charge. You'll be able to ask him sometime soon. Ask him to tie you up and screw you, I mean,' Barbara said. 'That's the real purpose of all this: being brave enough to acknowledge your needs and tell someone else. Ask him. He fancies you something rotten. When you know a man fancies you it's easier to ask him to do what you like.'

Jan blushed hotly. She didn't want to think of that. Barbara had somehow discovered her guiltiest secret. Jan's alter ego demanded to know why the secret was 'guilty'. Jan had no answer. It just was. She imagined Patrick as her lover on an official basis. Why not? Jan felt her heart leap with something suspiciously like joy at the thought.

'How do you know what Patrick thinks?' Jan asked.

'He talked about you when he came to pick me up the other day. I was really curious to meet the woman who had made him so interested. I was a little jealous, too. After all, I've known him for years.'

Jan felt jealous too. Patrick must have left her to go and get Barbara. But Barbara was speaking again.

'I'll tell Sam for you, next time I see him. Give him a chance too.' Barbara sounded serious.

You never thought about him at all, accused the red devil. But now you have to think about two men. Think you'll manage?

Jan didn't know, but she was making a tentative plan to try. James, returning, broke her chain of thought and brought her back to the present. With a smile at them both he announced to Jan that it was time for her to undergo sensory deprivation. 'A bit of silence and seclusion during which you can consider your progress, and your future,' he added portentously. But his smile belied the heaviness of the words. He untied Jan's ankles, unfastened her lead and assisted her to stand. 'Barbara is going to stay here and recover.' And to Barbara he added, 'Then we'll think of another diversion for you when I get back.'

Twelve

James led Jan back to the room with the swimming pool. There she saw that he had been busy while she and Barbara talked. The equipment for her sensory deprivation session was ready. It consisted of a diver's full face mask with the glass blacked over. Jan guessed it would serve the same purpose as a blindfold. There were air hoses attached to the mask, the ends buoyed so that they would float above the water like a long snorkel, she thought.

A chair stood near the edge of the pool, with what looked like an awful lot of rope lying on the tiled floor beside it. Jan thought of the witch's ducking stool she had seen in a museum. For my sins of omission, she thought, I'll get a ducking. She was partly right.

James led her to the chair and seated her.

Jan perched awkwardly on the edge of the chair, unable to sit back due to her bound arms. She watched with a curious detachment as he tied her ankles together again, pulling the ropes tight and knotting them securely. Next he bound her knees. When he bound her thighs together above the knees Jan admired again the contrast between the ropes and the smooth nylon tights. Definitely erotic, she decided. Why didn't I ever think of this?

I suppose you were too busy being neurotic, her alter ego replied, but in a gentler tone than before. Never mind, it added, you're here now. Relax and enjoy the ride.

And she did, surprising herself. The fear had gone. They were not going to beat her. Just a relaxing hour or so in the water. Rather like a long bath, only she had never bathed while tied up. Darkness descended abruptly as James fitted the face mask. The sunny day outside disappeared. Jan sat in darkness in the tight leather body-suit that encased her upper body and imprisoned her arms behind her back. Instinctively she tested the ropes that bound her legs together. James paid no attention to her reactions. He adjusted the hoses of her facemask. When he was done, he inserted plugs in her ears. Sounds became muffled and distant, and Jan felt as if she had taken a step back from the everyday world. The only sounds she could hear were the beating of her heart and the soft sigh of air as she breathed through the hoses.

Hands reached out of the surrounding darkness and removed her shoes. They lifted her from the chair. Jan knew she was being carried to the pool. The cool water rose up her legs as the unseen hands lowered her. James left her sitting on the edge of the pool with her bound legs in the water. Jan sat quietly as James made the rest of his preparations. She admired her own calm. A few days ago she would have been struggling and fighting.

The hands returned, lowering her into the water. Jan momentarily panicked as the water closed over her head. Suppose the hoses came loose, or sank, she thought wildly. The moment passed when she found that she could breathe normally. But the sensation of weightlessness was strange. She was disorientated. Up and down ceased to have any meaning. Blind, she could not tell where she was, whether she was standing or lying, on her side or on her back. Panic rose to choke her. Her chest felt tight, and she jerked wildly. The supporting hands disappeared, leaving her alone and helpless in her dark world. Jan bucked and fought, but could feel nothing around her. Her sense of balance was no good to her. The water held her weightless.

Jan had no idea how long she fought her bonds and the sense of falling, but when her breath was roaring in her ears and her heart was pounding, she had to stop. Gradually she grew calmer as she realised that she was breathing with no difficulty, and seemed to be in no danger. Nevertheless it took time for her earlier calm to return. She felt cut off from her body and from the rest of the world in her dark, silent pool.

When nothing alarming happened, she gradually relaxed in the cool water, not knowing whether she floated or sank. Jan entered a timeless darkness that allowed her no outside sensory information. It was curiously peaceful as her concerns receded. She gave herself up to the darkness and the silence. She no longer fought her bonds, welcoming them instead as a reminder of her helplessness and captivity. She was someone else's responsibility. She could do nothing for herself. That was curiously comforting. Only the pressure of the tight body-suit and the ropes that bound her legs reminded her that she still had a body. That was easy to forget as she drifted weightlessly.

Jan could not know if she woke or slept, so absolute was her isolation. She thought or dreamed that she was back at home, safe from the rest of the world, safe from the men who had abducted her and who now held her captive. She remembered Leslie's last visit, imagining she could hear her daughter going on about some bizarre holiday experience. Then she thought of Sam. Was he curled up in bed with another of his mistresses? Jan's mind, freed from her body, roamed back to her girlhood, her marriage and the birth of her children.

She had no way to judge how long she drifted in silent darkness, but at some point the comforting memories of the past faded and she felt the panic returning. She was back in the swimming pool, bound helplessly and breathing through an air hose. They had forgotten her. No one would come for her. How long could she endure the company of her own thoughts, with no other stimuli? She began to feel as if she were the last person in the world.

Nonsense, she told herself firmly. Someone put me here and someone will come for me. Are you sure? The tiny voice whispered to her from the fringes of panic. Jan fought once more, twisting and turning in the water, struggling against the body-suit and the ropes. And no one came. Oh God, I'm alone. No one will ever come. I'll be here forever. The panic grew to a shout in her brain, blotting out all rational thought as she struggled in silence. She heard her breath rasping. Her heart pounded. Jan thought she would choke on her fear. And no one came.

Exhausted, she drifted once more, waking, drowsing, a captive in mind as well as in body. Woke and drowsed, still in darkness and silence as if adrift in interstellar space, alone, beyond rescue. Jan had never experienced such isolation. She felt that she must return to the real world, to people and sights and sounds, to touch and feeling. She screamed within the facemask, as much to assure herself that she still could hear and make noises as for hope of release.

Jan felt as if she no longer had a body. The body that had been racked by sexual release only the day

200

before was now gone, and she longed for it to come back. She knew now why they had denied her the rubber cups over her nipples and the dildo in her cunt. She longed for them now. Even, she thought, shocked and disbelieving, the whip would be preferable to this eternity of no-feeling.

Sensory deprivation also included now, for her, deprivation of sexual release. She thought of how often she had denied Sam, and herself, this simple yet all-important experience. Jan understood the pent-up desire that drove him to other women. She didn't understand why he had stayed with her as he had. She vowed to be different. Never again the denial, if only she could get out of this . . .

Was this the transformation her captors were aiming for? If so, she was ready to admit the change in her ways. Even though so far she had been merely bound and penetrated by inanimate things, she was now ready for anything, even the real thing. Jan thrashed and moaned in her bondage. And she was beginning to realise that she was in another type of bondage too: she was gripped by the desire of a mature woman to have something filling the void between her thighs. She had scorned those women, even Leslie, who seemed obsessed with men and their cocks.

Her alter ego taunted her. Didn't take much time to change your mind, did it? And this time she admitted its existence, and the justice of its criticism. Oh God, just get me out of this and I'll be different from now on. Sam would not recognise the new Jan if she were only delivered from this void. The irony of her plea didn't escape her.

But deliverance did not come. In the end Jan thought she would go mad. Cut off from time and all her senses, she no longer knew where she was. Sensory deprivation was real deprivation.

When finally Jan felt the touch of hands on her body, at first she couldn't imagine what it was. Then she was flooded with gratitude. They had not forgotten her after all. They had come to restore her to the human race. She was lifted from the water and set onto the chair. The mask was removed. Light flooded in, dazzling her eyes after the absolute darkness of her immersion. She squeezed them closed in pain to shut it out. The earplugs came next. Sounds assaulted her ears after the silence. If she could have closed them, she would have. But most overwhelming of all was her vast relief at being in the company of people again, even if they were only her captors. Jan longed for someone to touch her, to validate her return from the limbo of silence and darkness and no-feeling.

If she had not been bound, Jan would have flung herself on them, rubbed her body against them, lost herself in the sensuous experience of holding her body close against another one. And especially Patrick's, she realised. Even with her eyes closed she could visualise his handsome face and lean, strong body. Jan knew that he was at least ten years younger than she was, nearer to Leslie's age in fact. But suddenly she wanted him with a fierce ache in her belly. Partly the result of her isolation, she knew, and partly the result of her talk with Barbara, but also the sudden crystallisation of a desire that had grown on her unseen and unacknowledged until now. Only her earlier shyness and aversion had prevented her from saying anything to him, and it did so again. Pride as well played a part in her silence. But she acknowledged the desire to herself: an important change for someone who had spent a large part of her life denying all sexual desires.

With her eyes closed Jan imagined herself bound to a bed, spread like a starfish, her wrists and ankles tied to the bedposts, waiting for Patrick to come fuck her. She imagined the door opening, the light flooding in to reveal his naked body and erect cock as he advanced upon her. Jan shivered at the image. She opened her eyes to slits and saw him bending over her, the man of her latest fantasy. For a moment she thought he was going to carry her off and ravish her.

And for a moment, before her normal reticence returned, she wanted him to do so. Then it all ended. She was encased in the dripping leather suit, her legs bound tightly together, safe from invasion and penetration, even if she wanted it.

'Would you finish her, Patrick? I need to see how Barbara is doing,' James said.

Patrick loosened the ropes that bound her legs. They left red indentations in her flesh beneath the tights. Jan spread her legs slightly, feeling the cramped muscles loosen. But she didn't want to try walking just then. She had been tied up for a long time.

She sat for several minutes in awkward silence. There seemed nothing to say that would fit the odd circumstances. Meeting Patrick's glance was too much. Instead, Jan looked down at the pool from which she had been plucked. The memory of her isolation made her shiver. Even though she was beginning to feel shy once more, she was glad to have Patrick nearby. The latest experience had been unsettling. She was glad when Patrick led her, dripping, from the pool room and up the stairs. She felt exhausted.

Thirteen

When, in the evening, Patrick came to her room with a carrier bag, Jan was not taken completely by surprise. She was in fact glad he had come, though she didn't want to say so. After the sensory deprivation in the pool, she was still pathetically glad for any human contact. That experience had taught her how isolated she had been, and she didn't like to think about that.

The bag bore the label of a famous department store, and Patrick joked that one could find anything in the world in that emporium. 'There was some hesitation when I asked for dildoes, but in the end they managed to find what I wanted.'

Jan did not find the joke funny. No matter where he had found the stuff in the bag, she knew that she would be the one to put it to use. But by now, Jan had become so accustomed to being tied up or otherwise restrained that she made no protest. She didn't even feel alarmed by the shiver of excitement at the prospect of yet another sexual adventure. Her alter ego thought that that represented progress. Jan tried to convince herself that she was merely bowing to the inevitable. She shivered again when he emptied the bag on the bed. Rope – quite a lot of it. There was a gag – a harness that would go over her head and face, and a ball that would fill her mouth. More promising (alarming, said her old self vainly), she noticed 'her' dildo, as she had begun to call it. Black and thick and threatening, it lay on the bed spread. Jan felt herself go damp inside as she looked at it, though as always she strove to conceal her reaction from Patrick. In addition, the familiar rubber caps were there. Jan looked at her breasts and saw that the nipples were growing taut with excitement. She blushed at the obviousness of her arousal, but there was nothing she could do to conceal it.

As it was evening, Jan guessed that she would spend the night tied up. She recalled her earlier experience of sleeping in bondage. It looked as if she was going to do it again. She caught her breath on a gasp when Patrick selected a length of rope from the bed and moved around behind her. She knew that she could stop all this simply by asking him to . . . fuck her. Jan brought her hands together behind her back without a word.

Jan Two gave her qualified approval. At least you're learning.

Jan stood still as Patrick bound her wrists together. It was not easy to conceal her excitement as he made her helpless once again. It's getting to be an addiction, she thought as the ropes drew tight. Her elbows came next, drawn behind her, nearly touching, causing her breasts to jut forward invitingly. She was disappointed when he did not accept the invitation. But he was not finished with them yet. He bound each of them around the base, against her chest, with short lengths of rope, pulling it tight, making them swell tautly and causing her nipples to tighten. Jan felt her legs go weak as the familiar tingle travelled from her bound breasts to her cunt. She knew that she was wet and parted, and before she could deny the thought, she wished that Patrick would put his cock into her and . . . But at this Jan reasserted herself. No, she said sternly. Stop thinking about that.

Not easy, Jan Two said.

Jan looked at her reflection in the mirror. The woman who stared back at her was a stranger with her face and body. She felt acutely as if she were two persons, both spectator and half-unwilling participant. How erotic, she thought. The bound woman in the mirror is . . . me.

Patrick brought the gag from the bed. He fitted the collar around her throat with the buckles under her chin. Jan opened her mouth at his signal and he stuffed the rubber ball behind her teeth, filling her mouth and making her cheeks bulge. Her tongue was trapped under the ball. Patrick secured the harness: a strap around the back of her head, under her long hair, pulled tight and buckled; a divided strap passed from the wide leather strip over her mouth, passing either side of her nose, over the top of her head, and buckling to the collar. The last strap passed under her chin and pulled her jaw closed around the gag. Jan made the ritual attempt to eject the ball, and was both relieved and excited to find that she could not. 'Ummnnhh,' she said, testing its effectiveness. No one outside the room would have heard her. It was now too late to ask Patrick to take her. Jan felt both relief and excitement.

Oh God, now I can't stop him from doing anything he wants to do.

And oh God, you don't want to stop him either, her alter ego added unhelpfully.

What he did next Jan found both arousing and alarming, in that order. First Patrick tied a piece of rope around her waist, in what Jan recognised as the beginning of a crotch rope. She immediately began looking forward, despite the urgings of her older self, to being aroused by the friction on her clitoris. She guessed (correctly) that he would insert 'her' dildo and secure it inside with rope running between her legs and tied to that around her waist. And indeed Patrick did just that. Jan held her breath as the thick, hard rubber shaft slid inside her, and made its presence known by the familiar full feeling she had come to enjoy so much. Jan clenched her vaginal muscles around the dildo, holding it in and savouring the feel of it once more. She had missed it during the session in the pool, and was glad to have it back now. The next thing was the alarming bit.

Patrick left her for a moment, going into the bathroom. Jan assumed he had gone to do the job for which one can send no messenger, and was content to wait for his return. He came back with a plastic squeeze bottle of body cream. Seeing it, Jan imagined how nice it would feel as he massaged it into her body, paying (she hoped) particular attention to her erogenous zones.

You mean your entire body, her alter ego quipped.

No, she replied, just my breasts and down there.

Tits and cunt, you mean.

Whatever, Jan thought, too excited to engage in internal debate.

When she saw the slim dildo Patrick took from his pocket her eyes widened in alarm. He lubricated it with the body cream and moved behind her. It didn't take too much imagination to guess what he was going to do with it.

Jan whinnied through her gag and retreated from him. Even though she knew there was no escape if he really intended to put that up her bottom (arsehole, her alter ego corrected her), she instinctively shied away from it. It wouldn't . . . couldn't fit up there.

Just another useless virginity to lose, her alter ego said. Jan disagreed, continuing her retreat until she reached the wall near the nightstand. There she put her back against the wall and clenched all her internal muscles against the second invader.

It won't help, her inner voice said. Remember what happened when you tried to resist the first dildo.

Jan thought of the whip. Would Patrick use the riding crop to force her to accept the anal dildo? She resolved to resist even if she was beaten.

Hey, that might be fun. Remember how Barbara came when James beat her?

Jan didn't need that reminder. She wished her mental state were less confused. Her mind as well as her body was divided against her. Nevertheless, she didn't move away from the wall, watching apprehensively as Patrick approached.

'I promise this won't hurt, Jan. Just relax and enjoy it.'

Patrick's advice did not calm her. It sounded too much like the Chinese proverb. Proverbs are sometimes based on truth, said her other self. Not this one, she replied.

Patrick laid the dildo on the dressing table. Jan couldn't take her eyes from it. The sight made her anal sphincter contract, while at the same time she couldn't help but wonder how it would feel to have two plugs inside her.

Attagirl! her alter ego encouraged her. Keep thinking like that!

Patrick came closer. Jan tore her gaze away from the dildo and looked at him, trying to read his intentions from his face. Patrick slid his arms around her waist and pulled her against him. Jan's erect nipples sent a delicious tingle southwards as they contacted his chest. One hand slid down to caress her bottom. Jan moaned, tugging against her bonds as he stroked her body. Arousal supplanted alarm. Nothing seemed more important than the sensations spreading from her breasts, through her belly and down her legs. She forgot about anal penetration and concentrated on her dildo and Patrick's hands on her body. When he kissed her over her gag, Jan wished that she could open her mouth to welcome his tongue. Before her old self had time to warn her that she should not be thinking about that, she remembered how excitedly Robin had received his kiss over her own gag. Being kissed without being able to return the kiss excited her. It was another aspect of being helpless, Jan realised.

The kiss drew out. Jan moaned, the sound muffled by the rubber ball that filled her mouth. She pressed her body against him. Only when he released her did she think of resistance, but by then her old habits were entirely too weak to make her draw away, or think of escape. It came to Jan in a flash of insight that she was again thinking of escape only after it had become impossible. Had she not been transformed by her sojourn, she would have been thinking of getting away all the time. This time it was not merely her bonds and her nakedness that made escape impossible. She desperately wanted to see how this encounter would turn out. She was momentarily shocked at her thoughts, but the shock too melted into arousal. The old Jan was surrounded on all sides, outmanoeuvred, helpless in the face of these new emotions.

She felt Patrick pulling a rope between her legs and tying it in front to the rope around her waist. It was time for her dildo to be secured inside her, time for the rope to rub her clitoris, time for orgasm and delight. When he slid the lubricated dildo into her anus, Jan stiffened in surprise, but could do nothing to prevent this second penetration. Immediately she felt stuffed full, uncomfortably so, but Patrick was already adjusting the rope between her legs so that it rubbed against her clitoris. Jan nearly forgot the loss of her anal virginity at the touch. Plugged front and back, she felt a wave of excitement sweep over her as she realised she could not eject those shafts inside her.

Told you so, her alter ego said. Enjoy it.

And, guiltily, Jan did, glancing at herself in the mirror. A woman with bound arms and breasts looked back at her, a white rope running tightly down between her legs. The bound woman felt the effects of that rope most acutely each time she made the slightest move. Jan moaned behind her gag. That's me, she thought with a touch of awe. Me in the mirror, me tied and gagged and wearing a crotch rope. I can't escape. She felt terribly excited. Terribly . . . adult. Grown up at last. If not exactly in control of her destiny, at least embracing it for the first time.

She saw also in the mirror that Patrick had an erection, obviously at the sight of her. Jan wished that it was his cock inside her instead of the rubber shaft, and then recoiled from the thought. The real thing was too much for her just then, though she had enough sense to realise that she was being softened up again for just that. But she was not ready. Later, she thought in a kind of panic. I'll face that later.

What's the difference between Patrick's cock and the shaft inside you now, her alter ego asked. Jan had no answer. Her continued aversion went beyond all reason. But she knew that she wouldn't be able to hold out forever.

She straightened her back as if to show her continued resistance. The movement made her breasts thrust forward, and she blushed all over in annoyance and embarrassment.

Patrick took her by the elbow and led her to the bed, seating her at the side with her feet on the floor. Jan felt the dildo in her anus stab her as the weight came onto her bottom. She squirmed, trying to stand again and relieve the unaccustomed pressure. Patrick held her down, and her squirming made her increasingly aware of her twin penetrations. Jan moaned, not entirely in pain. Patrick paid no attention. He quickly tied her ankles together. Jan was now unable to stand even if she managed to get to her feet. Her knees came next, the rope biting into her flesh as he pulled it tight and knotted it. More rope encircled her legs above the knees, this too pulled tight. Trussed and helpless, Jan squirmed and tugged at the ropes. But now she was trying out the new sensations rather than trying to escape. She already knew that, once bound, she would not be able to free herself. Now the realisation added to her excitement. She had allowed herself to be bound and gagged and stuffed without offering more than token resistance, she realised guiltily. But it felt so good, now that she was tied up.

Personality nearly transformed, her alter ego told her helpfully. Jan didn't dispute it.

Patrick approached with the familiar rubber caps. Again, Jan offered no resistance as he glued them over her nipples. She was mainly trying not to show how much she anticipated the pricking of those needles, and what would follow from that. She felt herself growing warm between the legs as she thought of being left bound all night.

Don't plan on too much sleep, said the inner voice.

Jan squirmed on the side of the bed, concentrating on the feel of the anal dildo being pushed deeply into her back passage. It was not painful or terrible as she had thought it would be. Jan was forced to admit that

211

it was *exciting* to have that shaft inside her, like nothing she'd experienced before.

Her alter ego was enjoying it too. Keep going, it advised her.

She glanced up and saw Patrick watching her. Blushing guiltily, Jan became suddenly still. She waited in mortification for him to remark on her reaction, and was grateful when he did not. A further glance at the mirror brought back the worry that *they* might be filming her, for purposes she dared not think about. When she reflected that Patrick was one of *them*, she felt slightly better. He wouldn't allow the tape to get into the wrong hands. But being gagged, Jan couldn't ask him if there was a film. And, she realised, she wouldn't want to know in any case. Knowing that she was going to be left bound through the night, Jan also knew that she would not be lying still. Couldn't lie still, now that she knew what responses she could expect from her newly awakened body.

Patrick bent and kissed Jan again over her gag. She felt dizzy. This was more exciting than a normal kiss, one she could return (if she chose) and control to some extent. She could do nothing about this one. Jan was acutely aware of her mouth, held wide open by the gag. He twined his hands in her long hair, keeping her head still as the one-sided kiss drew out. There was a roaring in her ears and she felt as if she might pass out under the combination of stimulus and anticipation. The phrase 'swooning with desire' came to her.

Finally Patrick released her and Jan tried to recover her poise. He went around the room putting out the lights. She knew he was about to leave her and wished that she had the courage to ask him to stay the night with her. Or the ability, come to that. Jan nearly made a noise through her gag to attract his attention, but stopped herself at the last moment.

Her alter ego was exasperated. I just . . . can't, Jan thought, defending herself against the voice that urged her to abandon all restraint.

Before he moved away, Patrick placed the control box for her dildo on the nightstand as he had done on the earlier occasion. Only this time there was no way for her to reach it. It occurred to Jan that he was telling her that whatever she did that night, she would do herself. He left the bathroom light on and the door open, so that the bedroom would not be completely dark. There was enough light to let Jan see herself in the big mirror on the wall. He went out, closing the door. Jan sat on the side of the bed in her bonds, trying to decide whether to lie down or to continue exploring the sensations from her twin plugs. She decided on the latter, reasoning that she could always lie down, whereas sitting up again might be more difficult with her hands and arms out of action. She felt a strong curiosity about the effects of the anal plug. Squirming once more, Jan found the sensation exciting. The knowledge that she could do nothing about her novel situation also excited her.

There isn't much that doesn't excite you now, her alter ego observed, with an overall tone of approval.

Jan felt the shaft in her anus shift as she squirmed on the bed. She was beginning to like the idea of being stuffed in all her orifices. There were more signs of approval from her cunt. She knew she was growing wet there from the warm sensation between her legs and from the smell coming from the same place. It was the odour of a woman in rut, which she had learned when Patrick had first held the dildo under her nose to allow her to smell herself. At first she had been embarrassed by her smell. Not now. There was a sharp pricking as her nipples erected and touched the needles in the rubber caps. Jan knew she was lost from then on. All her recent experience told her that she was going to come, and by her own efforts. And she was looking forward to it.

Jan relished the prospect of the night to come for a little while longer, then she lay down, raising her bound legs and rolling over backward onto the bed. From there she struggled to roll over onto her stomach, the task enlivened by the shifting of the two plugs inside her. That augured well for the future. The rubber caps pricked her nipples as they touched the bed. Lying on her stomach, Jan felt the dildo in her cunt more acutely. The one in her anus now was merely a presence and a full feeling, exciting enough, but nothing like as satisfying as the other. She ground her hips against the mattress, making the dildo bump her clitoris. That was more like it. Would they switch her on? But the control box was here, with her, out of her reach and theirs. Jan would have to see what she could do with her own limited resources and no longer so limited imagination.

The silence of the house closed about her, and Jan imagined that she had been abandoned, bound and helpless. The thought excited her. She felt that she was alone and unobserved. The earlier fear of being captured on videotape had lessened when Patrick put out the lights in the room. There was not now enough light to make a tape of whatever she did.

You mean your efforts to make yourself come, her alter ego suggested. That's what you're going to do. You know it. Why not get on with it?

And although she still felt vaguely guilty about masturbation, she knew that she *was* going to do it anyway. Being on her own would make it easier. For now, she hastened to reassure her alter ego before it could rebuke her for still being afraid of the real thing.

Jan reared up, arching her back and lifting her hips as far as she could before bringing them down against the firm mattress. She repeated the manoeuvre again and again, as if making love to the bed. She turned her face toward the mirror and saw a bound woman rising and falling as she brought herself to orgasm. The sight of the woman in the mirror aroused her still further. It was as if she were having an experience and watching another woman having the same one. The familiar signals were travelling from her taut nipples to her cunt. Jan gasped and moaned behind her gag, the sounds of rising excitement muffled but unmistakable.

Jan's partner in the mirror kept pace with her. Seeing herself gave Jan an added thrill. That's me, she thought. I'm doing this. The first spasm in her cunt made her moan loudly, her voice straining against her gag, her body straining against the ropes that held her captive. Then she was moaning continuously as she shuddered in a long rippling orgasm. The tight ropes intensified the experience as she struggled. Her imagination summoned up the picture of a bound captive struggling to escape, and the mirror echoed the image as Jan bucked and writhed on the bed.

Jan felt weary but still afire as she subsided, her breath sawing in her throat as she drew in great lungfuls of air through her widely flaring nostrils. Between her legs she felt the secret flow of her rut, seeping down and making the mattress damp. The smell of it inflamed her, and only the need to catch her breath prevented her from doing it all over again. Gradually cooling, Jan drowsed and woke, still captive. And she did it all over again. Through the slow hours Jan struggled and came, wearing herself out. Finally she drifted off to fitful sleep and lurid dreams. Unable to move, Jan dreamed that she was bound, helpless, forced to arouse herself for a cruel master who demanded that she wear herself out with orgasms. Which she had truly done.

Some time in the night Jan wakened again and saw her image in the mirror. She looked at the control box on the nightstand and wished she could get at it. Although she couldn't get at the control box, Jan could imagine what it would feel like to have the dildo come alive within her (within your cunt, her alter ego retorted). And in her imagination she felt her arousal begin again. Her first reaction was dismay. Surely her body wasn't going to make her do it again. But her dismay did not last for long. The familiar excitement rose within her as she imagined the familiar vibrations in her cunt. The needles at her breasts and the plug in her anus did their work too. Once more Jan struggled against her ropes, and felt the rising tide of pleasure in her body. This time she was not reluctant to arouse herself. She did it willingly, her mind and body aflame with the knowledge that she was doing something she always thought of as wicked. They had done this to her, made her think and act this way. You're doing it yourself, her alter ego told her as another orgasm swept through her. I can't help it, it feels so good. And with that thought she came again.

Her old self tried to tell her that she had been forced earlier. Her new self acknowledged that she had co-operated shamelessly with the sordid game her captors were playing. She should try to resist now, insisted her old self. *I can't*, she wailed mentally. Won't, insisted the old Jan. And so, torn between the conflicting halves of her personality, Jan writhed and bucked and came repeatedly. Her resistance was taking a beating. Jan found herself hoping it would be defeated, though she tried to thrust that idea away. I can't help myself, the new Jan declared silently.

Don't want to help yourself either, her alter ego said unhelpfully, but with a sense of ultimate victory.

She bucked and jerked for what seemed like an eternity of ecstasy. Jan was breathless and tired, but still she drove herself on, drove the dildo into her cunt, drove herself wild. Frantically she struggled in the bed, moaning through her gag as wave after wave of pleasure shook her helpless body. When finally she could do no more, Jan fell into a restless sleep, her body twitching from time to time as she dreamed luridly of sexual arousal and sexual slavery.

She woke sometime before dawn, still bound and gagged, and found herself revelling in her helplessness. She knew now that she would never be able to stop doing this. In the short time of her captivity they had indeed been able to transform her personality from shy, celibate, anxious woman to eager wanton. Yes, wanton, she thought with wonder and surprise. The two dildoes inside her were further reminders of her newly aroused sexual appetite. No return, she declared silently to the darkness, and to confirm her new freedom Jan rolled over onto her stomach with a struggle and began to grind her hips against the mattress, seeking once more the thrilling freedom of sexual release while her body remained captive.

This time, the orgasm building within her was a long time coming, but when it arrived Jan thought she would black out from the intensity. She bucked and jerked, her head thrashing from side to side, her face red and hot. Behind her back her bound hands twisted against the ropes. Her legs bent at the knees, her feet nearly touching her hands, her back arched, and then her body straightened out again with a jerk as she came. A long tearing moan signalled her climax. A small part of her was glad for the gag, for the inability to scream out her ecstasy and embarrass herself, while the larger part of her wanted the world to know that she was in the throes of sexual release the like of which she had never dreamed of.

Never dared to dream of, her alter ego reminded her. But this is better than dreams, isn't it?

After the last release, Jan lay quietly on the bed, still helplessly bound and gagged, still plugged in both orifices, but at peace. After this, there is only the real thing left, she thought. I'm about ready for it. I hope it is at least as good as this past night has been.

When Patrick came to untie her, Jan was nearly asleep. She woke as he took away her bonds, half wishing that she could remain tied. But she had to go to the toilet, and she had to have some sleep, so she knew that the ropes had to come off. She swung her stiff legs over the side of the bed, her cramped arms and shoulders protesting against moving after such a long immobility. The plugs came out, then the gag, and she was as free as she would ever be so long as she remained in this house. First the toilet, she thought as she nearly wet herself. And then a bath afterward. And then some sleep.

Jan dried herself and returned to the bedroom, wondering if Patrick could sense how intense the past night had been for her. In the light of the new day she felt embarrassed about the lurid night she had passed. But he never mentioned it, offering breakfast instead.

Jan was too tired. She refused food and lay on the bed again. Patrick seemed to understand. He undressed and lay beside her, taking her tired body into his arms. So she went to sleep cradled against the man she wanted as a lover. If the real thing was the next thing in store for her, she wanted it to be his thing.

Fourteen

Jan woke in the afternoon. There was a hand lying casually on her breast. The first reaction was alarm. Then she remembered, and felt immensely better. Patrick slept beside her, one arm under her neck and the other lying loosely over her breast. She flushed with pleasure at the touch. Patrick stirred as she moved. He kissed her shoulder and pulled her against him.

Jan rolled over to face him and offered him her lips. She held her breath as his mouth covered hers, reminding herself not to close her lips. The kiss drew out, and Jan felt her heart begin to pound with the excitement of lying naked in bed with a stranger and being kissed by him. And what was likely to follow the kiss was even more exciting. She was about to lose the last vestiges of her former self. She was, if not technically, then emotionally still a virgin, on the verge of her first real fuck. Both she and her alter ego were looking forward to it, in harmony at last.

Oh God, I hope he wants me as much as I want him. She didn't want to appear the complete fool, the older woman pursuing an unwilling younger man. It was one of the oldest clichés in romantic fiction, and now she was living it. A woman in heat can be such a fool, she thought. And she was in heat. The admission slipped past her guard. Jan felt her desire as a warmth (a fever, her alter ego amended) that pervaded her whole body, and this man was causing it.

Patrick held her for a long time, his hands stroking her back and bottom deliciously. Jan stifled a moan of pleasure.

'Bathroom?' Patrick asked with a lifting of eyebrows.

Jan nodded and rose reluctantly. A bath would be nice after the long hours in bondage. And it would give her time to think about what was coming. Don't think too long, her alter ego warned her. You might get cold feet. Jan bathed and dried in a flush of anticipation.

Patrick met her as she emerged from the bathroom. He took her into his arms and there was another long kiss. This time Jan's mouth was hungry for him. She did not draw back. She was both surprised and pleased by her ardour. At length he drew back and led her to the bedroom. There she waited while he laid out food for them with the easy grace and economy of movement she had come to admire in him. They were going to eat in this room, alone, intimate as lovers, even though they were not.

Yet, her alter ego remarked. But you'll get there in the end if you stop stalling.

'You must be hungry after last night and no breakfast this morning,' Patrick said.

Jan fought the urge to tell him not to bother with food, to take her instead. Lead me to my disordered bed and . . . and fuck me stupid. Robin's phrase came to her unbidden, and she used it with hardly any hesitation. Just pink arousal which she hoped would transmit itself to him without the need for the words she was reluctant to utter. Her stomach, however, rumbled loudly at the sight of the lunch he had prepared for them. She blushed and Patrick smiled.

'The body always knows what's best,' he said. 'Let it be your guide.'

Jan sat down in the chair he pulled back for her, feeling strange at the formality when they were both naked, but liking it nonetheless. The pleasures of postponing the final plunge appealed both to her old and new selves, for different reasons. Her old self urged her to resist, though without saying exactly how. Play disinterested, she supposed. Only she couldn't, for she was *very* interested in what was coming. Her body, knowing best, tingled all over at the thought of lying in bed with Patrick and . . . fucking. The word sounded more natural each time she thought of it.

They ate a real lunch this time: lobster, baked potatoes and salad. The wine was a fine champagne. Jan, who knew almost nothing about wine, nevertheless knew that this was something special, both in taste and in symbolism. She drank several glasses, no longer afraid of becoming tipsy with Patrick. When the bottle was empty and their plates nearly so, Jan knew it was time for the finale. She trembled with eagerness, though striving to conceal it.

Patrick got up from the table and looked at Jan with a smile. She felt as if someone were squeezing her heart when he beckoned her to him. She rose too and went quickly to him, hoping her eagerness wasn't too obvious. The reserve she felt even now was merely the vestige of her old habits, but it was hard to shed completely.

When she stood before him he embraced her again, holding her body against his. Jan knew he couldn't fail to detect the tremors that shook her. He kissed her forehead, kissed her eyes closed, kissed the corners of her mouth and the sides of her neck.

'Ohhhh,' she sighed, flushing with pleasure as he touched her. Everything else became of secondary importance.

But Patrick knew the effect of postponement, even if she didn't. He moved slowly. Jan responded with growing desire and impatience. When he stepped back at last, she looked at his erection for the first time. He wants me, she said silently, with a touch of awe and delight. Old stick-in-the-mud Jan Norris can make a man like him get erect with wanting her.

Told you, didn't I, the inner devil said.

Patrick sat in the armchair and pulled Jan down onto his lap. He arranged her, with her legs dangling over one of the arms and her back supported by the opposite one. She put her arms around his shoulders and moulded herself to him, very much aware of his stiff cock pressing against her bottom.

Jan told herself that she had known Patrick for only a little more than a week, and already she was ready for what it had all been leading up to.

That's what I mean, the devil retorted. Get on with it. Do something. Wriggle about. You've heard of lap dancing?

Jan couldn't. She looked at the mirror instead. The image no longer shocked her. She looked at it closely, seeing herself naked in the arms of a naked man whom she wanted rather badly, and whose cock was pressing against her bottom in a way that suggested that the desire was mutual.

She wished he'd take her now. For as long as possible. Now. In this room. On that bed, or even the floor if he preferred.

What would she do when they finally let her go?

Let her go. The thought brought a blank regret she could not have imagined at the beginning of her sojourn. From demanding her freedom she had gone to dreading it. She dreaded the loss of the virtually constant stimulation of her body and senses, the minute-by-minute enjoyment of her captive status. She did not want to forget that status nor be released from it. Jan knew that at some point she would have to resume her normal life. How would she cope without the means to gratify her new desires?

She might manage to keep the nipple caps to wear under her bra in public, or to obtain some of her own (though she shrank from the image of herself going into the local sex shop with its blacked-out windows and demanding a set). But they would only arouse her to no purpose without Patrick to tend to her when she finally made her way home frantic with desire. What about Sam? Available evidence indicated that he liked this sort of thing. Would he be an acceptable substitute for Patrick? Was there an acceptable substitute? Although she had learned a lot of new things about herself, it might already be too late for both of them. Sitting in Patrick's lap, being aroused by him, Jan tried to push aside these distractions.

Her old self retained enough influence to make that difficult. She tried to silence its voice by vowing to think it all over during the night. If she could think of anything then. All right, tomorrow.

Patrick's touch brought her back to the present. Gratefully Jan abandoned her depressing thoughts of the future as he touched her breast. He held her familiarly, cupping the full weight of her, and seemed to be waiting for her to give some sign of what she wanted him to do next.

Jan knew perfectly well what she wanted him to do next, or at least ultimately. But now that the moment had come she couldn't say anything. Damn the man, she thought. Why doesn't he just get on with it?

Get on with screwing *you*, you mean, the old Jan asked in horror.

Exactly, said the new Jan, and you can just shut up and let us get on with it.

Patrick tightened his arm around Jan's shoulders, raising her face and breasts closer and looking down at her calmly. His other hand, cupping her breast, gave her an encouraging squeeze.

Jan strained to raise herself still further, to raise her face to his, to kiss him and show him that she wanted him. She felt his arm tighten, helping her to rise while he smiled down at her. She managed the last few inches between them and placed her open mouth over his, preferring to let her body speak for her when words were too embarrassing.

In the mirror Jan caught another glimpse of herself. The image aroused her still further. She felt a burning in her cunt as they kissed. She tore her mouth from his and spoke in a tense, desperate whisper. 'Please, take me now!' She couldn't bring herself to be any more specific.

Patrick, understanding both the need and the reticence, helped her to stand, steadying her as she swayed and rising to stand beside her. With a hand in the small of her back he guided Jan toward the bed. She went blindly.

But there was one detail lacking. Jan had to tackle this matter head on, amazed and pleased by her directness, her boldness, as she thought it. I couldn't have done this a week ago, she thought. 'Patrick, I'm ready for the next step.' There, the words were out, and Jan only blushed faintly.

'But first . . . I want you . . . to tie me up.'

'Is that strictly necessary?' Patrick asked with a straight face.

'I . . . yes, it is.' This time Jan blushed more deeply, but she was glad she had forced it out. And it *was* necessary, as she had learned during the past several days. Essential, she would say. A *sine qua non*, as her Latin teacher would have put it, though she couldn't imagine Miss Harper using the phrase in just this situation. Nor indeed ever being in this position. Not many women would ask to be tied up before having sex. I'm in a very small group. Elite, if you like to think of it in that way. The prime of Mrs Jan Norris, that's what this is, she thought as she watched Patrick get up and collect some of the rope with which she had been bound all night. Would he use the gag as well? Jan didn't want to ask, preferring to leave that up to him. She had just about used up her supply of boldness for the day.

While Jan was thinking this through, Patrick took her in his arms. Jan felt her knees go weak as he kissed her again. She wanted to tell him that she wanted him badly, but stopped herself at the last minute. I can't, not again, she told herself. Instead she concentrated on enjoying the intimacy and affection, and the feel of him against her naked body. Her nipples erected and her vaginal muscles clenched as she imagined being penetrated by the cock that was making itself felt against her belly. Her chest felt tight as her breath caught in her throat.

Desperately she sought his mouth with her own. Words might break the spell. Jan allowed her body to speak its own need. Her old self looked on in fascinated horror as the new Jan welcomed her new lover with lips and tongue and arms. Her whole body ached for him to fill her, overwhelm her and the old hovering doubts with an eagerness that matched her own.

They embraced for endless minutes, drawing out the pleasure. Jan pressed herself against him, moulding her body to his lean angularity. Hurryhurryhurry said a part of her. Hurry before you lose your nerve.

The tiny devil-figure came to her rescue. Don't worry. I'm driving. We won't lose the way.

Jan now welcomed her as an ally. She relaxed, slowed, let the kiss draw out, taking the time to enjoy being Patrick's captive woman, almost his eager lover, hovering on the brink losing her lost virginity.

A wonder took her as she was lifted from her feet. I'm weightless, she thought, flying on the wings of this new sensation. Patrick laid her on the bed and began tying her. First her wrists, tied to opposite sides of the head board. Then her ankles, spread apart and tied to the foot board. Jan recalled her earlier image, in her kitchen as her abductors fondled her. Last week or a lifetime ago? Spread like a starfish, she had thought. And now here I am, among the echinoderms.

Giving her no time for thought or regret, Patrick got into bed with her and positioned himself between her thighs. His rude red cock was aimed straight at her cunt, and she was breathless with anticipation.

As she felt him slide home and fill her she moaned deep in her throat. The waiting was over. His cock inside her blotted out all regret and doubt and worry about the future. She wished she could use her arms and put them around his neck, hold him fiercely to her in welcome. That she could not, excited her terribly. Jan thought, I'm whole, a real woman now. And oh God, it felt so good.

Jan lay still for a moment, relishing the thick rude cock inside her, then she matched his rhythm, her hips rising and falling as he slid in and out of her cunt. The body remembered even if the mind forgot. As her arousal grew Jan raised and lowered her hips more frantically. This time, she told herself with fierce satisfaction, it's the real thing. And the real thing, she knew, was so much more satisfying than the various substitutes she had enjoyed so much only a day ago.

Patrick covered her mouth with his own, their breaths mingling as their bodies moved together in the old dance.

Jan moaned with her first real climax, but he did not let her rest. He kept on, sliding in and out of her as she came again and again. She was on fire. There was a fierce new heat in her belly. Her engorged nipples were pressed against his chest. Signals from cunt and breasts met and crossed, inflaming her still further. While Patrick covered her mouth with a long kiss, Jan began to keen deep in her throat, sounds that came from deep inside her. And when she felt him tense inside to begin his own climax, Jan screamed in pleasure and came with him.

They lay joined for a long time afterwards, breaths slowing, bodies cooling. Jan drifted in and out of sleep, waking always and taking pleasure in finding him still there. And later when she felt him growing erect inside her again she moaned in wonder and delight. Her newly awakened sexuality seemed boundless, her body shrugging off its post-coital lassitude as it prepared itself for more pleasure. How good it felt to be bound and naked and in rut.

Jan felt him move away as she was drifting to sleep.

'No,' she moaned softly. 'Don't go. Stay with me tonight, please. I need you here.'

And he did, lying beside her and holding her in his arms as she slept.

Jan woke to a new sense of joy and wonder to find him still there. This was what she had been missing, without ever knowing she was missing it. In the first light of day, she felt him stir beside her. She wanted to reach for him, to hold him back, but Patrick rose and knelt between her legs. He pushed them wide apart and bent to kiss her cunt. And this time she didn't even think of resistance. He used his teeth and tongue to arouse her once more. His cock was just above her face. Sixty-nine, Jan thought. What the girls used to giggle about. She lay on her back while her lover licked and kissed and nibbled at her labia and clitoris. Oh yes, she thought, as she crossed yet another boundary, as the delicious sensation from between her legs and in her belly rocked her yet again. No one had ever done that to her. She had never dreamed a man's mouth could bring such pleasure.

'Ohhhhhh,' Jan moaned, thrashing weakly as she came. He held her down, not allowing her hips to rise, and he stroked her belly, drawing her pleasure to a sharp point with his hands. And when it stabbed her again she screamed his name, twisting her head from side to side.

'Oh Patrick!'

And then Jan surprised herself. She opened her mouth and took his cock inside, using her own lips and tongue and teeth to give her lover pleasure. It was evident at once that he liked what she was doing, and this gave her courage to go on. When she came again, Patrick spurted in her mouth. Jan was taken by surprise. She didn't know what to do with the slightly salty fluid in her mouth. She swallowed, prompted by she knew not what instinct, and was not immediately filled with the horror that she expected to feel. Too weak to move, Jan felt him rise and lie down again in the bed beside her. He drew the covers over them both and took Jan in his arms.

The sun was bright in the room when she woke. Patrick was gone, and she was no longer tied to the bed. Jan panicked, then relaxed as she heard the sounds from the bathroom. She lay listening to the sound of her lover on the toilet and in the shower. 'Oh Patrick,' she sighed. 'My love.' It slipped out before she could think. She knew he hadn't heard her. But she had heard, and realised that she meant it. Jan felt a weight lift from her heart. It had been so long since she had felt like uttering those words. She couldn't even remember the last time she had thought about love. What a long dry time it had been.

She touched herself between the legs. Her fingers came away damp, and she smelled the mingled scent of their juices in the cool morning room. Jan smiled languidly as she remembered the night of arousal and release. Of passion, she said, savouring the word. No going back, she told herself, liking the sound of it.

The old Jan had her revenge. There's always a going back. Soon you'll be back in Godalming, back in your own house, and all this will be like a bad dream. You'll take up your gardening and maybe even write that book you've been thinking of.

Not a bad dream, Jan thought. More like a holiday, a glorious break from the daily routine, as holidays are supposed to be, but so seldom are. On holidays you always bring yourself along. But I've discovered a new self. And holidays can change the rest of your life, Jan told the shadow of her old self. I'll be bringing back someone new.

Patrick emerged from the bathroom to drive away the threatening gloom. She couldn't be gloomy when he was with her.

'Good morning, my love.'

Although he said it lightly, Jan felt her heart lurch. They ate a late breakfast. Naked, alone with Patrick, Jan felt as if she were doing something deliciously wicked. It had been a long time since she had allowed herself to do something wicked. Champagne after sex (and before it) compounded the wickedness. I'm becoming decadent, Jan thought with satisfaction.

About time, the inner voice said.

Jan's main worry just then was how to get him back to bed without having to ask. She was still having trouble with that. She wanted him to ask, so that she could be sure he wanted her.

Patrick suggested they go skinny-dipping. 'Otherwise why have an indoor pool?'

Jan thought that wicked too. The few times she had done it, mainly with her girlfriends, she had felt guilty and happy. She felt the same now. So when they finished the last of the champagne they went downstairs to the swimming pool. Jan felt slightly drunk, making it easier to stifle what was left of her conscience. There wasn't a lot left.

Patrick dove into the water ahead of her. Jan, conscious of his eyes and of the glass walls of the room, hurriedly slipped in as well. She felt better in the water. Long habits are not entirely broken in a day, or even a fortnight.

Patrick swam the length of the pool several times, Jan watching and not knowing what to do with herself. While skinny-dipping had seemed like a good idea up in the bedroom, it was not entirely satisfactory in reality. She swam out into the centre and trod water, slowly turning herself in a circle to look at the door leading into the demonstration room and then at the long glass wall. The sun shone brightly outside. It looked like a nice spring day. Jan realised with a start that she had not been outdoors in nearly two weeks.

Been too busy in here, her alter ego said with a grin.

Jan felt a hand on her ankle, and she was pulled under the water. Her long hair swirled around her face and head, partially blinding her. Through the floating strands she saw Patrick's laughing face floating before her. He put his hand behind her neck and pulled her close. They kissed underwater, Jan's long hair forming a cloud around their heads.

Laughing, Patrick broke away and surfaced. Jan came up beside him, smiling and breathless. He swam away toward the shallow end of the pool and, once there, stood up and beckoned Jan to follow. She swam slowly with the conventional breaststroke.

'How long has it been since you made love in water?' Patrick asked when she stood beside him.

'Never,' Jan said, thinking of the beach scene in *From Here to Eternity*. Her mother had thought it salacious. Jan had thought it rather tame, certainly nothing to make a fuss over.

'Then it's time you did,' Patrick told her. 'Come here.' He led Jan by the hand to the side of the pool by the ladder. There he turned her with her back to it and stood before her, his hands grasping the handrails on either side. 'We can't have you running away,' he told her with a smile.

'As if I would.' Jan returned his smile. Not waiting for him to make the first move, she put her arms around his neck and kissed him. My mother would be appalled, she thought happily. 'Oh!' she gasped as she felt his erection against her stomach. Once more Jan felt pleased to know that she could be that attractive to Patrick. She reached down and guided him into her. No foreplay, no slow arousal, no shame.

The water buoyed them, so that Patrick had to hold onto the ladder to keep himself in position, while Jan felt a marvellous lightness of limb and mind. Joined to him, holding him against her and inside her, she imagined herself afloat on a wide sea that would take her to distant and unknown shores. I've already visited some of them, she thought, and there's more to come.

Patrick began a slow in and out motion that made her feel as if she were being slowly rocked by gentle waves. Jan relaxed and concentrated on the sensations from her nipples and cunt, blanking out the glass walls and the daylight that would reveal them to anyone who happened by. And slowly he took her through her first climax, a slow rocking thing, not at all like the fierce shuddering ones she had experienced the night before. She floated with him, eyes closed while another climax washed through her. This one was more urgent.

Jan gasped and shook with it. And still Patrick moved slowly, methodically, driving her further from familiar shores with each climax. Jan imagined the onset of a storm at sea, the growing intensity as the centre approached. The waves grew in height and shook her body, each one more than the one before, and when she felt Patrick spurt inside her Jan screamed, her voice waking echoes in the big room. Then the still centre came, leaving Jan clinging to Patrick as the intensity slowly died away. She kept her eyes closed, holding onto him as if drowning.

'Well done!' Jan jerked back to reality to the sound of applause. She looked up and saw James and Antoinette on the far side of the pool. He clapped his hands, while Antoinette smiled her approval. Jan turned scarlet with embarrassment, unable to decide whether to push Patrick away and deny what she had felt, or to pull him closer and attempt to hide her nakedness from the others.

The little devil came to her rescue. Jan imagined the dusky red figure applauding too. Her embarrassment slowly ebbed, and she held onto Patrick, acknowledging the pleasure she had experienced.

Patrick was not embarrassed. He didn't speak, but his smile said its own 'Well done.'

232

He's proud of me, Jan thought, beginning to feel the same pride in him, in being seen with him. She kissed him as the applause died away. No going back, she thought again.

'Champagne for all in the winner's circle,' James said, leading Antoinette away. 'See you in the kitchen after you've dried off. No clothes,' he smiled at Jan. 'No cheating.' He indicated Antoinette, who was naked and had her hands tied behind her back.

'We're off today,' James told them when they were all seated in the kitchen. 'Antoinette and I think a visit to Paris in the spring is just what we need. Honeymoon and all that.'

Antoinette smiled pinkly as she drank from the glass that James held for her. In deference to Patrick, James had taken off his clothes. They lay in an untidy heap in the corner. In deference to Antoinette, Patrick had tied Jan's hands behind her before following the couple into the kitchen. She sat tidily on the chair across from him, blushing faintly whenever she caught his glance.

'She gave me my surprise early,' James told them, indicating the chain that led from between Antoinette's legs and trailed on the floor. His foot rested casually on the end of it. 'She was going to wait for some special occasion, but couldn't keep the secret. I think it's rather nice of her. Don't you?'

'What are you going to give her?' Jan asked. She was pleased with her new-found ability to speak in company and in the nude without being covered in blushes.

James looked down at his crotch and then up at Antoinette. She grinned. 'Fair exchange,' she said. 'What did Patrick give you?' she asked Jan.

'The same thing,' she replied, as steadily as she could.

Antoinette grinned broadly. 'I can see what you gave Patrick,' she said with a glance at Jan.

Jan managed not to look too much like the cat that had gotten the cream.

They all sat on while Patrick made sandwiches and James opened another bottle of champagne. It was getting on toward evening when James and Antoinette got up to go. He picked up his clothes and led her out to the car.

'Are they going to drive off like that?' she asked Patrick. She didn't think she was up to driving off in the nude.

Not yet, anyway, said her alter ego. Keep on as you are and you won't mind.

'Well, only as far as the airport,' he said with a grin.

Jan followed Patrick back to her bedroom, feeling slightly drunk and about to burst with happiness. Patrick brought along the bottle and glasses.

In the bedroom Jan felt a quiet satisfaction. It was getting dark outside. She and Patrick had been together for almost a whole day, both of them naked and at least one of them losing her last inhibitions. You've come a long way, she told the image in the mirror.

Fifteen

Finally it was time to go home. Too soon, both Jan and her alter ego thought. Neither of them knew how they were going to get along back in the real world, where neighbours and family would get in the way of their fantasy life, and where opportunities for the kind of sexual arousal they had become accustomed to would be scarce at best.

'Think of it as a holiday,' Patrick had told her the night before. 'Holidays have to end sometime, but you can always go on another one. And the time spent at home need not be a desert if you apply what you've learned here.'

What Jan wanted to say was that the time away from Patrick *would* be a desert. Sam might not be able to arouse her as he had done. Sam might not want to arouse her, after so many denials and refusals. Barbara (and his other paramours) might in the end prove more attractive than continued life with her.

Jan knew what she wanted but was unsure about how she could get it. Solve one problem and another arrives to take its place, she thought. She was waiting in her room for someone (she hoped it would be Patrick) to come to take her away, back home to the routine that had been broken so abruptly by her abduction. It was hard to imagine, here, her former life. She feared that, there, it would overwhelm her recent experience, and she would become the person she had always been.

Patrick had given her a telephone number and a promise: ring this number when the world is too much with you, and someone will come to take you away when you least expect it. We won't forget you if you don't forget us. With that Jan had to be content. Holidays always ended.

The clothes she had demanded be returned at the beginning of her captivity and conversion now lay on the bed: the cream-coloured dress, the pale blue bra and slip and underpants, the delicate sheer blue tights. Her high-heeled shoes stood side by side near the bed she had shared with Patrick just the night before. Jan no longer wanted her clothes; they looked foreign. But she had to get dressed. There was a present from Patrick: a suspender belt to match her other underwear, and a pair of long, pale blue stockings. She was to choose between the two. Would it be the tights or the stockings, the old or the new?

It was really no choice. Jan fitted the suspender belt around her narrow waist and sat on the edge of the bed to pull the stockings on. They came nearly to the tops of her thighs. As she clipped them to the suspenders, she remembered Robin in her long stockings and too-tight bra. Jan looked at herself in the mirror. The new woman looked back at her. She made a second decision. Jan folded the tights neatly and put them into the plastic carrier bag from Harrods. She shivered as she remembered Patrick coming into the room with the bag, full of rope and dildoes and delight for her. She folded the pants and put them into the bag too. Then she got into the rest of her clothes. This time she did not hurry as she had done for most of her adult life, anxious to hide her body away.

Jan felt both naked and deliciously wicked without pants. No one but her would know that she had none unless she was so uncautious as to stand on an air grating. Windy days might be a problem too, but Jan refused to worry about that. Let the wind blow, she thought.

The door opened to admit two of the women she had met in the last few eventful days. Barbara and Robin, come to say cheerio, not goodbye, they insisted. Since both were staying on for a few more days, they wore nothing but leg irons. Barbara's stripes were fading but still evident to one who knew where to look. Jan imagined that there would soon be more stripes. Robin's nipple rings looked fetching, and again Jan toyed with the idea of having herself pierced there. Later, maybe, she decided. Jan felt strange to be the only one wearing clothes.

They embraced, and talked, and wished one another well and promised to meet again sometime, somewhere. Barbara promised to call and visit when she got back home. 'Next time Sam is away,' she said. 'Call me any time.' Robin said she would come around soon: 'Next time I'm in the area selling double-glazing.'

Patrick joined them. Jan felt a stab of jealousy as the other women kissed him, and hoped he hadn't noticed. Her keeper with his arms around two naked women jarred with her. She concentrated instead on the Harrods carrier bag he had laid on the bed beside hers.

Barbara and Robin, now disengaged from Patrick, noticed it too, and took it as a sign that they should retire. Jan wanted to tell him to keep her forever, but knew she could not ask that of him. Instead, she showed him what was in her Harrods bag. It was the closest she could get to telling him that she was now 'transformed.' Patrick smiled at her and she felt her heart lurch.

Then it was time to go. Jan felt a tightness in her chest as Patrick tied her hands behind her back. This was so reminiscent of her abduction. Things had come full circle. Next he tied her elbows, making her full breasts jut out in the way that had so dismayed her the first time she had been bound. Jan regretted her clothes more than ever. For a gag Patrick chose her tights and pants, making them into a ball and thrusting them into her mouth when she opened it to receive them. He tied a scarf around her mouth and head, pushing the gag deeply into her mouth.

Jan looked at the mirror one last time. The woman staring back at her was herself, as she now was, no longer a stranger. Patrick took her into his arms and kissed her over her gag, and Jan felt once more the thrill of a kiss she could not avoid or control. She did her best to kiss him back, but her mouth was not hers to control. Nevertheless he smiled when he released her and stepped back. The leather bag came next. Before he closed her head in it she gave him a tremulous smile. Then the familiar room and the bright morning were blotted out. Patrick tied the strings tightly around her neck and Jan was ready to be transported.

He led her out of her room with a hand on one elbow, steering her toward the stairs she had descended and climbed so often during her stay. The breeze on her legs told her that she was outside the house for the first time since she had arrived. In public, she told herself. Panic. Suppose someone sees me? No one will know who it is, she thought. Yes, but what if they make a scene and call the police. I will die of shame.

Calm down, her alter ego told her. No one is going to see you. Remember Barbara and Antoinette walking around the grounds. You're just going from the house to the van. Nevertheless, it seemed to Jan that the short walk took several centuries, during any one of which she could be discovered and exposed to public scrutiny and shame. So it was with great relief that she felt Patrick turn her around and walk her backwards until she felt the lower sill of the door against the backs of her legs.

He helped her to sit on the floor, leaving her legs hanging down. A part of Jan wanted to get under cover at once. Another part of her relished the danger that had just caused such panic. When she felt the ropes around her ankles Jan knew what would follow. She would be exposed while he finished binding her. She was going to travel home much as she had travelled here, and that excited her. The outward journey had been made in fear. The return journey would be made in regret. But this time she resolved to enjoy the bondage at least. She had learned that much at the secret house.

When he had bound her legs, ankles, knees and thighs, Patrick rolled Jan onto the padded rear floor of the van and hogtied her. Her hands and feet were touching and her back was arched. Jan heard the door close, and she struggled on the floor to find a more comfortable position. She knew it would be a long journey. As before, she was helpless and would not be able to free herself. And she was excited. What would Patrick do when they got to her place? Surely he would not just dump her at her house bound as she was. Would he? Perhaps he would leave her in the garden, waiting to be found. Jan felt both fear and a certain thrill brought on by the many possibilities of her helpless state. But at the back of it all was the hope that Patrick would not be able to resist one last fuck before he left her. She clung to that thought as the van headed for Godalming. The ropes were uncomfortably tight, and her body grew cramped from the strain of her hogtie, but she relished it all in a way she had never thought she would on the day they took her.

Jan knew she was home when she felt the van stop. There was another moment of panic lest one of the neighbours saw her. She imagined Patrick carrying her over his shoulder from the van to her front door in plain view of everyone. Exciting and panic-making at the same time. Surely her would not risk discovery, both for her sake and for his.

Nor did he. He opened the doors and pulled Jan around to where he could undo the tight rope and unbind her legs. He helped Jan stand, supporting her as they crossed the short distance from the van to her back door. Jan did not relax fully until she knew they were inside her kitchen with the door closed. Patrick removed the hood and the light dazzled her eyes, as it had that first day.

As her eyes grew accustomed to the light Jan looked around the familiar kitchen where her adventure had begun. There was the chair to which her abductors had bound her, still turned away from the table as they had left it. The apron and the tea towel and the rubber gloves she wore while washing up lay neatly as she had left them to answer the door to Robin's summons. All the familiar things were in their familiar places, Jan realised with a shock. After the changes she had undergone, she had half-expected everything else to be altered too. But it was just the same and, now she was back, among the things she knew, she was sad.

Patrick removed her gag and laid the damp pants and tights on the draining board. Leaving Jan's wrists and elbows bound, he embraced and kissed her. This time she returned the kiss, a shade desperately, trying to let him know how profoundly she had changed, and how badly she wanted him to stay with her. She wanted him to take her away again, knowing he could not, that she could not go. She wanted some reassurance that he would not forget her, as so many women do.

The kiss drew out, and Jan felt her breath growing short and the old excitement rising. Patrick felt it too. His cock grew erect, pressing against her belly. His arms tightened around her. He too, she knew, could not just walk away. Jan drew her mouth away from his and said, 'Take me upstairs, please!' in a tearing whisper.

He released her and Jan turned away to lead him to her bedroom. She climbed the stairs steadily, her bound hands no longer impeding her. She wanted to get him to bed as quickly as possible.

Patrick caught her fever. Jan knew he was right behind her, ready to catch her if she stumbled, and to be ready when they reached their goal. Jan turned left at the head of the stairs, down the short upstairs hall and into the bedroom she shared with Sam. And now with Patrick, she told herself exultantly.

This time there was no question of untying her hands and arms. Patrick seized her from behind, his cock pressing urgently against her bottom and his hands cupping her full breasts. Even fully clothed, Jan felt a surge of excitement as he handled her through her dress. She lay her head back against his shoulder, and he kissed the side of her neck, her ear, hair, holding her from behind. Patrick released her breasts to unbutton the top of her dress. The pale blue silk bra had a front clasp, and he undid it, pushing the bra down and pulling her breasts out of the slip.

Jan gasped as she felt his fingers on her bare nipples, rubbing and squeezing and caressing. She trembled beneath his touch, barely restraining herself from telling him to hurry, to take her now, not to wait for anything. Her hands twisted against the rope that held her captive.

In the mirror of her dressing table Jan saw a woman with her dress open from neck to waist, her breasts spilling out of her bra as Patrick fondled them. The sight aroused her still further. 'Now, please now!' she gasped.

Patrick released her breasts and had her sit on the side of the bed. He knelt and raised her dress to her waist, exposing her full thighs in the long stockings. Spreading her legs, he knelt between them and put his mouth directly on her cunt. Jan felt herself go wet at the touch, and when he used his lips and tongue and teeth on her labia and clitoris she nearly fainted. Behind her back her hands and arms strained against the rope. She groaned as his mouth on her cunt aroused her still further. And then she came, shuddering, bending forward until her chin rested on the top of his head, her body racked again and again.

Patrick continued his attention until her next orgasm. Then he rose, undressed hurriedly and turned to her. Jan looked steadily at his erect cock, wanting it inside her *now*. He lay on the bed and drew her atop him, her breasts and belly against him and her bound hands behind her back. Jan opened her legs and felt his cock against her belly. She tried to move so that it could slide inside, but could not. She groaned in frustration.

Patrick helped her to sit up and to bend her knees so that she could straddle him. She rose slightly, and he guided his cock into her. Jan moaned as she felt him glide into her. Then she was full, impaled on his shaft, and he was helping her to rise and fall, guiding her with his hands on her hips. When she established a rhythm, he used one hand to stroke her belly and her pubic hair while the other fondled her breasts and nipples. Jan bent down to kiss him deeply, then sat up again to allow him access to her body. So she rode him, moaning and gasping and shuddering. In a haze of lust she had never been capable of before Jan came repeatedly, not thinking, only feeling. And this time when she felt him tense and spurt inside her she screamed as she felt the release in her belly. Afterward, amazingly, he was still with her. Jan lay down atop him and felt him growing again inside her, and she felt a fierce gladness as her body responded.

When the latest storm had finally passed she lay atop him, their breathing slowing, bodies cooling. Love in the afternoon suited her very well. Jan slept, and woke to passion again. Bound, half out of her dress, she felt herself lifted again to the heights of passion, and she revelled in her body's ability to give her such pleasure. Patrick held her on top of him as he thrust into her, and Jan was proud to know that she could give such pleasure to another. Especially to Patrick, who had taught her what she was capable of. Her screams filled the house as he filled her body.

Afterward she struggled to sit up. 'Bathroom,' Jan said as he lifted her off him. Jan squatted and peed. She felt none of her former embarrassment as Patrick wiped her dry and helped her back to the bedroom There he untied her wrists and elbows, and she stretched her cramped arms with only a slight grimace of discomfort. The old Jan would have hurried to tuck her breasts back into the brassiere and straighten her clothes. The new Jan took them all off. All except the stockings and suspenders. She felt delightfully wicked as she

243

stood before Patrick wearing the gift he had given her. His smile was her reward.

Jan insisted Patrick stay for a late lunch. A naked lunch, she said a trifle nervously. She was glad that he accepted, gladder still to see that he seemed to want to stay with her. They would have to make do with microwaved food from the freezer, she said. Patrick didn't mind. Jan nevertheless felt compelled to explain that, having been away, naturally she hadn't been able to shop . . .

'Stop apologising, Jan,' he told her, taking her hand as she bustled past and urging her to sit beside him. 'I want to stay with you. The food is not the attraction.'

Jan flushed with pleasure. She was attractive to him. He was more than that to her, but she didn't like to press her claim on him now. She knew that he had to go and she had to stay. So it was nice that he had said what he had said. It augured well for the future, she thought. Naked, they ate and kissed in the kitchen where her adventure had begun. I feel like a schoolgirl, Jan thought, liking the feeling.

The ringing of the telephone interrupted them. It was Sam, announcing that he would be home at ten in the evening. Jan wondered, without jealousy, if he were in bed with another of his mistresses. For the first time, she understood what it felt like to deceive a spouse. It felt awkward. But she would do it again as soon as possible. She smiled at Patrick as she chatted to her husband.

Hanging up the phone, she announced that they had the rest of the day to amuse themselves. And then blushed at her temerity. Maybe he had someplace else to go, she stammered.

Patrick rose and crossed the room to her. Taking her in his arms, he bent his head to kiss her mouth.

Her knees felt weak.

'Upstairs again?' he suggested.

Jan didn't think she could go through yet another . . . fucking, she thought, relishing the vulgar flavour of the word. Not just this minute. Later.

'What happens now, Patrick?' she asked, sitting at the table dressed in just her stockings and suspenders. The future was going to be different from the past, and she needed to accommodate the changes.

Ensure that you get regular sex, you mean. Call things by their proper names. Things like that, her alter ego insisted.

Patrick saved her from having to quell an internal mutiny. 'We'll go on as we have, of course. As often as possible.' He paused. 'As often as you wish,' he amended. 'You have the telephone number. Call whenever you want to. Someone will come for you. That's a promise we make to all our *alumnae*. We take their further education very seriously,' he said with a smile.

'But what about Sam?'

'Well, what about him? He knows where you've been while he was away, if not precisely what you've been doing, but maybe Leslie has filled in the details for him. I imagine he will be eager to see how you've changed.'

Jan was silent. *Leslie* telling Sam about her? Then . . . Leslie must know about the 're-education' programme too. But how? The possibility that her own daughter had been to one or another of the courses, and maybe had nominated her own mother for a session, caused Jan some confusion. How can I face her or Sam?

Don't say anything. Just do what you've learned comes naturally, advised her alter ego.

Jan would have to think about that. But meanwhile there was Patrick. Patrick. Had her new-found lover been shagging Leslie too?

Probably, her alter ego said. So what? Plenty to go round for everyone.

Jan was shaken. She barely felt Patrick urging her up the stairs again. She found herself in her bedroom again without knowing how she had got there. Her discarded clothing lay on the floor where she had dropped it: dress, slip, bra, shoes. The old Jan would have tidied it all away at once.

Or never have gotten undressed in the first place, her alter ego suggested.

Jan had to concede the point. The new Jan turned to her lover and embraced him. When the long kiss ended she picked the rope off the bed and turned to Patrick. There was no need to speak her desire.

This time he tied her wrists together in front of her, but surprised Jan by drawing her hands up and over her head until her hands were behind her neck and her elbows were beside her ears. He led the rope down behind her back and tied it around her waist, leaving Jan with her hands held behind her neck. She tugged against the ropes and found that she was again helpless to escape. Standing in her stockings and suspenders, Jan shivered as she knew that her entire body was exposed to his gaze. And to his hands. Patrick moved behind her to cup her heavy breasts.

Jan gasped as she felt herself held and fondled. Her nipples engorged themselves in record time, the veins standing out against her flesh as she had noticed them when she and Robin were together at the first 'demonstration'. As then, this visible evidence of her excitement excited her still further. Jan wanted this afternoon to go on forever, even as she was aware it must end. But not yet. Not yet. She moaned when Patrick pinched her erect nipples.

He moved his hands to her stomach, rubbing and stroking, moving lower and lower until her knees bent and she thrust her hips forward, opening herself to him. A finger slid between her parted thighs and into her wet cunt, unerringly finding her clitoris. Jan was sure she could feel it swell at the touch. Behind her neck, Jan's bound hands twisted and tugged against the rope. She could feel Patrick's erection pressing against her bottom. 'Please! Take me now.'

Instead Patrick eased Jan to her knees among the scattered clothing on the floor. He bent her from the waist until her elbows and head rested on the floor and her bottom stuck into the air. She spread her knees and thighs to him.

Patrick knelt over her from behind. Jan gasped when she guessed what he was going to do. This is how dogs do it, she thought with a shiver. His cock lay between her thighs. She felt it brush against her pussy from behind. Craning her neck, Jan could just see the tip of his erection nearly touching her cunt. She saw his hands as he reached under her belly to open her labia. Then his finger was again on her swollen clitoris and she lost track of things.

Jan gasped in surprise when he spread her labia and slid inside her. Dogs knew what it was all about, and now so did Jan. 'Ohhhh!' she moaned as he began to thrust in and out. Constrained by her position, Jan could only hold still as he fucked her. But movement wasn't important. The waves of pleasure that spread through her belly and down her bent legs were the only things she heeded. With his cock fully inside her, Patrick reached around under her belly to tease her clitoris. Jan heaved and came at once. Patrick rode her easily as her body bucked beneath him. Her bound hands clenched behind her head as she fought the ropes in her ecstasy. When Patrick came, Jan screamed and nearly fainted with the pleasure of it.

She was only dimly aware of being lifted to her feet and taken to the bed. She lay on her side gasping and shuddering in the aftermath of her orgasms. She drowsed, contented.

Patrick finally got up to get dressed. She knew he had to go. Taking comfort in repeating to herself the telephone number he had given her. The emergency number, Antoinette had called it. The next emergency would probably occur the next time Sam had to take a business trip.

Dressed, Patrick smiled down at her. There were no more words to say, Jan thought.

Her alter ego disagreed. Get yourself ready for Sam. When he gets home it isn't likely he'll want a quiet game of Monopoly.

'Leave me tied here, Patrick. Sam will be home soon. I want him to find me here.'

He nodded smilingly as he untied her hands and stretched her out on her back.

Then he tied her wrists and ankles to the four bedposts, leaving her as a present for Sam. She would much rather he were merely leaving her helpless while he stepped out for a bit.

Patrick bent to kiss her as she lay on her back. 'You make a pretty starfish,' he remarked. He kissed her once more, thoroughly, on the mouth before replacing her gag and blindfolding her with a scarf from her bureau. The last thing Jan saw before the darkness descended were her clothes lying in disarray on the floor. She moaned when he planted a lingering kiss between her widespread thighs.

Then he was whispering in her ear. 'Remember the number.'

As if I could forget, Jan thought.

Her alter ego smiled happily.

Jan now faced the uncertain hours until her

husband returned, but she was easier in her mind. She had seen his regret at going as plainly as she felt her own. He would come back for her when she called. Maybe even before then. Between now and then she'd think of what Sam would do when he found her.